Also by Janine Boissard

A MATTER OF FEELING
A NEW WOMAN

CHRISTMAS LESSONS

Janine Boissard

CHRISTMAS LESSONS

Translated by Mary Feeney

LITTLE, BROWN AND COMPANY   BOSTON / TORONTO

FIRST ENGLISH LANGUAGE EDITION

Originally published in French under the title *Claire et le Bonheur*
by Librairie Arthème Fayard, Paris, 1979.

Library of Congress Cataloging in Publication Data

Boissard, Janine.
Christmas lessons.

Translation of: Claire et le bonheur.
I. Title.
PQ2662.O54C513 1984   843'.914   84-12537
ISBN 0-316-10097-8

BP

Designed by Jeanne F. Abboud

Published simultaneously in Canada
by Little, Brown & Company (Canada) Limited

PRINTED IN THE UNITED STATES OF AMERICA

CHRISTMAS LESSONS

❧ I ❧

The Feast of St. Aimé

IT was the feast of St. Aimé, a nice-sounding morning to
start back to school. The yard was the same as yesterday,
fragrant and golden with its sudden showers of leaves; the
pond had been emptied and cleaned, and if you walked unhurriedly beneath the tall walnut tree, you'd feel the first
nuts, still in their brown shells, cracking under your feet. It
was all open space and freedom, but for me that was over
now. Five mornings a week I'd leave before the clock on the
village church's steeple struck eight. I would no longer be
sent to pick up warm bread for lunch, and every morning
when I left, it would be a little darker, a little colder.

Straddling my moped, I looked up at the still-drawn curtains at Claire's bedroom window, and for once I envied my
older sister, "the Princess," her idleness.

I'd made a point of dressing the same as the day before,
even though my pants had walnut stain on the pockets, or
maybe because they did. But I hadn't gone so far as to put
my bathing suit back on under my clothes. Last year's bookbag would make it through three more terms, and I knew
when I felt inside it there would be old chewing-gum wrappers and pencil shavings, composting into memories. No

pencil pouch, because I hadn't used one for ages. No note-books either, just a huge folder.

Cécile, my little sister, over twelve and starting sixth grade — not exactly "ahead of herself" — had been ready for several days.Every year she demands a complete new set of school supplies, makes a big fuss over them for a week, then forgets all about them. She can't forgive Mom for buy-ing her used textbooks. In her shiny green bookbag was a new transparent plastic pencil pouch, showing off her col-ored pencils, ruler, compass, eraser, and pen. She also had a box of stickers, but not the self-stick kind because "what's your tongue for?"

The sight of her all excited over her new gear made me envy her, too. I remembered feeling the same near-certi-tude: that the carefully sharpened pencils, the untouche ' eraser, the straight ruler, the blank pages would make schoolwork (and good marks) come easy.

But for two years now I'd been hanging on to my old things. I'd beg the shoemaker to make one more repair on the game bag I use for my books. The leather smells of fish and is cracking at all the seams. And my favorite pencil was only three toothmarked inches long.

Fall was on the damp brown road, in the morning light, but most of all in my heart. Riding toward the suburban train station, toward my last year of high school, I thought how much I hated the word *senior*. This year would mark an end to six years of secondary school. Then what? The saving grace was that I'd be back together with Beatrice — Béa — my best friend.

Every year on the night before school started, ever since we were kids, Daddy would pay us a visit in our bedrooms. He hardly ever set foot in them otherwise, unless we were sick, and he seemed almost shy. First he'd look around and try to find something nice to say about the room. Cécile had rugby posters plastered everywhere, so he'd talk scrum, try, tackle, until he made a subtle connection between the athlete in training and the pupil beginning a new school year. Cécile had to realize she was working for herself and not her parents, even if good grades would make said parents very happy.

For the last two years, over my protestations, Cécile (her nickname is "the Pest") had hidden a cassette recorder in her top dresser drawer, leaving it slightly ajar so she could tape the parental state-of-the-union speech, solely for the edification of her future offspring, she claimed.

Daddy didn't pay a call to Claire last night, because, as the Pest put it, the Princess was in her second year of post-secondary Leisure Studies, and there was nothing left to say on the subject. But he did go in to see Bernadette, who'd just gone back to her riding-school job.

What he told her, big surprise, was not to overdo it. Bernadette's fiancé, Stéphane, would leave soon for Toulon to do his year's service in the Navy. Daddy was afraid she'd compensate for his absence by working harder than ever with the horses. I don't know what he said to her, but Bernadette's laughter practically raised the roof, and her room is in the basement.

Then Daddy went up to see the Pest. He begged her to change the "could do better" comments she was always bringing home to "well dones." Why not? Cécile showed him her cheerful bookbag, her pencil case and new notebooks, and eagerly promised to do as he asked. Daddy, by the way, apparently wasn't known for collecting "well dones" until his last year in school. And yet he already knew he wanted to be a doctor and had started his practice on a number of unsuspecting girl cousins.

When he came into my room, I was sitting at my desk writing. I'd arranged a superb bouquet of autumn leaves to give him an opener. As I expected, he complimented me on it and said that given his choice of rooms, he would have taken my garret.

He lingered over my favorite painting, a Brittany seascape. The sea is methodically assaulting the shore but doesn't manage to disturb the small white house huddled in the broomflowers in the background.

The white house is me. It has only one window, enough to enjoy the sky when it's not too dark. The waves and foam are all the beautiful and terrifying forces we sense at work around us.

I went to my father's side and looked at the picture with him. I told him how much I love Brittany even if it scares me a little. The boulders are rough with barnacles and sea snails, and sheets hung out to dry there end up smelling like mainsails.

Daddy was amazed. As far as he knew, we'd only gone to Brittany once and I was little then. . . . But someone special had told me so much about it I felt I'd just been there.

Charles — that's Daddy's name — looked at me for a few seconds and I think he understood.

He had no advice to offer me about my schoolwork: steady as she goes. He asked me what I planned to do after graduation. The answer spilled out: "Write!" Once I said it I felt peaceful. I saw where I was headed.

"Write what, darling?"

Poems, short stories, novels, all that you can't say out loud, that sleeps within you, blooms without your knowledge, and about freedom, suffering, the end, and the beginning — everything.

He gave me a look that seemed to see me differently, not quite so clearly, not so well into the future. Then he told me that except for a lucky few, even very gifted writers don't make money, and that I should think about finding another way to earn a living. But that didn't mean I should give up on the idea of writing, certainly not. And he'd be happy to read my work and offer me advice if I'd let him.

I said I would, but later. When I was ready for criticism. He stood up to go, and when he kissed me I felt like he was telling me how he'd like to let me know more clearly and more often that I was part of his life.

I heard him going down the stairs. The third step creaked, as usual. When he was back downstairs, I stretched my hand out in front of me, sideways and slightly curved. I looked at it so hard it seemed like a fine plaster cast executed by a great artist and lover of literature.

In front of the plaster cast was a nameplate made out of something rare and noble. It was engraved, "Hand of Pauline Moreau." And hovering over the name was renown.

❦ 2 ❦

The War of the Primroses

*I*N the meantime: cows!
    Ten o'clock at night. We'd been back to school for
three days and already felt like we'd never had a summer
vacation.

When Cécile shouted from the window, "There are cows
out in the yard!," no one paid any attention. We were on
to the Pest's practical jokes. From her armchair, Mom sig-
naled her to shush, pointing at Daddy immersed in a phar-
maceutical journal, reading what must have been a deadly
dull article, since his head was bobbing and behind his
glasses his eyelids fluttered. And anyhow, Daddy prescribed
drugs sparingly. He'd rather let nature do its work.

But when Cécile, after another few minutes with her nose
to the windowpane, defied the maternal warning and yelled
at Charles, "They really look like they're enjoying your wil-
low tree!," Daddy woke with a start, dropped his journal,
and joined the Pest at the window, walking over calmly to
show us he wasn't falling for anything.

He peered out where Cécile was pointing and instead of
bursting out laughing, turned to Mom and said accusingly,
"I see three of them."

Then we were all at the window, even Claire, who'd been

looking like a martyr all evening — I wondered why, since she was the only one whose life hadn't changed a bit that September, when millions of students and workers had to go back to the daily grind.

We could see the cows in the light of a streetlamp a little farther up the road.

"They're from the dairy," said Cécile. "That's Marie-Toulouse, you can tell by the spot the shape of Ireland on her back. The other two are heifers."

The Matons, an older couple, own the dairy farm at the outskirts of Mareuil, our village. We buy our milk there. Sometimes they have rabbits, and their potatoes are much better than the ones in the stores. In late fall, I'm sorry to say, they sell what are supposedly excellent Brussels sprouts.

"It looks like they're settling in for the night," Bernadette said with a loud and delighted laugh.

She opened the window and a breeze ruffled the pages of Daddy's journal. Fall is even more palpable at night.

"How on earth did they get in?"

"Madame Cadillac is letting the Matons use her field," Cécile informed us. "They were bringing the cows over there when I went to get the milk. I ran into them. That Marie-Toulouse is really lame."

Madame Cadillac runs the bakery; her field is next to our yard.

"I'll run over to the farm and tell them," Bernadette said.

Daddy followed her out to the front steps. When he turned on the front light, a sort of floodlight we mostly use when we eat outside, the cows stirred in surprise.

By that time Daddy was genuinely upset. He eyed his English mixed border.

"If they come over this way, they'll ruin everything."

And he looked sadly across the yard to the Taverniers' window.

The fact is, there's an undeclared war between Daddy and Monsieur Tavernier, the next-door neighbor we call

Roughly Speaking because that's what he says every other word. The war is over their flowerbeds.

It started when Roughly Speaking gave his mournful analysis of our soil, not rich enough, it appears, to grow anything that isn't hardy. The ultramodern tiller our neighbor bought didn't help matters any, despite the sophisticated irrigation system Daddy installed. But what brought it to a head was the aphids.

When the aphids had infested our Dutch tulips three months before, Daddy applied an insecticide according to directions. It killed the few surviving tulips; then the aphids, stronger than ever, attacked the lupine. When Roughly Speaking got wind of this, he had the audacity to tell Charles he hadn't mixed the spray right — you could tell from the lumps left in the nozzle — so Daddy decided to shut him up for good. He secretly grew some cape primroses in his cold frame, then transplanted them by night into the mixed border.

The cape primrose is a sumptuous flower, with a wide throat and wavy edges. Tavernier quickly spotted its unusual blue from his window and turned green with envy, according to Charles. He'd been green for a week now.

And tonight the cows were grazing on the lawn between the pond and the cape primroses.

Bernadette got her moped out of the garage, made the mistake of starting it in the driveway, and sent the cows galloping into the flowerbeds.

Oblivious to danger, Daddy took right off after them, in his old velvet slippers, yelling so loudly he drove the cows a little deeper into the flowers.

"Get the hell out of there, you idiots," Daddy roared. "You stupid beasts!"

Cécile fell down on the steps laughing. Mom tried hard to give her a stern look.

"Do you know how much time your father has invested in those flowers?"

"I know," gasped the Pest, "I know! That's just the point."

Daddy got the cows to beat a retreat. Out on the road they stared at him, puzzled.

"Thanks a lot for your help," he shouted at us.

"What do you want me to do?" Mom yelled.

"Use your head and bring me the lantern," he hollered.

Cécile ran to get it in the basement and brought it to Charles, going around the back of the house to stay clear of the cows.

He didn't want to use the lantern to scare off the culprits, but to assess the damage. The whole town must have heard him groan.

"Believe me, old Maton is going to hear about this. When you keep cows, you keep track of them."

Claire had returned to the living room. Cécile was back on the front steps.

Then the three cows, flank to flank, were edging toward the concrete pond where the grass is thicker and also very slippery. Every year some much lighter and less awkward visitor falls in and we have to furnish hot drinks and dry clothes.

"If they fall in, it won't be any trouble," Cécile pointed out. "At least you won't have to lend them your bathrobe."

"Very funny," Daddy said. "Really. Very, very funny."

Finally we heard the whine of the moped coming up the road, followed by the whinny of the Matons' old car. The cows turned nervously toward the front gate. If they backed up now, they were sure to fall into the pond.

A dreadful-looking dog came hurtling into the yard ahead of the Matons, who looked as sleepy as their cattle. She had a scarf on over her curlers; the next day was Sunday. The dog headed straight for Daddy, barking up a storm. He jumped backwards.

"Go ahead, Zero. Let 'em have it. Show these trouble-makers your stuff."

Marie-Toulouse recognized the dog. Mooing in terror, she disappeared into the darkness, the heifers at her heels. There was a racket of rustling leaves, crackling branches.

"Not over there," Daddy howled. "My cold frame!"

"Wouldn't you know," old Maton said. "Wouldn't you know."

He came over to greet Daddy, dumbfounded.

"Our gate's broken down, and it must have been Marie-Toulouse," his wife was explaining. "When she feels like a snack, there's no stopping her."

Over by the fruit trees, Zero was barking louder and louder.

"Do you think he'll be able to herd them?" Daddy moaned.

"In nothing flat," old Maton promised. "Back to the barn, the party's over, and no dessert."

"Maybe you've noticed, Dr. Moreau," Madame Maton interrupted, "what a terrible limp Marie-Toulouse has. Well, the vet swears her leg is sound as a dollar. He says it's all in her mind. That she does it to get attention."

Madame Maton looked proud of her speech. Daddy had no diagnosis to offer. Cécile was in seventh heaven.

"Maybe she needs a shrink," Bernadette suggested.

Alerted by Zero's barking, Roughly Speaking then emerged from his house, at the very moment the three perpetrators where straggling back into the streetlight.

He strode over, a crimson velvet dressing gown topping his suit pants. At a glance he took in the family, the Matons, the cows, Daddy.

"Going into livestock, my dear Doctor?" he gently inquired.

Old Maton thought this was a scream. Tavernier went to check out the cape primroses, but Daddy, one step ahead of him, switched off the lantern.

"And organic fertilizer, I see," Tavernier added. He gestured toward Daddy's right slipper, and only then did Daddy see what he'd put his foot into.

Harassed by Zero, who seemed to be all over the place, the cows walked by us in single file. Cécile gave them a friendly look.

"I've heard that during the war the cows dropped like flies because there was no one to milk them," she explained. "Their udders were hard as rocks and scraped on the ground. How awful not to be able to milk yourself!"

Old Maton loved it, couldn't stop laughing.

"I wish you'd teach them to. Then we'd be able to sleep in!"

Once the cows were herded out the gate, Maton shook Daddy's hand.

"About your cold frame: see if there's any damage and we'll talk about it tomorrow."

Roughly Speaking's ears perked up at the mention of "cold frame."

"Don't worry, it's just an old thing I never use," Daddy said pathetically.

Marie-Toulouse gave one last regretful look behind her before disappearing down the road. Madame Maton, who's never managed to pass her driver's test, started up the car and took off with a roar.

"You really have all the luck," Tavernier told Daddy. "One day it's aphids, the next it's cows. I don't think those cape primroses would have made it anyway. Flowers are like sick people. They don't always do so well when they're moved."

Daddy didn't even have the strength to answer. Our neighbor closed the gate very quietly, as if someone had died. Suddenly everything was quiet again, and when we turned off the outside lights we could hear the wind rustling in the trees.

Mom timidly suggested that her husband leave his slippers on the doorstep. He did so without a word and went directly to their bedroom. He seemed like a child being punished.

We heard strains of Mozart coming from the living room. The Princess was curled up in her chair, eyes closed. Cécile went and stood in front of her, incredulous.

"Mozart you can listen to anytime, but this was a once-in-a-lifetime thing. You don't have any idea what you missed."

Claire opened her eyes and looked at Cécile as if returning from somewhere far, far away.

"Is anything wrong?" Mom worried aloud.

And as I watched the Princess try hard to smile, heard her voice say no, no, nothing is wrong, no problem, I saw clearly that in fact something *was* wrong with her, terribly wrong.

But what?

3

Claire's Silences

You notice a problem, promise yourself you'll do something about it, and the next day you forget or maybe ignore it, who knows, out of selfishness or laziness. . . .

But then we were so used to Claire's silences, her self-contained ways, her ups and downs.

It was Bernadette who nicknamed her the Princess. Even as a little girl, apparently, she was already different: quieter than most children, always neat and clean, silently weeping when she didn't get the ring on the merry-go-round, the tail on the donkey, Boardwalk, all the aces when we played War, or, of course, to be King of the Hill.

Later, when she was attending school in Paris with Bernadette, she always bought first-class commuter tickets, leaving our horse-loving sister behind in second class. And then there is the fact that she's very pretty and stands straight, head high, as if the sky's the limit.

Some people couldn't understand why she was allowed to stay home, doing nothing. That's just the way it was. After she ran away, our parents gave up. If people didn't like it, too bad. It was too hard on us when she was gone. And that's that.

It often seemed to me that Claire's refusal to work simply had to do with the fact she couldn't do anything that wouldn't be truly fulfilling, anything "average," which was exactly what she didn't want to be. But what *did* she want?

In the meantime, she read a lot, listened to music, went on long walks, and when we all got home, there she was. She had a knack for using the bathtub just when everyone else wanted to, even though she *was* home all day. She didn't seem to have many friends. She said she was just living.

And that Wednesday when I got home, a conference on Claire was being held in the kitchen.

Bernadette hadn't even taken off her riding boots or the pants she wore in the stables, which certainly created atmosphere. Some people like that, I guess. A few weeks earlier she had taken a bad fall. Her head had been shaved for her operation, and her hair was growing back slowly, very thick. She looked a little boyish but in a way it was becoming, or at least sexy. You weren't quite sure who she was. You wanted to keep looking at her to check. And from the way Stéphane looked at her when he took her in his arms, he seemed to be keeping close tabs.

Straddling a chair, Bernadette looked intently at Cécile, who was sitting by the stove with a stack of cookies.

"Well, first she asked me to lend her the money I got for my birthday, said she needed it right away," the Pest told us. "I promised I wouldn't tell anyone."

"Nice work," Bernadette said. "We'll be sure to tell you our secrets, too."

"You two aren't anyone," the Pest shot back.

After we said thanks, she continued: "Right after lunch she said she was going for a walk, but she went into the city."

"How do you know?"

"Madame Cadillac dropped her off at the station."

"I don't see anything so unusual about that," I said. "Claire can go into town and see her friends if she wants to."

"What about the money?"

"Maybe she went to the movies or something."

"Well, it must not have been a very funny one," the Pest said, "because when she got home her eyes were all red, and when I asked her if she had a good time she didn't say a thing and walked right down to the river like she was going to jump in."

Bernadette and I exchanged glances. What bothered me was hearing that Claire was crying. Claire never cried. The last time she did was after she ran away, when we went to bring her back home. And then she cried because she was so happy when we said we'd let her be.

"If you ask me, it's a man," declared the Pest. "When you're in love, you're attracted to water — rivers, lakes, that kind of stuff, like Lamartine. She's in love and it's not working out."

"If she's in love she must have fallen pretty fast," Bernadette pointed out, "unless it's still that guy in San Francisco."

"I really doubt it," Cécile said, "except maybe if absence makes the heart grow fonder. She didn't seem like she was in love with him when we were there."

I agreed. The guy in San Francisco was Jeremy, a young lawyer with a beard. Claire liked him, but that was all. A fling. And a nice little fling wouldn't leave her with a broken heart.

"You two are weird," Bernadette said. "Why does it have to be love? Is that all anyone ever cries over?"

"Easy for you to say," retorted Cécile. "You've found somebody. But when you haven't it's always on your mind."

And then she added, "We're having a soufflé for dinner tonight. The acid test."

"What do you mean?"

"If she doesn't scrape out the dish, we'll know it's serious."

She looked out the window. "Here she comes. Let's break it up, okay?"

Claire appeared at the far end of the yard. Under a rock there we hide the key to a rusty old gate that opens onto the banks of the river Oise.

It's a place where the water flows slowly along the steep concrete banks, slapping against them when a barge goes by. No one fishes there anymore, because of the motorboats, and the wooden piers are rotting. When we first moved to La Marette we could still swim in the river without worrying about pollution. I remember how the water felt on my shoulders and that delicate moment when you hoist yourself onto the muddy banks to get out.

Eyes to the ground, the Princess walked unhurriedly toward the house. With her coat and purse, she looked like a visitor.

"Girls are too damned complicated for me," Bernadette sighed as she took off for her room.

I left Cécile by the stove, trying to put on a trustworthy face, and went upstairs. Mom's door was open a crack. A familiar smell wafted out. I went in.

She was painting. I think she liked to paint even as a girl. She'd started to do it again two years before. Oil paintings, collages, a little of everything. My mother believes things have "vibrations" we can sometimes glean: one of the things we have in common.

I went closer. She had to have heard me come in, but she didn't turn around. It was a painting she started right after we got back from California. It must be about the good times we had there, the sudden return. I saw a spot something like a sun, different shades of brown, a strand of gray like the wind. Was the piece of dark blue cloth the Pacific? I shouldn't try to figure it out. You're not supposed to. If you look for something, it's no good. You have to let your-self go. If there's life in the painting, it will hit you.

I tried to empty my mind, but it was reeling. I saw Claire in her coat, her shoulder bag, walking toward the house as if she were under a death sentence.

I wanted to talk to my mother about it. If I spoke, she wouldn't send me away. She'd put down her glue, scissors, brushes, and listen, but her eyes would still be somewhere else for a moment and there might have been a sigh in them. . . .

So I went to my room instead. I left my window wide open that morning on purpose. I was in no rush; I wanted to postpone the moment when I found my favorite view again. I wanted to want it, hold back so I'd enjoy it more.

The first thing you see out my window is the chestnut trees. It was the time of year when they're at their most beautiful, russet, brilliant. Then farther off are the roofs of the village, mostly slate. Soon I'd see nothing but rooftops and sky; as winter came they'd blend together more and more. Sounds match the view: a dog, a rooster, a car going by, loud voices.

Then there's the steeple. When I stare long enough, it seems entwined with a light that could be the hope or desire for God.

I put down my bookbag and went over to the window, a low one because my room is in the attic. To see out, you have to kneel down, lean on the sill, rest your head on your arms, and then you can let yourself go.

But once I got to my window, I saw my father's car slowly pull in. Someone was with him. Oh, Antoine! He got out and shut the gate naturally as if this were his own home. He was wearing a turtleneck, corduroy jacket, stoop-ing slightly, probably because he's so tall.

I was happy to see him, and as if he could feel it, he looked up, saw me in my window, spread his arms, smiled, and bowed deeply.

4

The Soufflé Test

A T first we called him "the substitute." He took over
Daddy's general practice in Pontoise when we left for
California in July. If Bernadette hadn't fallen from her
horse, we'd never have gotten to know him. But fall she
did, we came running back, and Antoine stayed on at the
house until the end of August.

If I thought of him at night with my eyes closed, I saw
his eyes, and they showed all of him: a questioning expression, deep, a mixture of gentleness and harshness. No, not
harsh, demanding. Eyes that look at you but keep to themselves. We really knew practically nothing about Antoine
Delaunay.

He was thirty and living in Paris. He was one of those
rare doctors who still made house calls; he thought they
were part of the job and helped people get well faster. He
believed in the importance of breathing correctly. Most
people, he claimed, are selfish breathers, taking in more air
than they give back, which is bad for everyone. You can
always inhale enough air. The trick is to exhale completely,
sending your spirit into the world.

The day he left us at the end of August to take his own

vacation I felt that something important was leaving with him.

And tonight he was back!

"With some good news," Daddy said.

He looked at us all, eyes shining behind his glasses. Mom smiled, touched to see Daddy so happy and, as always, unable to contain it, like a child. You almost expected to see him start clapping.

We were in the living room. The smell of the soufflé drifted in from the kitchen. Antoine would be staying to dinner. He'd taken his favorite place near the fire, standing by the hassock where I like to sit and watch the flames.

"I've taken a job in Pontoise," he announced.

Cécile gave a whoop and flung herself at him. Bernadette's face lit up. Claire's face showed only astonishment. I was so happy I hardly dared look up.

"Will you be working with Daddy?"

"Part-time," Antoine told us. "I'll be on staff at the Center, too."

We knew he meant the Center for Disturbed Children in Pontoise. Claire looked interested.

"Will you commute from the city?" Mom asked.

Antoine's eyes sparkled.

"Not on your life. I've found an old farmhouse with a huge fireplace and a yard just about the same size."

"Very far from here?"

"Within moped range. Éragny."

Éragny is no more than five miles from La Marette.

"Why?" Bernadette asked abruptly, chin resting on her hand, with a serious expression.

"Do you know how it feels to be fed up with the city? And then fall in love with the Oise, the dusty roads, and the sound of horseshoes?"

"Horseshoes, sure," Bernadette said. "And the rest of it, too, I guess."

"But will you have to live all alone?" asked the Pest.

There was a brief silence. Leave it to Cécile to ask the nosy questions.

Alone? Antoine hadn't had anyone with him in the summer. But that didn't mean nobody was waiting for him in Paris.

He didn't really answer.

"I'm not afraid of being alone. And I'm counting on all of you to keep me company."

"It's a deal," the Pest said.

Claire got up quietly and left the room in a natural way. We were used to it. She suddenly seemed to need more breathing space. Or be called away. That night I wanted to tell her to stay, but I knew it would be no use.

Antoine watched her go.

"Is the house in good shape?" Mom asked.

"Not at all. Hasn't been lived in for years. There are a few sticks of furniture, lots of cracks in the walls, missing windowpanes, but the roof is supposed to be good."

"We'll help you fix it up," Bernadette said.

Then everyone was talking at once. Cécile wanted to wash the ceilings. The part she likes is when you get down from the stepladder and feel dizzy, like you've just been riding around the paddock. Daddy was asking serious questions about the yard. What could he put in the garden?

"Cape primroses," Bernadette suggested.

Even Daddy laughed. He really seemed happy that Antoine would be working in Pontoise. He was certainly hoping he'd spend a lot of time with us. And so was I.

"And what have you done with your Stéphane?" Antoine asked Bernadette.

"We're all going over tomorrow night to ask for his hand in marriage," our equestrienne muttered. "Then he goes into the service."

She was toughing it out, but we could tell she'd miss him.

And we wouldn't feel sorry for her after all the trouble we went to to patch things up between them.

The next night we were invited to a sort of farewell party at the Saint-Aimonds' — Stéphane's parents' — in Neuilly. Townhouse. Old money. Well, we'd see.

"Now I wonder," Antoine teased, "who'll have the real regulation haircut, you or Stéphane?"

Bernadette groaned, running her hand through the thatch on her head. Through the window I saw Claire go by, on her way to the pond. What or whom was she thinking about? Was she asking time to suspend its flight, à la Lamartine, or did she want it to whisk her away? I remembered a conversation she and I had had. Love and passion had no place in Claire's plans. They get in the way of freedom. Was someone threatening that freedom? If so, who?

Mom stuck her head through the kitchen door.

"I'm taking the soufflé out. Time to eat."

"I'll go get the Princess," Antoine said, "and see what's new in the garden."

He was already out of the room, as if afraid someone might stop him. Mom called me to help her. Through the kitchen window, I saw Claire standing by the pond. She didn't even look up when Antoine came to her side. She stood still, looking at the water.

A minute before I had been so happy. Now I felt gray all over, lost, alone. Antoine looked at the water too, speaking to Claire. An autumn garden is such a sad thing. The colors of nostalgia, a stifled cry responding to another distant cry within you. What was he saying to her? Why wouldn't she look at him?

Mom took the risen soufflé out of the oven. I opened the window.

"Hurry up, you two. The soufflé will fall."

They both looked around at the same time. Antoine laughed.

"We're coming."

Cécile was at my side.

"They look good together."

"Do you think so?"

Still, Antoine sat next to me. And as he unfolded his napkin, he whispered: "There's something for you in my new house. Will you come see it?"

"What is it?"

"You'll just have to keep guessing."

I was happy again. The look in his eyes was the one I remembered. Yes, I'd come.

The soufflé test was conclusive. When Cécile went to set the empty soufflé dish on Claire's plate, the Princess pushed it away. No, thanks, she was full.

It didn't necessarily mean anything. After all, there was an unexpected element that night.

A few days before, I'd bought a dress in Pontoise. I was starting to feel less like wearing pants all the time. Daddy would be happy; he was always complaining about our "blue jeans uniform." The dress is a floral print, periwinkle blue, with an old-fashioned gathered yoke. My body feels freer in it. If I'd known Antoine would show up, I would have worn it for the first time that night. I'd even have worn it to school so it wouldn't look like I was all dressed up just for him.

5

A Calendar of Hearts

I fell asleep thinking about Antoine and when I woke up
he was still with me. It wasn't at all like being in love
with Pierre the previous winter. With him everything was
so strong, self-contained, that happiness and pain were in-
terwoven. With Antoine, I felt at peace. No longer at sea, I
was in the harbor. Coming home. At last. I realized that up
to now my whole life had been a kind of waiting. That's
what's so confusing about growing up: all the different
roads you can take. And I still haven't chosen.

Antoine didn't stop by again. I made some discreet in-
quiries. He was moving in! He had two weeks before he
had to start his new job and he was fixing up the house
before he shipped his furniture out from Paris. It's funny. I
couldn't imagine Antoine having furniture. But everybody
needs a bed, and there was no reason why Antoine should
sleep on the floor.

The village nearest his house is called Moutiers. I like the
name. It makes me think of a man with a beard, a solid type,
some kind of craftsman wearing an apron, the kind you
could love like a father but that was all. A nice, kind man.
Must be something I got out of a novel.

I kept making wishes that the weather Saturday would be nice, and I got my wish. Of course it was only an autumn reprieve for the sun, but warm enough so I could dry my hair outside. It's better than a hairdryer. Brings out the highlights.

I washed my hair right after I got up, and I was in my new dress by breakfast time. "Going out with someone?" Cécile asked. I said no, though I'm not sure she believed me. But it was true. No one had asked me anywhere.

I was walking on air all morning. I felt lightheaded, not quite all there. That's probably why I felt I had something to make up to everyone. Mom wondered what had come over me when I grabbed the vacuum cleaner away from her and did the whole downstairs.

I waited until four to say I was going out for a ride. Sometimes I just take off like that. I need a new perspective, room to think about something besides myself. Cécile ran after me. Could she come with? She wouldn't bother me, she'd ride behind.

I turned her down flat, and when I saw her looking so small beside the front gate, holding her old bike, I felt guilty again.

Once I got out of Mareuil, I took the first side road and found a place to pull over and undo my bra. At the Saint-Aimonds' the other night, as we sat on the terrace, I'd felt a wild desire to bare my breasts to the night, the breeze, the season.

I know it's not a particularly original idea and everybody goes braless, starting with my friend Béa jiggling merrily away in her tight sweaters. But for some reason the Moreau sisters still wore bras. Bernadette needed one for riding. Claire had practically nothing to show. And until then I didn't dare not to.

I stuffed the bra in my bag. The wind whipped my dress around me. It told me to unbutton the first few front buttons, and that felt better. I could have ridden like that for hours.

I ran into a wedding party in the village of Moutiers. Some moron was standing in the middle of the street, flapping his arms, trying to make me stop. I had to brake hard. They probably couldn't tell about my bra, but I felt myself blush, and until I turned off the street I hummed to keep myself together. All of a sudden it wasn't fun anymore.

It took me a while to find the house. No one in the neighborhood knew Dr. Delaunay yet, apparently. An old lady had heard a doctor was moving into a house down the road. She was just as glad, and even gladder when I told her what a good doctor he was. I felt like talking to her. I was in no hurry.

The setting wasn't at all what I'd imagined. It was much more like the country than our house. In a tiny yard with a huge field behind it, the house was long and low with square windows and a roof of weathered tile.

The buzz of my motor alerted Antoine. He came out with a big, welcoming smile. He was in shirtsleeves, as I thought he'd be. His jeans were paint-spattered and he was holding a sponge.

"I was sure La Marette would come calling today."

It wasn't La Marette, it was me. Thanks a lot! I leaned my moped against his car and followed him into the yard. My dress was buttoned back up to the neck and I hunched over a little so my breasts wouldn't be too obvious. I noticed that he smelled good. Of the sun, physical labor. Manly. I liked that.

He dropped his sponge.

"You're the first person who's seen this place and your dress is too nice for me to put you to work. So why don't we have some apple juice and then I'll show you around?"

While he went to get the juice I paced the yard, trying to look at things but not really seeing anything, waiting again.

Then Antoine was back, holding a container and two glasses and smiling. He had some kind of dog with him, short-haired, a sickly cream color. It looked naked.

We sat down on a bench set haphazardly in the yard. He filled a glass and handed it to me. His gestures were natural, right: probably the same as if he were all alone. I've always admired people who don't change the way they act just because you're with them. It makes you feel you can depend on them.

After he poured some for himself, he put the juice container down between us. It really did smell like apples. I didn't know where to start the conversation. We'd spent almost three weeks together under the same roof. We'd had talks with him in his pajamas, me in my bathrobe; we'd spoken freely, and now all of a sudden there was this wall between us. Not a wall, but distance, a separation, perhaps because we were in a different setting. New places always take some getting used to.

He showed me around the yard, the house.

"I can hardly believe all this is really mine. I didn't know I'd feel this way about being a homeowner. There's something moving about it. It must be a little like having a child. You feel responsible in a way."

He closed his eyes, breathed deeply. "Let me tell you something else. When I breathe, I feel like the air belongs to me too. Here it's 'my' air."

I laughed. "Selfish breathing, huh?"

The dog came over and put its paw on Antoine's leg, wanting to be petted, as if the dog belonged to him, too.

"I don't know whose dog this is. It comes and spends the day with me."

First Antoine patted its head, between the ears, then its back. Finally, when the dog lay down, he stroked its side.

The best I could come up with was, "I guess you got tired of Paris."

"Paris and everything it represented to me. And know when I realized it for certain? Living at your house this summer. The good life!"

He set his glass on the ground in front of him and stared at it. He looked like a child.

"And look! Being able to set your glass on the lawn whenever you feel like it. . . ."

"Lawn" was stretching it a bit if he meant the few shoots of green pushing up through the gravel. Of course I snickered without meaning to. What I wanted to know was what Paris represented to him.

I finished my apple juice. At least I was doing a little better now. I sat straighter, and if he'd been interested he could have seen I had nothing on under the top of my dress and that I was nervous. But all he did was fill my glass again, though I wasn't a bit thirsty anymore.

"How's school going? Start your philosphy class?"

I told him about our first class. Especially the teacher: a woman of about thirty, small and crisp, who seemed to be on fire, eager to communicate her burning. Maybe that's what philosphy is all about. A different way of burning up your energy. Watching the sparks you make and the way they burst in the universe. Béa and I had summarily taken our places in the first row. I liked the way the teacher talked to us as if each one of us was important, each of us able to learn, understand, feel, do, everything. Sometimes it seemed that her words were lifting the veils from truths that had always been in the back of my mind. They only needed to be brought to light. And how many veiled truths does everyone carry inside forever? And do they have to remain half-hidden?

After the first class, Béa went up to explain her personal philosophy to the teacher. I didn't dare. Mine was still too unclear. First of all, freedom. I wanted it and feared it. I was the prisoner of my fear.

"Prisoner?" Antoine said. "That reminds me. Come see!"

He got up and motioned to me to follow him into the house.

Inside it was dark and cool. The walls were thick old farmhouse walls and the low ceiling reshaped the sound of our words.

"Look at the floor," he said. "That's what made me buy the place."

It was made of soft-colored quarrystone veined with rose and honey. There was also the huge fireplace he'd mentioned. It took up one whole wall. For a minute we breathed in the smell of old stones, the smell of peace.

"Now come on and I'll show you the surprise."

He led me into a small bedroom at one end of the house. There was very old floral paper on the walls and the window was open.

He pointed to one corner: "The bed must have been over there."

I went closer. I imagined an old iron bed with a gilded ball on each bedpost, like the ones at my grandmother's.

At the head of the phantom bed, he showed me something like a calendar that had been drawn around the flowers on the wallpaper. Inside each flower was a heart. Some of them were crossed out, some not.

"Can you tell me what it means?" Antoine asked. "I'm sure you know."

I looked at the crossed-out hearts, the others. It meant waiting. It could mean what I sometimes sensed at night: that the best years of your life, the time for hearts and flowers, can be fretted impatiently away without your really stopping to enjoy it.

I said: "She was waiting."

He smiled. "She?"

"Of course."

"And who was she waiting for?"

"Who knows? You!"

I couldn't manage a laugh. I didn't say anything.

"Why did you think this was something for me?"

He walked away. "In a way this room reminds me of you. And you just mentioned prison. Crossing off days, hearts, is something a prisoner would do. I thought you'd understand it."

The dreadful dog came in, wagging its tail and sniffing around. I walked to the mirror. Why was he telling me all this? For no reason?

The mirror had been soldered to the wall. I suppose that's why it was left in place, while everything else had been removed, even the pictures, or posters, you could tell had been on the walls where the paper was less faded.

I went up to the mirror. I always hope mirrors have a secret spot where they store the image of the people who've looked in them. I saw a young girl like myself. For once she was wearing a dress. She had flyaway hair, but it looked all right. Except she looked a little too hungry, a little too hurried, and unable to say why.

Behind her, I saw Antoine walk up, smiling. My head started to swim. It was the best time of day, as I'd imagined. Outside, the countryside throbbed. I couldn't speak, so I looked at him and called his name.

He put a hand on my shoulder.

"Pauline."

His voice was full of emotion. I leaned against him. I felt his arm tighten around my shoulder. I felt myself being led away.

My legs followed his, but I didn't. *I* was still in the bedroom, watching him walk toward me. Everything was still possible.

The yard, the bench. My glass full of juice was in my hand again, his on the ground. He was telling me how he wanted to fix up the house. White, everything white, wouldn't that look good? With darker trim around the windows and doors like an English cottage. That would make it look warm, comfortable, maybe a little theatrical, but why not? He was counting on me to come help him, and he hoped my sisters would follow, even Claire. She could do the trim.

I heard both of us laugh. The only painting the Princess ever did was with a lipstick brush. He looked straight at me and I thought about the idiotic bra stuffed in my bag. There were only two things I could do: stop on my way home and put it back on, or go straight to my room when I got home. It didn't really matter. I'd lost.

The sky was the color of the wallpaper in the girl's room, the color of the hearts, of everything faded, lost opportunities, foolish notions. The dog was stretched out at Antoine's feet. Once in a while it raised its red-rimmed eyes to him, as if begging for pity.

Walking me out to my moped, he told me in a firm voice how happy he was to have me for a friend. He was very fond of me and hoped I'd feel free to come to him for help if I ever needed it.

Come to him!

6

Aux Délicieuses

AND then it was Sunday. Bernadette was spending the day at the Saint-Aimonds': Stéphane was leaving the next day. Claire said she'd go with me to see the original *King Kong* in the Latin Quarter. I told the Princess that Fay Wray looked like her; she liked that. I'd pay her way. Apparently she'd used up all the Pest's birthday money.

We aimed for the four o'clock show. I like to get to the theater when the house lights are still on and people are finding their seats, talking quietly, expectant. I don't mind the previews. They give you time to get ready for the feature, work up to it. With something to munch on, it's heaven.

There weren't many people on this subway line at that time of day. Even so far into the fall, people leave town for the weekend. And it was hunting season. The sound of gunshots woke me up that morning. At the end of the day, our village café would be full of rifle-toting men with serious faces. Killing is serious business. When the victim puts up a fight, it's more exciting. When it's afraid, the meat tastes even better, I hear. Yuk!

The couple sitting in our car could have been anywhere from forty to sixty. They weren't talking, but looked fairly happy. Used to each other. On another seat was a woman with a little girl who looked too well-behaved, as if she didn't dare move in her immaculate outfit. So there still are little girls like that! Nearest to us was an old lady. I like old people. They're frail and snowy, their faces a pale reflection of their past. I always feel like thanking them for still being around. This particular old lady was very short and occupied a minimum amount of space. She wore a gray herringbone suit. Her shoes looked too big, but it must have been because her ankles were so thin.

Afterwards I'd tell myself I noticed her. I'd remember the details, no matter how quickly I looked her over: gray stockings, the strange chignon stuck all over with combs even though she didn't have much hair. And her old-fashioned handbag. Long and flat with a clasp that goes click. Some of the girls in my class carry bags like that. When they fish for their comb or Kleenex, they seem to be hoping they'll find something extra inside. And one more important detail: on her lap the old lady had a bakery box printed with the name *Aux Délicieuses*.

Claire saw it too and smiled. *Aux Délicieuses*. We'd remember it.

They got on at Duroc. Three of them. With the same sleazy, slicked-back hair that made it seem like they were trying to look ugly. All three wore leather jackets and pointy boots with metal toes. One had his eyes hidden behind dark glasses.

They checked out the car. Chose the old lady. One beside her, two across from her. Near us. As they sat down, I noticed that the one with dark glasses had a chain around his waist. The ends of it dangled between his legs.

The doors closed and the train left the station. The old lady turned her head toward the window, but she could still see them anyway. Subway windows are like mirrors.

I turned to Claire. She gave me a reassuring smile and

looked away. Maybe I was just imagining things, and they'd chosen their seats at random. The other people in the car looked our way. Cautiously. Not really looking us in the eye, just glancing over. The middle-aged woman seemed to draw closer to her husband. The one with the little girl got up almost immediately and stood near the door. Was that really her stop? She held on to her little girl, who turned to look at the newcomers' boots. They looked like weapons; perhaps they were. The woman leaned over the child and she stopped staring. At the back of the car was another man who'd just gotten on; he was reading a newspaper.

I got out my movie guide and looked up *King Kong,* trying to act natural. As if the new passengers were just like anybody else, though I was afraid they weren't. Mustn't egg them on. But when the one with the chain started twirling it, I saw that I wasn't mistaken. They knew we were afraid, and wanted us to be.

Once again I turned to Claire. She stared at the old lady, who still had her face to the window. You could tell how frightened she was by the way she clung to the wall of the car, as if she were trying to disappear. The guy with the chain knew she saw him. He knew she was afraid. He slowly took off his dark glasses and put them in his pocket. His face was very ugly: squashed, slack, and colorless, with two lifeless eyes. Almost hydrocephalic. He must have had a hard time when he was little, but now he was making up for it. He was on top of the situation, the leader of the pack, with his swinging chain and two snickering cohorts.

It was one of them who started it. The whole bottom half of his ashen, sick-looking face was covered and scarred with acne. He pointed to the bakery box.

"Hey, guys, look what Grandma brought us. Nice of her!"

My heart started to thump when he reached out and hooked his finger through the loop of gold cord and lifted up the box marked *Aux Délicieuses*. He didn't stop smiling or eyeing his prey; now she could no longer ignore her seat-mates or conceal her fear, her quivering lips.

"She brought us a treat," the punk continued.

I felt dizzy. I knew I ought to do something for the old lady. I knew I should. I studied the alarm signals. They were all over, on each side of each set of doors. But if I pulled one, what would they do? How long would it take someone to get there? Wouldn't it just make things worse? And they hadn't touched her box yet.

We came to a station, lights, walls plastered with ads. Not many people on the platforms. Suddenly the old lady made her move. She abruptly stood up and without reaching for her box tried to get out. Even said excuse me, I think. Murmured it.

The three punks stretched out their legs to block her way, and the one with the chain started twirling it again.

"I'm sure this isn't your stop, Granny. What's the matter? Scared of us?"

She sat back down and turned to us with eyes pleading "Help!"

The woman and her little girl got off. At the last minute, the middle-aged couple followed suit. I looked at Claire. She didn't budge. She stared at an advertising poster out on the platform. The only other person left in the car was the man behind his newspaper. Two stops left for us, I calculated in a daze. I was aware of every part of my body — my knees pressed tightly together, my hand holding on to the movie guide — as if the three young thugs were staring me down, which was not at all the case.

If either one of us interested them, it was Claire. The pimply one kept looking over at her. She ignored him. No one does it better.

Nobody got on.

The bell signaling that the train would leave the station

was already sounding; now we'd be prisoners again. If only the car were full, everything would have been different.

Just before the doors closed, a boy and girl slipped into the car. They were out of breath, laughing because they'd made it. We took off. I could see the ageless couple on the platform. They'd stopped near the exit and were trying to pick out our car. Would they call for help? Call whom? And what would they tell them? I started to feel desperate. Maybe I should have pulled the alarm. But now it was too late.

The guy who took the box opened it with his stubby fingers. It was full of jelly thumbs. They looked good.

The old lady tried not to look at the cookies. She seemed to have stopped breathing. He held out the box to his buddies, who licked their lips as they took the cookies. Then he offered them to Claire and me. I shook my head. Claire didn't move a muscle. Looked right through them. The awful part was that they seemed to be in no hurry, convinced nobody would get in their way. They were relaxed. Enjoying themselves.

"You don't know what you're missing," the guy with the chain told us, his mouth full. "These cookies are great. Even better than my mother's."

The other two laughed. The fact that he mentioned his mother made me even more frightened. There was no pity in him.

"How about a look at your purse, Granny?" the third one suggested.

He hadn't said anything yet and I was hoping he'd be different from the other two. He was the only normal-looking one, I mean not outstandingly ugly. But his voice was horrible: the voice of someone words couldn't touch.

The teenagers who had just gotten on took in the scene: the hunched-over old lady, the three guys, the two of us. I tried to catch their eye, but it was too late. The boy took the girl's hand and they walked to the other end of the car. They didn't sit down; they'd be getting off at the next stop.

Now the old lady's purse was on the chain-twirler's lap. She tried to say something but couldn't get the words out. She reached out. They laughed. Their outstretched legs, six identical denim-sheathed legs, completely blocked her path.

Claire got up. I did the same. My body wasn't my own. It was wooden. And my head was buzzing. "You've got to do something," I kept saying to myself. But I kept putting it off until later, in a while, in a minute, the very next thing.

I always thought that if I saw someone being attacked I'd help. But had they actually attacked her? For the time being, she hadn't even been touched. The jelly thumbs were no big deal. They'd give back her purse. They were just fooling around. If someone tried to interfere, it might get worse.

This wasn't our stop; it was the next one. Would Claire get off? She didn't head for the door. She looked at the old lady and I could see her concentrating.

Then it was the station, the posters, the people who wouldn't help us.

The teenage couple got off. We didn't. A few people got on. They looked in our direction, seemed to sense something wrong and without undue haste, so it wouldn't look obvious, settled in the other end of the car.

Some people relate their experience saying, "It was like a nightmare." It wasn't like a nightmare. Quite the opposite. I was taken, bound, plunged into reality.

Why did Claire get up if she wasn't planning to get off? The train left the station. This time the next stop would be ours.

They finished going through the purse. Looked disappointed. A ten-franc note, her identification, a letter. The pimply-faced guy pointed to the old lady's earlobes.

"Check this out, guys. Think they're the real thing?"

They were two small pearls. They looked like they were

part of her flesh; must have been there forever. When the kid reached out as if to yank at them, the old lady squirmed away, frantic. She put her hands over her ears. They laughed.

"Leave her alone," Claire said.

They weren't expecting it. An order. Ice-cold. When Claire uses that tone of voice, we all know it's no use contradicting her. Then there were her eyes: piercing blue, blue contempt. Something fantastic flickered in her eyes, a breath of hope. I'll never forget her expression. The other people in the car heard her, they had to. Claire spoke up so they could. But everyone stared out the windows.

Claire said, "Leave her alone," then did something else they weren't expecting: calmly picked up the purse and held her hand out to the old lady.

"Come on. We're getting off."

She didn't give the three punks another look. For them it was all over in her book. They weren't worth noticing.

They looked at one another with sickly smiles. The one with the chain had cookie crumbs at the corner of his mouth. I was standing near the door. I should have gone back, shown I was with Claire, but I hoped beyond hope they'd just let the two of them get off.

The old lady did get up, looking at Claire, who smiled encouragement. But the three boys got up at the same time. The box fell to the floor, the jelly thumbs scattered.

"Just look what you've done to Granny's cookies," the one with the grating voice said to Claire. "She's going to be mad about this."

As if she hadn't heard, Claire reached for the old lady's hand again and said, "Come on."

Now all three of them faced my sister. They looked her over from head to toe, the way they'd seen TV bad guys do.

"I didn't hear her ring for you," the pimply one said. "She's staying with us. She likes being around the younger generation. You go ahead and get off if you want to. No one's stopping you."

The old lady fell back in her seat. She was crying. They looked at her and laughed. That was when Claire said it. She looked each one of them right in the eye, clear and direct, and spat it out:

"You little creeps. You make me sick."

Everything happened fast after that. A fist flew toward her face, my sister's face. A girl who could only be Claire grasped for the seatback, slowly fell into a heap they rammed with their pointy boots.

I screamed, "Stop, stop it!" They didn't even hear me. They beat her. Couldn't they see that she was pretty, delicate, wouldn't hurt a fly? Everyone in the car stayed clear. So did I. Claire's skirt was up around her waist, showing everything. The old lady howled in a strange, high voice. What was happening was simply impossible. Like death. I planned to do something. That minute. Right away. But then it was too late. They were gone.

And people ran out on the platform, yelling for the conductor to wait, stay in the station. I heard the words "Help. Someone hurt." People crowded around to see. It's amazing how many people there actually were in the subway. I crouched beside Claire; she'd uncurled herself but looked dazed. I pulled her skirt down. There was blood on her face. I was afraid they might have hurt her with the metal tips of their boots. There was a ton of bricks in my throat. It was so painful. Just a thin stream of air whistled in.

Two men helped Claire get up and practically carried her to the row of seats on the platform, where they made her lie down. She was very pale. Blood seeped from the corner of her eye, her mouth. They asked her if it hurt anywhere. "Over here, kind of," she said, pointing to her side. She seemed to have trouble talking, as if she were chewing something. "She may have broken bones," someone said. "Is there a doctor around?"

There were no doctors. The old lady sat down next to my sister, took Claire's head in her lap the way old ladies do in movies. She took a handkerchief out of her bag and dabbed at Claire's face. She kept repeating, "She saved me. She saved me, you know," as if she still couldn't believe it. To Claire she crooned, "Don't move, dear, just lie still." Her tears came and went.

Now everyone was talking. Now everyone wanted to do something. And it had been so silent in the car for those last three stops. They took the box of cookies, rifled her purse, toyed with the old pearls anchored in her ears . . . how heavy the silence was, until Claire.

The word *ambulance* was mentioned. Claire tried to sit up. She said, "No, don't bother," but she obviously wasn't all right. She was trembling all over. A man covered her with his jacket.

I didn't see the train pull out, but now there was another one, and I saw all the faces staring out at us. *They* were still safe in thinking they would have done something.

"Do you know her?"

The question was addressed to me. I answered, "She's my sister." I felt ashamed to be intact. I was still clutching the movie guide. Hadn't even lost my place.

Claire's eyes searched for me. I wondered if she'd ever forgive me. She made a face; I think she was trying to smile. I leaned over. In her muddled voice she ordered, "Call Daddy. He's got to come. Understand? He has to. I've got something important to tell him."

❧ 7 ❧

Emergency for Charles

THE phone rang at least ten times before Cécile answered. I asked for Daddy. Of course she knew who it was, but she said, "He's outside. May I take a message?" I said no. She prodded, "What's going on? Aren't you supposed to be at the movies?" I mustered all my strength to say, "Please just go get him, and hurry." I heard her breathe. I felt her waver. I repeated, "Hurry up!" Finally she said, "Okay."

I heard the thud of the receiver being set down and her voice yelling, "Daddy, Daddy, it's Pauline. Hurry!" She must have been yelling out the window. Then she was scurrying down the steps and running through the yard. And where was Mom? I hoped she wouldn't pick up the phone. I wanted my father. Cécile was running in the yard, in the peaceful sway of autumn. Cécile was galloping in happiness.

Words crowded in my head, my throat. First I'd say, "It's nothing serious, don't get upset." I'd say . . .

Daddy's voice: "Hello?"

He was out of breath. He must have run, too. Maybe Cécile was beside him. And Mom?

I stammered, "Claire . . ."

"Yes," he says. "What is it?"

But I couldn't go on. Everything that had built up inside me during those terrible moments in the subway came rushing into my throat, damming up the words I wanted to say. It was from hearing my father's voice, seeing La Marette. No one there knew yet.

"Hello, Pauline?"

I tried again, but only a kind of croak came out. Great! He probably thought she was dead. But it was also from telling myself nothing would ever be the same. Ever.

"Calm down," the voice on the other end said. "Take a deep breath. Take your time. What's happened to Claire?"

Of course his "take a deep breath" nearly made me strangle. But there was so much concern in his "what's happened?" that I managed to squeeze out a "nothing serious." My knuckles turned white as I stumbled through the rest of it: subway, old lady, hoods.

"Can you tell me exactly what's wrong with her?"

"She lost a tooth. They think she swallowed it. And she probably has a couple of broken ribs. But she wants to see you right away. She has something important to tell you. That's the first thing she said when it was over. It's urgent."

There was a silence when I finished. Then in a calm voice my father said, "I'll be right there. And stop worrying. Cochin is an excellent hospital. All right?"

"All right."

I hung up. The old lady was waiting for me in the hall. Everyone thought she was our grandmother, so no one said a thing when she got into the ambulance with us, still holding on tight to Claire's hand. Her name was Louise. She'd be seventy-nine in three days. She was a great-grandmother. The raspberry jelly thumbs were a treat for her great-grandchildren. She went to the phone now to call her son, a journalist.

We waited for him outside the emergency wing where they'd taken Claire. Walkways with no memory led to the hospital's various buildings. Everything was still and uniformly gray, but even here you could tell it was Sunday: something in the air.

A man of about Daddy's age approached us. He was short, with a beard and glasses. He looked anxious. He hopped along like a bird.

As he held her, the old lady broke down again. He didn't let go of her to shake my hand. "What happened?"

"Three men attacked her in the subway."

Between her sobs, she kept repeating, "Nobody moved! Nobody lifted a finger! As if they were all blind." She kept asking me to agree: "Wasn't it? Isn't that right?"

It seemed she didn't lump me in with the cowards because my sister had acted.

We went back to the small waiting room. I remember seeing some vials of blood on a counter. After a minute a nurse came to get us. We could go see her now: Room 42. The X rays showed she had two broken ribs. That was all besides the tooth and quite a few contusions. Nothing serious. She'd been given a shot and bandaged up. She'd just taken a tranquilizer. We mustn't tire her out.

There was another woman in the room, gray hair, eyes closed, sick-looking. From her pillow, Claire watched us coming up to her bedside. She was wearing a stiff white gown like something from an orphanage. Her left eye was swollen shut, her upper lip had puffed up even more. Her left cheek was turning several different colors.

The first thing she said was, "Daddy?"

"He's on his way."

She sighed deeply.

The old lady introduced her son. He took Claire's hand and simply said, "Thank you." It was a profound thank you. He tried to make it say all he felt.

The Princess answered with her eyes, or rather her eye.

She seemed less alert than in the subway. Maybe it was the tranquilizer. Or the hospital gown.

She pointed to her purse.

"Hand me my mirror."

It was a tiny one, luckily. She could only see portions of the damage. First she looked at her eye, then her mouth.

"In two weeks," the old lady's son said, "you'll be good as new."

How could he know that she considered it her duty to be as beautiful, as perfect as possible down to the last detail? She repeated "two weeks" as if it were the end of the world, and asked me to brush her hair. I went very slowly so I wouldn't hurt her.

The woman in the other bed was awake now and looked at us as if she'd known us forever, or rather as if she didn't see any difference between us and anyone else. There was one question I had to ask Claire, an important one for me. I waited until the old lady was talking to her son.

"Were you scared?"

She looked over at the window and I knew she was seeing the three punks, their boots, the chain.

"To death," she said.

I was hoping against hope she'd say no.

I went back outside to watch for Daddy but mostly because I was smothering.

There were a few people on the walkways. Visitors and patients. Two girls strolled arm in arm. Their wrinkled nightgowns hung below their bathrobes; their hair was messy. They seemed to have given up on appearances, and I saw that as the final proof that the hospital was removed from real life.

I also saw a young man in a wheelchair. He stopped just below the hips. He was smoking and laughing with his friends. What struck me the most, for some reason, was that he'd let his beard grow. It seemed like with no legs it wasn't worth the trouble.

I spotted my parents a long way off. Mom had come too. They parked the car. Daddy literally jumped out. He was still in his gardening clothes.

"How is she?"

I told them about her ribs and the tooth. I had trouble getting it out. They walked ahead of me toward Claire's wing, almost breaking into a run. Did I know which doctor she was assigned to? I couldn't remember.

When we got to her room, the old lady and her son stood up. The other patient was gone.

Our parents went to Claire's bedside. She looked at them, breathing carefully. Mom touched her forehead to the backrest. Daddy wore a changed expression, one of tenderness and concern. I stopped feeling sorry for the Princess. Not the tiniest bit of pity. I resented her being there instead of me. That was all.

Charles finally found his voice: "So you won't even let your old Dad just spend all day Sunday in his garden?"

Claire sighed gingerly and looked at the ceiling. Now Mom was having a good look at her, the bandages, the streaks of antiseptic, the mottled bruises. And she smiled gamely.

"I'm sorry," the Princess said in her pathetic voice.

"Silly goose," Daddy muttered, and bent over to kiss her.

We'd completely forgotten the old lady. She came over and started her spiel again.

I'd just about had it. In the subway I felt sorry for her, with her heavy stockings, cookies, pearls encrusted in her earlobes. But now it was all over. She'd been rescued. She might have had the tact to leave the family alone.

Her son got her to go. Before she left, she came back to take Claire's hand.

"Is it all right if I come to see you?"

"Anytime, as long as it's not in the subway," the Princess answered.

As he ushered his mother out, the son said mysteriously that we'd be hearing from him.

"Does it hurt?" Mom asked when they'd shut the door behind them.

"A little, when I breathe. But not much. I'm not supposed to cough or laugh."

"I'm going to try to find the doctor who took care of you," Daddy said. "I'd like to have a look at those X rays."

He was almost to the door when Claire stopped him.

"Daddy!"

There was something new in her voice. My heart stopped. I knew this was going to be serious. What was it she said in the subway? "I need to see him right away. I have something important to tell him."

It took her a long time to get it out. Daddy waited by the door, uncomprehending. She sighed as she sometimes will, resigning herself to fate. But not too deeply because of her bandaged chest.

"Okay. I did get kicked in the stomach, so I think I'd better tell you. I'm pregnant."

8

It Never Rains . . .

DADDY froze, goggle-eyed, as if expecting the burst of laughter that usually followed a good joke. It didn't come. Claire studied her left hand; one of the nails had been chipped and she had trimmed it. Mom was floored. She slowly lowered herself onto a chair. There was an immense silence. And as they always do when one of us pulls something on them, our parents turned on the innocent bystander — me, in this instance — as if she must be in on the prank and should have warned them.

I wasn't in on it. I hadn't suspected a thing and I couldn't believe it, either, but suddenly everything was clear to me. The dark circles under Claire's eyes, Cécile's birthday money, the trip into the city. So it *was* love after all. Cécile was right. But maybe not the Lamartine variety.

Daddy practically dragged himself back to her bedside.

"Pregnant? What on earth . . ."

Another resigned sigh from the bed.

"Are you sure?"

"I had a test."

"How far along?" Mom asked in a very small voice.

"Six weeks."

America. California. Jeremy. A lot of good it did her to visit the home of the Pill.

Claire closed her good eye. She seemed almost relieved. It must have been hard keeping it to herself. But to lay it on them that day . . . it never rains but it pours.

I pictured her on the floor of the subway car, curled up in a ball. To protect her baby? The Princess's baby. I felt like laughing. The Little Prince!

Now Daddy was at the window, in his funny old pants that were flared at the hips and pegged at the ankles, out of fashion for ages.

He turned abruptly and paced back to Claire's bedside, his face a grimace.

"You're pregnant and you don't even tell us."

He could barely keep his voice from shaking. The color of his face showed what an effort it was to control himself. Even his neck was turning red.

"I haven't decided what to do about it," Claire said.

"What do you mean by that?"

"You know what I mean."

She spoke evenly and seemed a little distant. The tranquilizer, I thought. Everything must have seemed fuzzy to her. It would have been funny if she'd fallen asleep.

Mom had apparently come to her senses. "Jeremy?" she asked.

"I don't see who else it could be," Claire answered with a little smile.

"Maybe you think it's funny, but I don't," said Daddy.

I did. There's one thing for sure: if you lose your sense of humor in a situation like this, you've had it.

Once again there was an immense silence. Words were too small.

Claire opened her eyes again. Her eye.

"A basin," she groaned. "I'm going to be sick."

There was a second's panic, then Mom dashed into the

bathroom while Daddy pressed a button near the bed that turned on the lights but didn't ring for anyone.

"Try to hold it in, honey," Mom said as she brought Claire a receptacle clearly destined for another use. "It'll hurt if you cough too much."

Claire stared in revulsion at the object now being held under her chin, as if she didn't know what made her feel sicker. Daddy seemed torn between anger and pity. He looked at Mom as though she was from another planet. It was the way she said "honey." The way she'd already accepted the situation. Claire was pregnant. Fine. Bring her a basin.

"We can talk about all this later," she said. "Don't you think she ought to be examined again now?"

"Obviously," Daddy said. "I'll see to it."

"Not you. Please!" the Princess bleated.

We all hate having Daddy examine us. Even Mom. We really have to be at death's door, our defenses down, before we let him.

"Don't worry," he said. "I have no intention of assessing the damage."

We could tell what he meant by damage. From the doorway he wheeled around, took in all three of us with one wounded look. As if he really felt we'd ganged up on him.

"Sometimes," he said, "I wonder if abstinence wouldn't have been better."

With these kind words, obliterating our existence, from Mom on down, he flung open the door and found himself face to face with the icing on the cake. Antoine!

I'll never forget Antoine's face. Stern with worry. He looked right through Daddy. He brushed past him and headed straight for the bed. He bent over Claire, scrutinized her, breathed her in, devoured her with his eyes. Then he lowered his lids and it was as if only then could he catch his breath. It all took a few seconds. Then, in a voice that didn't sound like him, deep and rough, he said, "Clever!

Very clever to be brave like that. Defending old ladies when no one else will."

Daddy was back in the center of the room. Claire looked at him, wild-eyed but demanding. It was easy to guess what she was asking for. She didn't want Antoine to know what she'd just announced. About the blessed event, as it's called when it happens in wedlock. If not, replace "blessed" with "blasted."

"Clever," Antoine repeated.

"It was the only thing I could do," Claire murmured.

Antoine's expression softened. He leaned even closer to her. For a minute I thought he was going to kiss her, but he settled for gently brushing his fingers across her cheek. There was still no one else in the room for him.

Daddy had to clear his throat for Antoine to realize he wasn't alone with Claire. He straightened up and gave us a strange look, almost triumphant, as if to say, "I've been telling you all along what a wonderful girl she is!" Then he started barraging Charles with questions.

"Did they take X rays? Who was her doctor? What about a tetanus shot? Are you sure they did everything right?" I forget the rest.

Daddy answered: the tooth, ribs, shock. Antoine went back to the heroine's bed and ordered her to open her mouth. She protested, saying it would hurt her side. He didn't give in. He studied the hole and promised she'd get a magnificent new tooth. She'd look even better than before.

Claire's breathing was shallow.

"How did you find out?" Mom asked Antoine.

The Pest, of course. He'd stopped by the house to say hello, found Cécile in tears. The way she talked, the Princess must be dead. That reminded him. We were supposed to call her right away. He'd promised.

I went out to call. Down the hall, down, down. I felt as if I'd lost something. I was empty, nothing but air. I dialed without thinking. Cécile must have been waiting by the phone because she answered before I even heard it ring. She made me promise not to spare her feelings, to tell her everything.

I told her to dress for the funeral. That calmed her down. When I'd filled her in on everything, except the most important part, she told me Madame Tavernier was there, yes, in Daddy's chair. She'd just called her sister the nun in Angoulême. I could tell Claire the whole convent was praying for her.

Cécile wanted to know more but I couldn't go through it again. I told her she could call Bernadette at the Saint-Aimonds'. She could tell the whole world for all I cared.

When we were through, I dialed Béa's number. She was there. I asked her if I could invite myself over to spend the night. No problem. In fact, it was a good idea, since she felt like staying home. She'd be there when I got there. If I really wanted to, we could go to the movies. *"King Kong?"* She didn't understand what made me laugh. Until I cried.

Only Claire and Mom were left in the room when I got back. Antoine and Daddy had gone out looking for the doctor, the X rays, all that. Mom was holding the Princess's hand.

"Do doctors have to withhold confidential information from one another?" Claire asked anxiously.

"Of course," Mom said. "I don't see why your father would go telling Antoine our secret."

I took note of the "our." I said I was going over to spend the night at Béa's. Mom didn't object. She understood I needed to get away. They'd certainly spend a while longer at the hospital, where Claire was to be held overnight.

Claire looked at me. I went over to kiss her. On the spot Antoine had stroked so tenderly. She smelled antiseptic. I sensed she had something to say to me, but I didn't give her time to.

As I walked toward the door, Mom remembered that I had been in the subway car, too.

"Are you sure you're all right?"

I answered yes with a smile. She could see that I was fine. I had all my teeth, no broken bones, and as far as I knew I was not expecting. Quite all right.

"We'll see you tomorrow, then."

"See you tomorrow."

I ran until the hospital was out of sight. I was running away from what had brought us there. People were walking a Sunday walk, slower, wearing a freer expression. Nobody knew. I sat down on a bench and closed my eyes. I couldn't read my feelings anymore. I was scared. Guilty. Then Antoine swept everything else aside. All I could see were his eyes, his concern, his hand on Claire's cheek. Now I felt nothing but jealousy, rage, an overwhelming powerlessness. I was the one he should have looked at like that, his face strained to the point of harshness: the face you wear at crucial moments. Something like Pierre's face just before we made love for the first time. A face I'll never forget.

He loved her! For him I only counted in terms of her. When I'd gone over to see him, he was seeing her. I was ready to love him. He'd treated me like a child. A glass of apple juice. Thank you, Doctor!

I got up. Well, Claire was pregnant. Claire wasn't free. And that was that.

❧ 9 ❧

The Courageous 1 Percent

*I*T was sunny at Béa's. She greeted me in a Japanese kimono. The color went with her hair, her still-tanned
skin. There were circles under her eyes. She must have been
up until all hours again. Béa does as she pleases. She doesn't
have to answer to anyone.

Right away she guessed that something had happened.
She sat me down on the big bed her parents will never share
again, the bed where they made her, as she likes to put it.
By chance. Or maybe luck.

We stretched out on the guanaco spread. The guanaco is
a wild llama with very soft fur. It's even nicer to be on it
than under it. Rolling up in it naked is heaven, I'm told.

I'd promised myself I'd say as little as possible, but it all
came pouring out. Minus Claire's pregnancy, of course. Minus Antoine. They got into our car. I knew right away. I
froze. . . .

They could have killed the old lady and Claire, and I still
wouldn't have done anything. I kept telling myself "in a
while." If I'd been alone, I would have gotten off at the first
possible stop like the other people did. And I still hadn't
told her the worst part: that when they offered us the cookies, I turned them down with a smile.

Lying on her back, arms behind her head, Béa listened silently. To her credit, she knows when not to talk.

When I was finished, she turned to me, her kimono opening to reveal just about everything.

"What's the big deal? In a situation like that, you either can or can't act. That's the way it is. There's the kind of person who jumps off bridges to save someone from drowning, or runs into burning buildings. And then there are the others. You're one of the others. You acted the way ninety-nine percent of all people do. It's nothing to get all worked up about."

"What about you? What would you have done?"

"I'll tell you when I've been through it myself."

Still, she thought it over. Her forehead wrinkled. "Off the top of my head, I think I just would have wiped them out."

The expression made me laugh.

"But not right away," she sighed.

She went to get a bottle of Muscadet and some *crème de cassis* to celebrate my resurrection. With the dry white wine and black currant liqueur we made ourselves two huge *kirs*. I was in the 99 percent who stayed on the bridge or outside the burning building. The cowardly 99 percent. I felt lighter now that I'd admitted it, now that I knew. I could live with myself. What I didn't want was to go home, not tonight, not tomorrow. I didn't want to be with the other 1 percent, with the congratulations, the shiner, missing tooth, tender gazes.

I felt good at Béa's. In a sort of no man's land. Or rather a free country. That's how it was in her apartment. I didn't bump into memories every few feet. No hints of my child-hood lurked here. The objects told only their own stories. Just a few well-furnished, livable rooms with a view on the sun-filled Luxembourg gardens. You could convince your-self that the strangers strolling below had the same feelings as you but didn't make a federal case out of it. And it was an apartment with no parents. With parents, there's no way you can feel completely innocent.

In short, after two *kirs* I loved the place, Béa, the relaxed way she displayed her anatomy. I saw it as proof positive of her freedom.

We decided to have dinner in front of the TV, no matter what was on. She lent me a kimono. She was in command, and I didn't mind at all. She could tell I didn't, and laid it on thick. "Move over. Take this pillow. Finish the salad."

At times Béa's gestures seemed masculine, a bit brusque, sudden, decisive. So that you wanted her to soften them for you. She also had a masculine way of brushing aside the unimportant details girls sometimes attach too much importance to. It may have been my emotional state, but I was lost in strange thoughts, as if the day had opened a new door to me.

I told myself it wouldn't take much for my friendship with Béa to turn into something else, for me to want her to love me as a man would, somehow stronger. That night there was just a thin line that a move from either one of us could have broken through. And instead of making me feel guilty, the thought filled me, I'm not sure why, with a sort of happiness.

The positive thing was all the different paths I was starting to sense, branching off from the road I was supposed to follow. For so long I'd thought it was the only one. One more *kir,* please!

Of course, in a way it hurt a little to discover there's no one straight line, that we go forward trembling, blindly or wearing blinders, crossing fragile bridges suspended high above us, above all our possibilities. But how amazing it is to be moving along, carrying both your own sunlight and night inside you.

I could have said "your own courage and cowardice," but after my third *kir* I decided all that was behind me now.

The Tea Party

*B*UT only temporarily. It was back when I woke up, though I didn't want to talk about it. I had a headache and everything was gray, including the sky. I would have had a hard time expressing my feelings, but my life had changed. It went deeper than the guilt over not doing anything, the jealousy of Claire for doing what I should have. My anger had ebbed. This morning I only felt very tired and a little sick. I think I'd had enough of myself. That was all.

Béa and I ate breakfast together. In silence. When you've aired all your feelings, the next day there's nothing left to say.

All we had was instant coffee and some stale toast. Béa can't get anything down until she's had her first five or six cigarettes. That depresses me. Breakfast is important: the first step into the day. Skipping it gets you off to a bad start.

At school I had to manage without my books and notes. Monday isn't a hard day. The teachers are perfectly aware that we're good for nothing after the weekend, so they assign the most work for Tuesday and Thursday. By Friday we're already thinking about the weekend again.

At any rate, it seemed ridiculous to be there calculating vectors or learning that in 1969 there were six goats per capita in south Kazakstan, when a few hundred yards away there are creeps with metal-toed boots cruising around, frightening old ladies and giving you a chance to prove you're a coward.

Everything my teachers said went in one ear and out the other. Now all I wanted to do was get back to La Marette.

I got off my moped before the gate to the house, which I closed quietly behind me.

What I wanted most of all, the way you crave a cool drink of water when you're thirsty, was to walk alone for a while before I saw anyone. I felt like I was coming back from a trip. It always takes a minute to feel at home.

I walked out under the tall trees. The yard was like a fresh burn, red with leaves and with pain, at the foot of the house with its scarlet honeysuckle bushes. Beautiful as it was, it was still a last gasp. Nothing could be done to stop it. And much as I love them, I resented the big, calm trees, the tranquil lawn, the walkway, the breeze with its scents I know by heart, everything that once protected me but could no longer offer shelter from the world that existed beyond the gate.

I heard someone running up behind me. Cécile.

"I saw you come in."

"I guess you did."

She had on a long plaid shirt, the latest fashion. She must have traded something of her own for it at school. Mom can't keep track of her wardrobe. Half of it is stuff she gets from other girls, and she doesn't usually come out ahead in the deal.

I kept walking. She tried to look at my face.

"Were you really afraid?"

She wasn't saying it to taunt me; she simply needed to know, as if she wished she'd been there instead of me.

"Of course I was," I said very naturally, with a shrug

of the shoulders that could have passed for bravery.

"So was I," she said, "respectively."

"You mean *retro*spectively."

I turned around and as we headed back to the house she told me about the Princess's homecoming.

When Bernadette told them what had happened, the Saint-Aimonds offered the use of their car. Daddy was on call at Pontoise, so he took them up on it.

It was a sight to behold: the chauffeur opening Claire's door, doffing his cap and respectfully placing the plastic bag containing the Princess's soiled garments in the trunk. Madame de Saint-Aimond was waiting with a bouquet of flowers.

The flowers were on the breakfront now. Claire was lying on the couch, Bernadette sitting cross-legged on the floor next to her. I still couldn't believe my sister was pregnant. And Bernadette and Cécile still didn't know.

I learned that the police had come to question Claire in the hospital that morning. It seemed she gave a very vague description of the three guys and refused to press charges.

"So they'll be able to go out hunting again next Sunday," Bernadette said, "and I hope they really bag someone next time."

"You mean you would have told on them?" Cécile asked reproachfully.

"You bet I would've," said Bernadette. "They ought to be put away. When you have a nasty horse, you break it. Because if you waste your time finding out about its grand-sire and trying to sweet-talk it out of being mean, before you know it you're knocked for a loop."

"Well, what if society made them turn bad?" Cécile continued.

"If you don't mind, just let us defend ourselves while we're waiting for you to build us a society where everyone is rich and well-behaved."

Cécile was wearing her left-wing expression. I didn't

know what to say. I didn't feel I had the right to say anything.

"And all those jerks in the car who looked the other way," Bernadette scolded.

There was an unbearable silence. My heart thudded.

"Like me."

All three of them turned on me. That squeaky voice couldn't have been mine.

"You stayed by me," Claire said.

"Big help."

"More than you think."

"I didn't lift a finger."

"I'm glad you didn't. The only thing I was afraid of was that you'd make a move. Where do you think that would have gotten us?"

Bernadette stared at her shoes. Cécile seemed to wonder what I was getting at.

"Well, it would have gotten *me* somewhere. How do you think I feel?"

And I left the room. I had nothing more to add. Besides, I couldn't have said anything.

I went into the kitchen and drank a big glass of water. Two. At first I could hardly get it down. Had to gulp. Now that I'd said my piece, I felt both relieved and hopeless.

The door opened but it wasn't any of them; it was Mom. She was carrying groceries. I whispered hello and went to the window to look out at the yard.

She put the bag down on the table.

"How was Béa's?"

"Great."

The water hadn't helped my voice any. Mom came to my side. I turned away.

"What's the matter, honey?"

She'd said "honey" to Claire yesterday after she told us she was expecting. What to expect . . .

"I can't take it."

One: not being able to keep from crying. My tears seemed to be on the tip of my eyelids. Two: being so colorless, inconsistent. In school we studied about ego and superego. But I had no personality. If I did, I'd be braver. Three: I couldn't take Claire.

Mom was over looking out the window with me. She smelled good. I liked the way she was dressed, like us, in jeans, a shirt, a crewneck sweater. At first she didn't say anything. I squinted over at her. She looked a little worse for the wear. There were circles under her eyes. Just what I needed.

"How about some tea?"

While she lit the fire under the kettle, I got out two cups.

"Last winter in Pontoise," she said, "I saw a boy attacked at knifepoint by two others. Right across the street from me."

Sugar, milk, two spoons. Mom scalded the teapot. Steam rose to the ceiling.

"I kept telling myself it must be somebody they know. As if that meant I shouldn't do something."

"Did they kill him?"

"They left him on the sidewalk. Some people came by and got him up. When I saw he could walk, I went the other way. And that was all."

Bernadette came in, frowning. She barely looked at us, opened the refrigerator, took out a beer, opened it, sat down, and waited.

The kettle was already whistling. Mom put three spoons of loose tea in the pot. I poured some milk in the cups.

"Two sugars for the ladies, as usual, I suppose," Bernadette said, putting it in the cups for us.

Cécile came in next. She looked at the three of us, sat resolutely down next to Bernadette, and stole a sip of her beer.

Mom poured the water into the teapot.

When Claire walked in, holding herself stiffly, Bernadette gave her the captain's chair with the rush seat, the one we sit in when we're studying and watching something on the stove at the same time.

"What's going on?"

"They were talking about you," Cécile said, "about yesterday and everything."

Mom poured our tea.

"I was thinking," she murmured, and her low voice matched her face, "that all you hear about these days is violence. And yet no mother is sure what she should tell her daughter to do in a situation like the one you were in."

Bernadette didn't say anything. Cécile looked at Mom, shocked.

"But aren't you glad she let them have it?"

Mom's eyes closed for a second.

"I think so."

Her voice wavered. She seemed to be saying it in spite of herself.

"If you can't say no," Claire spoke up, "even if no one else in the world goes along with you, then life isn't worth living."

And she added, "I always feel like saying no."

We were still thinking over her unexpected statement when she went on:

"And besides, they were just too ugly, with their greasy hair, their clown boots, and their gang outfits. I can't stand guys like that."

She wasn't finished yet.

"When I was little, Jelly thumbs were my favorite cookies."

She looked so serious that we couldn't even be sure whether or not we were supposed to laugh. Cécile was practically choking with laughter. Claire had put her life on the line for jelly thumbs.

At that point Daddy appeared.

He stopped in the kitchen doorway, amazed to find this late-afternoon tea party, before he set the open newspaper down on the table. Right away we spotted the article in a red box.

"It happened yesterday, Sunday afternoon, in the subway. A young woman . . ."

There were two columns. Two columns of praise, a paean to the young woman's bravery and beauty. Claire's modest expression showed us it affected her. The article was signed "L.B.": Laurent Boyer, the old lady's journalist son.

"He thought you'd rather not have your name mentioned," Daddy said.

"Too bad," said Claire.

A funny thing happened after dinner. As always, Cécile put her horrible orthodontic retainer down on the table. As always, Daddy told her to get it out of his sight, and she covered it with her piece of bread. She'd been wearing the disgusting thing for a month by then, and it was turning up in the strangest places: on the mantelpiece, the bookshelves, and once in the middle of the fruit bowl.

The Pest's teeth are too big for her mouth, so they're trying to fix them. The dentist will never forget her first appointment. She opened wide, but when he got his fingers inside her mouth she bit him. Drew blood. Fortunately he was a friend of the family. He said it was one of the risks of the job.

So Cécile hid her retainer under a piece of bread, along with her chewing gum. And when the table was cleared, it was nowhere to be found.

It had to be in the garbage. As luck would have it, Bernadette had just emptied the kitchen garbage into the large trash bag in the garbage can out back.

Apparently the retainer wasn't worth much, but the fitting had taken several appointments with Dr. Dutil, the dentist Daddy's friend had referred her to. It's a long trip to his office. Time is money. So we hauled the trash bag onto the grass and started looking for the thing.

I held a napkin under my nose. Mom put on plastic gloves, and Bernadette used the silver sugar tongs. Daddy, still in his hospital clothes, stayed to one side. From the window, holding her nose, the Princess said she'd like to help us but with her ribs she really shouldn't.

The skeletons of yesterday's fish dinner were tricky; Cécile yelled "I've got it" at least ten times, but she didn't have it. The more we dug, the more odors we uncovered, but no retainer. Daddy protested loudly when his beloved velvet slippers appeared, covered with spaghetti. Poor Mom had decided to sneak them into the garbage the day before despite the fact he warned her not to throw them out.

Finally, just as the Taverniers started coming through the yard to see what was going on, we found it, still stuck to Cécile's chewing gum.

Afraid she'd lose it again, Cécile shoved the whole mess back in her mouth. Daddy covered his eyes. We didn't notice until the next day that the silver sugar tongs were missing. But by then it was too late. The garbage men had done their job.

❦ *II* ❧

The Choice

I went up to my room. I stopped in the doorway and looked at yesterday.

Yesterday, I threw those pants on the bed next to my open book. Yesterday, I set the books I'd need to study after dinner on my worktable. Yesterday, only yesterday, I held that brush and debated whether to wear my hair in a ponytail or a twist to go see *King Kong* with my sister.

Not for a minute did I doubt I'd be back in my room that very evening. Not for a second did I imagine that the bed would stay empty, the book unread, the homework in drydock. It was a Sunday like any other. And yet, somewhere in Paris, three young thugs were on their way to entering my life, Claire's and mine.

The most upsetting part was the way things can happen to you without warning, without leaving you the time to prepare your defenses. It meant that someday my mother or father could say their last words with nothing to alert me to the fact. Or that another day I'll inevitably shut the door to this room behind me for the last time, without necessarily being struck by lightning on the spot.

I went back out into the hall. I closed the door. I walked to the stairs and came back. I grasped the doorknob and turned it, concentrating as hard as I could, then went back into my room.

At least I'd made it through closing the door one more time. For the hell of it. I wished that from now on I could be warned in advance of life's little surprises. I might suffer more, but I'd never have something important sprung on me.

It was a little after nine and pitch-black out. Starting at six now the birds began calling each other into the tree by the garage. Since the leaves had thinned out, their songs rang clearer, as if announcing the coming frost.

Below, in Claire's room, I thought I heard Daddy's voice; I strained to catch a few words, but couldn't. Mom was down there too. Easy to guess the subject of the conversation.

I lay down on my bed. Out loud I said, "Claire is pregnant." It sounded like nonsense. It sounded impossible. As if I'd said, "Claire is somebody else."

Inside her she carried a kind of threat: to her, but also to us, La Marette. Our harmony. My heart ached. I didn't want her to have this baby. I knew it would turn everything upside down. But on the other hand I couldn't imagine her not having it.

And downstairs, so near me, her future was being decided. I couldn't stand it. I went down to Bernadette's room.

She was in her pajamas, or rather Stéphane's, beautiful beige silk ones with a mandarin collar, a keepsake he'd left her. On the pocket were three letters, two S's and an A. Her own clothes, worn and patched, were neatly laid out on a chair, her boots beside it. Sitting on her bed, she was trimming her toenails, one of her favorite activities. Whatever turns you on!

She was surprised to see me. I closed the door and dropped my bombshell.

"Claire is pregnant."

"What the . . . are you out of your mind?"

"Jeremy. San Francisco."

She dropped the nail scissors. Stretched out her legs. Looked at me wide-eyed.

"You aren't kidding, are you?"

"Not on your life."

She flopped back. "And she had to pick an American!"

I sat down on the end of her bed.

"Do Mom and Dad know?"

"She told them yesterday at the hospital. They're talking it over right now."

"Just what Mom and Dad need."

She did some quick figuring and sat back up. "At least it's not too late."

"Too late for what?" I knew but I wanted to hear her say it.

"To get rid of it."

I bristled. The way Bernadette is always ready to make everyone's decisions for them gets to me.

"I'm not sure she plans to."

She gave me an incredulous look. "But what will she do with it?"

"I don't know, but it's her choice, not yours."

She jumped to her feet. "That may be, but I'm going to let her know what I think."

She headed for the stairs, tripping over her pajama legs. I ran after her. We were both barefoot, so they didn't hear us coming. She didn't even knock.

The drapes were drawn. On the dressing table there was an absolutely pathetic bunch of dandelions, Cécile's welcome-home present to Claire. Cécile says we're unfair to flowers, that they all deserve to be loved, that even the ugly ones are beautiful.

The Princess was in her bed, the covers drawn up to her chin, flanked by our parents. Things looked grim. No one was talking.

Daddy got up when he saw us. "Isn't there any way to have a private conversation in this godforsaken house?" he roared.

Bernadette paid no attention. She went right up to Claire, looking her over as if she were searching for proof of what I'd just told her.

Proof of Claire's assault was about all she could see. Claire looked into Bernadette's eyes. She looked tired but happy to see us.

Daddy turned his angry look on me now. I never could keep a secret.

"So it's true," Bernadette said.

Claire nodded.

"And you weren't going to tell us?"

"I would have had to eventually."

"So what have you decided to do about it?"

"Look," Daddy broke in stormily, "this isn't your problem, it's your sister's. And it's not an easy choice."

"But you'll go along with it regardless, I suppose?"

There was a challenge in her voice.

"That's what we were just telling her."

"You too?" Bernadette asked Mom.

"Claire knows what I think," she said in a firm voice. "But I don't want her to keep it because of me. It's too serious a decision. I can't advise her. All I wanted to tell her tonight is that no matter what she decides, I'll stick by her."

"She shouldn't do what she wants to *or* what you want to," Bernadette said crisply. "She should do what's best for the baby. Period."

Claire looked up from under her covers.

"I know," she said softly. "But don't you see what it means when you're already calling it 'the baby'?"

There was a silence. It was awesome. She called it "the baby" and it was alive. No matter that it was still shapeless and unseeing inside her, the minute she called it that it grew arms and legs, it laughed and moved. Had a soul, Mom would have said. A soul, she was surely thinking. There ought to be another name for what it's legal to get rid of for the first three months. Only after that should you say, "She's expecting a baby."

"Until yesterday," Claire said, "I wasn't sure what to do. Then, in the subway, something happened . . ."

She broke off. It looked like this was going to be hard to get out. Not just because of her split lip, either. Daddy stood at the foot of her bed and looked at her intensely, but she was talking to Bernadette.

"When those guys attacked the old lady, I stuck my neck out for the baby. I did it for him. I kept thinking, 'You can't stand for stuff like this and then bring a child into the world.' "

Something swept through the room. Once she said those words, we knew it had been decided.

Mom looked out the window. Maybe she tried not to let her smile show her approval, but it broke out anyway: a sort of light that came from deep within her, welled up from everywhere. For a second, she was luminous with relief.

Claire was going to keep her baby. We'd seen him in this room. We'd heard his laugh. He was here, climbing all over us and causing all kinds of problems. Claire already had him to thank for her black eye, puffy lip, mottled cheek, not to mention the gap in her teeth.

"Looks like it'll be a real peacemaker," Bernadette said in a husky voice.

"Exactly," Daddy said.

And he tried hard to keep from smiling too.

He got out his pipe. He lit it and paced the room drawing big puffs to get it started. I looked at the smoke that made a picture of yesterday, at Bernadette in Stéphane's pajamas, at the pathetic bunch of dandelions, closed up for the night, and I said to myself, "See, here we are at a turning point in our lives." I tried to make myself aware of it, welcome it as best I could, and I had a brief feeling of exaltation.

Daddy came back to the foot of the bed.

"What about Jeremy? Does he know?"

"No, and I wasn't planning on telling him."

We were completely taken aback. The way Claire said it, we knew it was a final decision. She fell back on her pillow.

"This has nothing to do with him."

"The Immaculate Conception, huh?" Bernadette teased.

"So you've decided," Daddy said slowly, "to have this child without letting him in on it."

"That's right."

"Do you think that's fair to him?" Mom asked.

"He doesn't believe in marriage. We don't love each other and he thinks it's stupid to have children because of the threat of nuclear war."

"Actions speak louder than words," I pointed out.

I don't know what came over me, but I felt myself starting to giggle. The minute Claire decreed she wouldn't marry Jeremy, looking as stubborn as Bernadette, who now looked at Claire with something bordering on respect, I felt liberated. What had I been afraid of?

Daddy sat back down on the bed. He absentmindedly picked up a bottle on the nightstand: Claire's homemade suntan lotion. Take your mother's olive oil, your father's cologne, mix together, shake, apply, it's free!

I knew what he was going to say. I wished he'd wait awhile. At least until tomorrow. It was coming even faster than I'd feared.

"Do you plan to bring it up by yourself?"

"Yes," she said, watching the bottle Daddy was holding upside down, a container of motion in green and gold.

"How will you support yourself?"

"I'll manage to somehow," Claire said. "If we get in your way, I'll rent a place near here."

"Great," Bernadette said. "I'll call the Ritz right this minute and reserve a suite for you."

Mom and Daddy looked at each other, completely bewildered.

Claire pulled her covers up a little farther. "I'm sorry," she said softly.

"No," Mom said, leaning over the Princess. "You don't owe anyone an apology. You don't have to answer to anybody but yourself. Have this baby. Love it."

"I already do," Claire sighed.

Daddy circled our sister's delicate wrist with his hand. That was all. Except in Claire's eyes were the tears that said no matter how she made it look, it hadn't been so easy to make up her mind. And there was something else in her eyes. Someone else.

"Let's not tell anyone yet," she whispered.

Antoine. She turned to me. "Anyone" was him. She was asking me not to tell him.

I turned away.

"It's up to you to decide when we should start telling people," Mom said.

Daddy got up.

"Why don't we all go to bed? We have . . . seven months to talk about all this, if I'm counting right."

"One hundred and ninety-three days," Claire said.

In the hallway Daddy seemed to notice Bernadette's resplendent nightwear for the first time.

"Where did you get those pajamas?"

"I bet you'd like to get your hands on them," Bernadette joked. "But don't even think about it. They're Stéphane's. Pure raw silk."

"I don't see why your father couldn't wear raw silk," Charles retorted with a smile. He added, "All in all, I'm glad you two came up. But you can see how I was starting to feel things were getting out of hand."

"You bet," Bernadette said. "Maybe you can see why it's

so refreshing to deal with horses."

"I'm just surprised we didn't find the Pest hiding behind the curtains or underneath the bed," Mom laughed.

"The Pest is down in the living room," Bernadette said. "Don't you hear her?"

That was when we noticed the music downstairs.

The window was open and it was rather cool. Cécile was lying on the couch, in total darkness, her tape recorder set on her stomach, still running.

She turned it off when we came in.

"You don't have to spell it out for me," she said huskily. "First she started throwing up. It could have been indigestion, but every morning at the same time? You guys didn't hear her because she'd cover her mouth with the beach towel we got in Houlgate, the one you use, Daddy, the biggest one. Then she tried the test you do at home and it turned the wrong color, because that's when she started crying all the time and borrowed my birthday money to go have a doctor do it again. I think it's kind of nice because Bernadette will be leaving and we'll have room. I just hope it's a boy for a change."

❧ 12 ❧

Bonjour, Philippine

I took out the big green notebook I supposedly use for science class, and my favorite pen. I pulled my table out and pushed it in front of the open window. I breathed the way Antoine says you should: exhaling to the limit, mixing my own energy with the universe's. I closed my eyes so that all I'd be was one star in the midst of this greater energy, taking part in it.

The wind wrote on my face. It wrote all we'd lived through here. It felt painful but good: a summons I was afraid I wouldn't be able to answer.

When I opened my eyes again, things seemed changed. The silence had never been so clear. There for listening to myself. In the middle of the page, I wrote firmly: "Chapter 1."

My hand drooped. Where to begin? When? I knew only one thing. I wanted to go back to when our family was intact. Before Bernadette met Stéphane. Before the trip to California where a certain Jeremy awaited our Princess. And for me, before Pierre.

A lot of novels begin, "I was born on the tenth of April, at this time of day, in that city." Never. That was going too far back, totally lacking in interest. In my life there must have come a point when things made a strong enough impression on me so that they could be described in full color.

Almost automatically I wrote, "I never liked my name." That was hard to say, a little like admitting "I never liked myself." And perplexing as a first line when naturally you want to have everyone love you. But that sentence opened the way to others, about liking your name and loving yourself and others, about my parents and sisters. I got them down on the page. I captured them in my sentences, bound them in my words, with their quirks, good and bad points, their warts, their way of talking, the color of their eyes, their feelings. At times I pressed so hard with my pen that it went through the paper.

I didn't stop writing until my hand was frozen. The first chapter was finished. I let my hand rest on the notebook for a minute, then shoved it in the bottom of the drawer and locked it. Enough.

Thursday was the day a strange caller came for Antoine.

It was six o'clock. Claire was feeling better but her ribs still bothered her. She couldn't cough or laugh yet. It took her fifteen minutes just to get up to her room. She took advantage of her condition to monopolize the bathroom for hours. We forgave her everything. For the time being.

We were in the living room, where we'd lit one of the first fires of the season. A tall, mild-looking young man, blond as the Princess, was teaching her how to play backgammon. Now that she was stuck in the house we realized she did have friends after all. This one was like her: calm, quiet, a bit distant. He didn't seem surprised about how she'd acted and said he wouldn't have pressed charges either.

Claire had just pulled off what was apparently an impressive play for a beginner when we heard the bell ring from the gate.

Our regular visitors come right in so it had to be someone we didn't know. Cécile went to answer it.

Mom always tells us not to leave people standing in the doorway. Last winter I ended up letting in a complete madman who didn't want to leave without the fireplace screen, swearing it belonged to him.

Now the Pest, her face telegraphing a hundred unreadable messages, led in an amazing-looking woman who asked to see Dr. Delaunay.

Amazing-looking because of her Hollywood clothes, tangle of necklaces, makeup, bleached hair, her walk, her perfume drifting through the living room as she went up to Mom. Amazing and attractive. Very. More than the four of us put together, for sure. How old was she? Hard to say. Under thirty, anyway.

I'd seen her somewhere. Where? I knew that face. So did Cécile; she couldn't take her eyes off her.

"Dr. Delaunay hasn't lived here since September," Mom told her with a hint of regret in her voice.

The woman's face fell and she looked at each of us warily, as if she suspected we were lying. Over on the couch, the backgammon game had come to a standstill. Claire's young man seemed stunned by the beautiful stranger, too. A completely different world had waltzed into our living room.

"Well, then, where can he be?" the woman asked, talking to herself. She turned to Mom again. "I've been in the States since July. When I got back I found out he'd moved."

"We were in the States too," Cécile announced proudly. "In California, with a heated pool and everything."

The newcomer was not impressed in the least. "You don't know his new address?" she asked.

"I believe Dr. Delaunay plans to settle in the area," Mom answered, sounding as though Antoine might be no more than a casual acquaintance of ours.

Cécile looked at Mom, astonished. She was about to say something when Mom went firmly ahead.

"He does stop by once in a while. Would you like to leave a note for him?"

The woman hesitated. She seemed completely at a loss. Why didn't Mom just give her Antoine's address? Perfectly poised, she handed the strange woman a pad and pencil, told her to sit down and take her time.

As she wrote, we marveled at her white hands with midnight-blue nails. She wore rings on every finger. I'd never pull that off. Cécile and I must have looked like absolute blockheads, staring at her. From the couch, frowning, Claire motioned us to move back.

The stranger folded the paper and handed it to Mom.

"May I ask who it's from?" Cécile said.

"Philippine Legrand."

Philippine? We all froze. Of course we knew her face. She hosted a variety show, "Bonjour, Philippine," every Wednesday at six. A very popular show. What was her connection to Antoine?

In the wink of an eye, the Pest tucked in her shirt and smoothed her hair, hoping, I guess, that Philippine would discover her. Claire showed no emotion. I couldn't help being impressed. It's not every day that TV stars walk into our living room. It's silly, but suddenly the room looked tacky to me, dark, dusty, small, and shabby, with all the furniture like tired old friends.

"We all enjoy your show," Mom said.

Philippine murmured a feeble thank you. She got up, gestured toward her note on the table. "Can you give this to Antoine as soon as you see him?"

Antoine? So it *was* personal. She looked so sad; all of a sudden her glamorous name didn't fit her anymore. But she still looked beautiful. Even more beautiful. Beneath the stage makeup there was a soul.

"I'll be sure to," Mom said. "It should be soon. May I offer you a drink?"

The Pest's eyes lit up. "There's scotch," she said, "hundred-year-old scotch."

But she said no. No thank you. And then all that was left of her in the room was a whiff or two of perfume the Pest inhaled as intensely as if it were incense.

We heard a car start out on the road. It looked like the backgammon game had had it. The blond friend, too; Claire announced that she had a headache. If it weren't for the folded note lying on the table, we might have thought we'd dreamed the whole thing.

What was Philippine Legrand's connection to Antoine? They didn't seem to go together; in fact, they seemed like opposites. But she was so beautiful. Perfect.

Mom slipped the note into an envelope, sealed it, and wrote Antoine's name on it. She put it next to the phone.

"If he doesn't come by tomorrow, we'll mail it to him."

"*I* would have read it," said Cécile.

But we had to wait for the cocktail hour before she revealed her theories to us.

The cocktail hour is one of our sacred institutions. Daddy can't stand sitting right down to dinner when he gets home. First he changes, then goes out to his garden to forget the suffering he's seen all day. Even though he always says he loves his work and would never want to do anything else, by the end of the day he's had enough.

The cocktail hour is also when we talk. After dinner there's TV, homework to do, and everyone's tired.

Of course, we only get real cocktails on special occasions, much to the regret of Claire and Cécile. But we have juice and all kinds of munchies Mom buys in bulk.

Daddy noticed the envelope by the phone. Mom gave him a brief account of our caller. Cécile concluded gravely, "So that was Antoine's secret."

Charles didn't react. He seemed slightly embarrassed, as if he knew something he couldn't tell.

"Who told you anything about a secret?" Claire attacked.

"It's easy to see that Antoine doesn't like to talk about himself," the Pest said. "You might even say he avoids it."

"Some people are discreet enough not to want to discuss their personal affairs with everyone," the Princess protested.

"Well, he had a pretty good one to hide! I never did understand why he wasn't with someone. At his age it's not normal. People don't realize it's a problem for men."

Bernadette snickered. "And now that you're a woman you can help them solve it."

Cécile heaved a most serious sigh. "I don't think so. Not after all the flashers I've been seeing."

Understandably, this bit of information threw us all off balance.

"Oh?" Daddy inquired.

"The last time was in the cemetery," the Pest explained. "They show up in the strangest places."

"But what were you doing in the cemetery?" Mom exclaimed.

The village cemetery is outside town, surrounded by high walls. Still plenty of plots left. I prefer the cemeteries in the south of France; from a distance they look like bouquets of cypress trees.

Cécile took a handful of almonds.

"It's quiet there. No cars, no mopeds, flowers everywhere, lots to read and look at. It's nice."

"Doesn't what's under there bother you?" Bernadette asked.

"What's under there is happy to have a visitor more than once or twice a year."

The other day, she'd gone to sit on our young friend Jean-Marc's grave and have a talk with him. A guy in a raincoat came up, with a pious expression on his face.

"I thought he was probably looking for a marker, but he was looking for something else."

"What happened?" Claire asked in the voice she uses when Cécile, eager to please, brings her a present from the garden, like a slug, an earthworm, a slimy snail.

"Then he opened his raincoat, and it really wasn't worth the trouble," Cécile sighed. "It's enough to turn you off for good."

She looked at our sole representative of the masculine sex as if he'd understand. Charles was nonplussed.

"Wasn't there anyone else in the cemetery?" Mom asked anxiously.

"No, no one else you could *see*. I thought I'd reason with him, but there was only one thing on his mind, you might say. It wasn't till old Madame Lepine came by with a potted chrysanthemum that he closed his coat back up."

Daddy came over and perched on the arm of Cécile's chair. He put his hand on her shoulder.

"Now listen . . ."

We'd all heard this lecture before. Especially when we were still living in Paris. Exhibitionists are sick, but they can be dangerous. The only thing to do is get away. Or scream if there are other people nearby.

I didn't dare do either. In the subway, where you usually saw them, I'd simply freeze. I don't know how Claire reacts. She doesn't discuss such things.

And not everyone has Bernadette's nerve. When one guy decided to display his wares to her in public, she took a good look and announced loudly, "Hope the next show is better."

✥ 13 ✥

A Basketful of Walnuts

*B*Y the next evening, the note wasn't next to the phone anymore. Claire put it in the mail, it seemed. At lunchtime, eating a sandwich in the Luxembourg Gardens, I told Béa about the Princess, even though I'd promised myself I wouldn't say a word about the baby. All Béa had to do was ask me, "How is she, her eye and all," and what I'd been able to keep to myself the other day just tumbled out.

Béa, whom nothing surprises, was flabbergasted. That was a start. But pessimistic! Found it touching that Claire wanted to keep the baby. Great that she already loved it. Not in the least important if it didn't have a father, since a mother and father are bound to conflict. But how was Claire going to "bring home the bacon?" I didn't have an answer.

A couple lay on the grass in front of us. There was still a feeling of warmth in the air; the trickle of the fountain, the smell of the sun. The sun does have a smell. Of gold, the inside of a straw hat, summer vacation, so many things already long gone.

And suddenly I was in California, at the university I toured with Claire and Jeremy. All three of us stretched out on the grass. Claire looked up at the sky. Her face was full of serenity. "She's in her element here," I thought to myself. Surrounded by beauty, affluence, freedom. And carefree, besides.

Well, it was all over now. "Bring home the bacon." No more options. She'd slammed the door to freedom behind her.

"What's the matter?" Béa asked. "Don't be upset. Nobody's *making* her keep the kid. She's doing it because she wants to."

I changed the subject.

In October, our favorite thing when we get home from school is to go out in the back yard and check under the walnut trees. The wind had been blowing so hard lately that pretty soon we wouldn't have to bend over to pick the nuts; the'd still be on the fallen branches.

This year's crop was huge. Baskets and baskets. Walk slowly on the grass and dead leaves, feel something round and hard underfoot, and your mouth starts watering. Though I don't take a personal interest because I'm allergic to walnuts.

This afternoon I found Mom hard at work on the nuts. She already had one of the big baskets three-quarters full. She was wearing gloves because the shells stain your hands black as coal. She had on Bernadette's clogs.

"Help at last," she exclaimed when she saw me. I wondered if she'd timed it, knowing I'd be home soon.

I already had my hands full. The minute you pick up a nut, you know from the weight of it whether it's a good one or if you'll find something blighted, twisted, blackish inside. Or the clear powdery stuff worms leave.

"Don't pick the small ones, they're hollow."

Now we could see the Oise through the trees, the sound of barges like an echo in an empty church. Sometimes I think that there are "churches" everywhere, an appeal, prayer, or plea to God or some other higher order. I have a hard time believing in God but can't convince myself there's nothing up there, either. Everything reaches upward. It must be toward something.

Out under the walnut trees Mom told me Claire had found a job. She'd just told her about it when she got back from the dentist's. A friend had recommended her to a florist in Pontoise. She would start the next week.

"She's going to sell flowers?"

"Why not? She seems happy about it. The important thing is for her to get used to working again. It's hard to go back when you stop for a long time."

"What does Daddy think about it?"

"We'll find out tonight."

She stood up straight and looked back at the house with its thinning cover of vines. Not to mention the section of gutter that had fallen off two nights before. The repairman had been called. Panic in the budget department.

Something soft flashed across Mom's face.

"The other day your father suggested that Claire might do some secretarial work for him. Do you know what she said?"

"Thanks but no thanks!"

"No! She said, 'If you hand me everything, how do you ever expect me to make it on my own?'"

Three nuts under one set of leaves. Béa was wrong to be so negative. The Princess was going to face her responsibilities. Without compromising her principles. A flower shop was just right for her. She'd be selling beauty, life, fragrance.

The basket was getting full. Last Sunday Bernadette and Daddy had taken turns out here with the scythe, and the rough grass scratched our ankles. The bugs were still biting, too.

"If you hand me everything, how do you expect me to make it on my own?" Claire had said it all. I didn't feel like talking anymore. Everything I could see around me had been handed to me, my life had been handed to me. "How do you ever expect me to make it on my own?"

I cracked a nut with my teeth. A feeble attempt at independence. I was surprised Mom didn't yell at me. And so what if I was allergic.

We headed back to the house.

"What about Jeremy?"

I felt like he'd been given short shrift. I could still see him with his beard, his silences, his calm and generous approach to life. I saw him studying law with no idea that here in France his child . . . and in a way I hurt for him.

"It's really up to Claire. And since she doesn't want to get married . . ."

But what about him? The young man who might never know that somewhere a new person would breathe something like he did, have his walk or his eyes? Would he have been completely indifferent to that? Feel no attachment? Could anyone be that superficial?

"What will she tell the kid?"

"We'll have time to think about that," Mom said.

In my mind's eye I saw the students I'd watched earlier in the day in the Luxembourg Gardens, especially the couple on the grass.

"I think it's all too complicated. She really shouldn't keep it."

Mom gave me a hard look.

"You're just saying that."

Maybe. Or maybe I didn't know what I really thought. I chomped on another nutshell.

"I guess you don't care if you ruin your teeth!" Mom said.

Daddy took the news well. His only concern was that being on her feet all day would tire Claire. It wasn't a good idea to go from one extreme to the other. Since she'd decided to keep the baby, she'd better take good care of herself.

Claire was sarcastic: "So now that I want to work you're going to object?"

Charles backed down. Except for Claire's moped. She

could forget about that; he'd give her a ride to work.

It took us a minute to understand why Bernadette thought all this was a riot. Then she acted out an imaginary scene at the Saint-Aimonds' for us.

High tea in Neuilly. Elegant ladies and petits fours on silver trays, uniformed maid, white-gloved butler. Mrs. Fine Old Name asked: "Does your future daughter-in-law plan a career?"

Madame de Saint-Aimond: "She works at a riding stable. Head groom."

Embarrassed silence. Sips of tea, discreet clearing of throats. Bernadette is a good actress.

Mrs. Fine Old Name number two: "She has sisters, I believe?"

Madame de Saint-Aimond: "Oh, yes. The eldest sells flowers. She's expecting a baby soon. The youngest one collects snakes. The other sister . . ."

Bernadette turned to me, laughing so hard she had tears in her eyes.

"I don't know what you have in store for us, but it had better be good."

Even Mom and Daddy couldn't stop laughing now. But it was a different laugh, with a little hurt in it, remembering the carefree laughter of the past. They were laughing in spite of themselves. Not Cécile, though.

"I was just thinking," she said, her eyes shining, "that maybe we could start telling people about the baby. What do you think?"

"Forget it," Claire screamed. "I don't want you to say a word to anyone." She shot a dirty look at us and left the room.

"Geez," said Cécile. "If it was up to me, I'd tell people right away. I'd say, 'Here's some good news . . .'"

I think it was then I noticed Philippine's note wasn't by the phone anymore. Mom told me Claire had mailed it that morning.

We wondered why, since Antoine was coming to lunch the next day.

❧ *14* ❧

Smelling Like Roses

*H*E arrived at noon with a plum tart and a bundle of books he immediately dumped on the Princess's lap.

"I hope you'll read these, I'd like to discuss them with you."

Claire glanced at the books, leafed through one, slightly tense.

"Thank you," she said, "but I won't have much time for reading anymore. I found a job."

He looked at her, amazed.

"At a florist's in Pontoise. I start Monday."

She spoke quickly, as if to get it over with. Antoine still didn't seem to understand.

"A florist's?"

"If I have to work," she replied with a half-smile, "I'd rather smell like roses than typewriter ink."

Antoine didn't look at all enthusiastic. He stared at our silent parents, then turned back to the Princess.

"Don't you think you could have found something more constructive?"

I liked his "constructive." It was better than "lucrative," at any rate. Or he might have mentioned "a future." Whatever her future might be . . .

Daddy came up and eyed the books with interest. If he didn't have at least four books going on his nightstand, he felt like something was wrong.

On the Princess's skirt lay Queneau, Alain-Fournier, Hemingway, Cocteau. My own favorite authors are like friends. Sometimes I even hear them talking to me.

"But this is so sudden," said Antoine.

"A one-time opportunity," Claire explained. "And my parents don't think it's so sudden when I've had a year and a half to make up my mind."

She stood up, and to show the subject was closed to discussion, she followed Mom into the kitchen, supposedly to put Antoine's tart on a plate. What next!

Antoine watched her go, bewildered. Daddy launched into a lecture on how much Alain-Fournier meant to him as a teenager. Antoine replied listlessly that Alain-Fournier made a big impression on him, too. I wished I could shout out the truth: "Claire is pregant. Yes, pregnant. She has to think about supporting herself and the child she's carrying. Now her own childhood is over for good. Life is really beyond our control. Except maybe when you're old, and it doesn't matter anymore, and life is so slow, so heavy you drag it behind you like a lame animal."

Lunch started out with a strained, heavy atmosphere, full of Claire's baby and Philippine. Mom had threatened Cécile with dire consequences if she mentioned our mystery caller. It was obvious that the Pest was looking at Antoine with new eyes. He was the man a TV star tracked to our house.

Luckily, we had a hot topic of conversation going at mealtimes: ecology.

"Beefy," the Pest's geography teacher, had assigned a report on ecology. She couldn't have known what she'd let us in for: we couldn't eat, drink, or breathe anymore without hearing what we were wasting or killing, or how we were digging our own graves.

With a worried look, Cécile studied the water in her glass.

"Do you know how many gallons of water one person used to consume in a day? Three! And now it's . . ."

"Three million!" Bernadette interrupted. She didn't look like she was in a very good mood.

Cécile let her have it.

"Twenty-five! For one little person, twenty-five gallons of water per day!"

"Well!" said Claire.

"Maybe it doesn't matter to you," the Pest went on, encouraged, "but every time you pee, let's say a cup, when you flush you're stealing a gallon of drinking water from the Third World."

Claire turned scarlet.

"I'm stealing a gallon from the Third World?"

"You're finally getting it," said Cécile.

"We're all guilty," Daddy chimed in, coming to the aid of the Princess. "What do you suggest? Should we go in the garden?"

"It wouldn't hurt," Cécile said. "And we could try only flushing every other time. That would be a start."

"If you do," Bernadette said, her eyes flashing, "I'm warning you that I won't flush once all day."

Even Antoine laughed. Outraged at her family's callous attitude, Cécile quit talking for a minute and we started telling Antoine about Christmas, about Montbard, where we were lucky enough to spend our holidays.

"Will there be a tree for sure?" Cécile started up again.

"Your grandmother said so in her last letter," Mom answered. "A big pine tree, right up to the ceiling."

"A big tree, proud and happy to be uprooted so it can hold decorations and stand over your presents," Bernadette muttered.

"Grandmother always plants them again," Cécile said. "You know she does."

She turned to Antoine. "Come with us. We'll show you Burgundy."

He didn't reply directly to her invitation. "Would I have to eat *escargots à la bourguignonne?*"

"Of course not," Mom said. "Then I won't be the only one who doesn't like snails."

She liked them well enough when she was little. Then one day when she was fifteen she was invited to Monsieur Clairet's, a friend of Grandmother's, to try his special recipes. To her horror, she realized you could still see the snails' feelers. She stopped eating, slipped what she could into her pocket to pretend she still was, and soon let out a scream. They were creeping right down her thigh. Actually it was only the sauce.

"Pauline, where are you?" Daddy asked.

Everyone looked at me.

"On vacation," I said. "Way back when."

Antoine cut the tart he brought us. Beneath the knife, the plums splayed, offering up their golden bellies. I liked his precise gestures. As his cuff pulled back, I could see his wrist, the dark hairs. I have a weakness for men's wrists. And I'm very sensitive to the way they smell. I have to know things and people by their scent.

The Pest had shelled a heap of walnuts and covered her piece of tart with them. When she offered some to Antoine, he didn't refuse.

"Nothing better than walnuts from your own tree," he said.

"It's a special basket, too," she added. "From the Philippines."

The silence made me realize what she'd worked in. Claire froze. Mom's eyebrows knit. The Pest bit into her tart. We'd never know if she'd mentioned the name on purpose. Antoine's face betrayed no emotion.

After lunch, Bernadette hurried back to the stable. Claire disappeared. As if that was all he had been waiting for,

Antoine steered the conversation back to Claire's job.

He sat down next to Mom. Didn't she think Claire was acting a little too hastily? This wasn't quite what he imagined her doing.

And then he started to sing her praises again. Our Princess had a way about her, a presence, a light. We shouldn't think of her refusal to work as laziness, but rather a rejection of mediocrity. And inside she was very strong. Look how she'd acted in the subway.

"I've had it with the subway," Cécile whispered.

But Antoine seemed to picture Claire in the subway like a Christian martyr facing the lions, staring them down with only the force of her faith to help her. Enough is enough. The wildcats in the subway had given Claire a shiner, and plenty of saints ended up inside the lions.

When Mom was a little girl, every night Grandmother would read her and Uncle Adrien a chapter from the Lives of the Saints. Their favorite illustration was a big arena with Christians being thrown to the lions like fodder. One night Mom's brother suddenly burst into tears. They were touched. Such a sympathetic little boy. Then he pointed to the lion in one corner of the picture: "That one didn't get a Christian."

So Antoine was confusing Claire with a Christian martyr, making it hard on her sisters. He asked our parents if they couldn't get her to change her mind. He'd thought of something for her and he'd like to talk to her about it. It would mean going back to school, if they had no objection.

Daddy looked very uneasy. He cleared his throat.

"But Claire has already made a commitment."

"Maybe this florist would understand if she changed her mind," Antoine insisted.

Charles never has been a good liar. He started to hem and haw. Not quite that simple . . . a commitment to a friend, too . . . as for going back to school, this didn't seem like the right time . . .

Suddenly a total change came over Antoine's face. He'd been so happy when he came in with his books and his plum tart. Now he was closing up before our very eyes. Turning back into the man we'd seen when he first came to stay with us: a man we could tell had been hurt. The change was painful to watch.

Cécile looked at him, at me. . . . If she hadn't understood at first, she did now. Mom and Daddy saw it too, and trying to make things better, Daddy dug himself in even deeper.

"Don't you think school is another way of staying dependent? Claire has to take charge of her life now. It's time. She's the one who accepted the fact she couldn't go on this way."

"Are you trying to tell me," Antoine asked slowly, sadly, "that Claire has met someone?"

We didn't expect the question at all and there was a silence: a silence that might have meant yes.

"That's not it, exactly," Mom broke in, looking terribly unhappy.

"Girls are so complicated," said Daddy.

Antoine turned away. He took his pack of cigarettes out of his pocket. It took him two tries to get one lighted. His hand shook. And I'd thought he was so strong! We all looked the other way. The truth burned on my lips. Damn Claire! She had no right to keep it from him. Nor the fact she'd decided to form no attachments, that she wanted friendship, affection, but not the kind of love that ties you down. To think that it was probably on her account that Antoine had moved near us, because of her Philippine was searching high and low for him.

I couldn't stand the silence. I felt Cécile trembling at my side, trembling like me with anger and the urge to speak out. If she told, it would be fine with me.

"What a stupid mess," she whispered.

Then Antoine got up without a word. Without another word, he nodded goodbye, and we didn't know how to show him with our eyes that it wasn't a lost cause. Perhaps. He left.

Cécile jumped up and ran to the door.

"Why don't I tell him? All right?"

Mom wavered.

"No," Charles said firmly. "We promised Claire . . ."

"Claire is a bitch," I said.

Later we noticed Antoine hadn't taken his car. I guess he just walked right off into the countryside he was growing so fond of.

About twenty minutes from here, if you keep up a good pace, you go by big brown fields full of twisted apple trees. If you walk through them, you send up sheaves of birds.

After the fields come the woods with their pungent smells, ferns like tongues of fire.

When you walk a long time, there comes a moment when you fall into a rhythm and feel a kind of deliverance. The earth, the horizon dance before you. You'd like to go on, go farther, always farther. I've often wished I could lose myself. But the deepest fields, the hugest forests, inevitably lead you back to roads, milestones, traffic signs.

Unless you suddenly, without even knowing why, turn around and go back the way you came.

❧ 15 ☙

Waiting for Montbard

I started waiting for Montbard, for Burgundy, our Christmas vacation, almost desperately. Everything seemed like a mess to me. A hopeless mess.

Every morning at 8:30, Claire left with Daddy. Every night a friend brought her home, usually the same one, the backgammon player. She had circles under her eyes. She went up to bed right after dinner. Her pregnancy was going fine, apparently. But hadn't we said we'd welcome the baby? Not the way it was going.

Bernadette wasn't in such great shape either. She hadn't realized how much she needed Stéphane until he wasn't around anymore. A classic case of absence making the heart grow fonder. And one being more in love than the other at different times was classic too. In the meantime, it was as if she were no longer with us.

Antoine came back twice. The first time was on a Sunday. Almost at once, the Princess went up to her room to show she didn't want to see him. The second time was one evening before she got home from work. She came into the living room with the tall blond guy who'd driven her home, as usual. It just so happened she asked him in for a drink that evening. I knew she'd done it on purpose when she saw Antoine's car.

Antoine took one look at this much younger man the Princess was being so nice to, and that was the end of it.

School was all right. But it wasn't very exciting. Except during French and philosophy class, I wondered what I was doing there.

To make Mom happy, I joined a youth group. We met every two weeks, had dances. Mom thought I didn't have enough friends. I agreed. But with people my own age I feel strange, different. I'm not interested in the same things. I'm afraid they won't like me.

How far away that September day seemed, when I'd gone to Antoine's house hoping he'd take me in his arms. I decided I'd never loved him. My body wanted him, that was all. I'd get over it.

Sometimes I'm afraid I'll never meet the man I'll feel right with. I want him to have known suffering so I can console him. It will make his eyes look deeper, his arms hold me tighter. I won't hide anything from him, but he'll love me in spite of it. And love me — why shouldn't he? — for things that are hard to describe. I want him to take life for what it is, yet still be optimistic. Because of the damp grass that seems, with the first rays of light, alive with birdsong. Because of the spot where a pine branch, bent with snow, weds the earth with its touch. Because of the tune you keep hearing in your head, then hear a stranger humming a little while later.

That day, December 15, while I was looking for the nail scissors Mom ordered me to find before Daddy got home, I discovered something I wish I hadn't.

Fishing in the drawer of Claire's night table, I felt a piece of paper stuck in the back and took it out.

There were just two lines in a large, bold hand. I couldn't stop myself from reading them: *"Call me. Right away. I'm sorry. I love you."*

It was signed *"Philippine."*

❧ 16 ❧

The Gift of Silence

WITH her long, slightly thin, white hand, she selected six tea roses, arranged them with the tulips, added some greenery, wrapped them in cellophane, tied them with gold string, pinned the edges, stuck on the label, handed the bouquet to the customer, took his money. Thank you, come again.

A bell rang briefly as the door closed, and we watched the customer walk past the shop window, holding his flowers, looking a little awkward.

"I like waiting on men," she said. "They almost seem intimidated by flowers. A lot of them ask for advice. And they're always for women."

She ran a brush through her hair, slipped on her jacket. "Where are we going?"

I named a café in the old part of town. I chose a quiet street and a restaurant with no jukebox or games, where we could talk. As we left, Claire's eyes checked everything once more. All those flowers! It was like leaving behind a sort of mysterious breathing.

She locked up. The sign on the door said *"Back at 3."* It was a small shop I'd never noticed before. Until she hired

Claire, the owner ran it herself. She'd just had a baby. Now she could stay home with it.

Claire took a big gulp of air: "I know you won't believe it, but the smell of flowers is nourishing. Like sunshine."

That morning when I had asked her to have lunch with me I was sure she'd say no, but here we were walking side by side.

I was confused. I'd wanted this to happen, but now I wished I were somewhere else. There are times when you feel like going out of your way. And then, there are the other times.

We crossed the bridge. The Oise was down there, flowing toward La Marette. And toward freedom, since here she'd been boarded, domesticated. Landings, houses, restaurants.

Claire walked slowly, staring at the water. Suddenly, without turning her head, she said, "I can feel it move now."

Something rushed through me, stopped at my heart. It moved? This was the first time Claire had mentioned the baby to me.

Without looking at her, my voice as neutral as possible, I asked "What's it like?"

"A big bubble sloshing around."

I felt like laughing. For joy. She must have sensed it. Our eyes met and she ventured a smile. I moved closer. Should I take her arm? I couldn't. Though there are women who can walk together touching, close. I peeked at her stomach. Bubble or no, you couldn't tell yet. The only thing that had changed a little was her bust. She'd always complained about being flat-chested. And now there was one more jar of skin cream on her dressing table: especially for pregnancy.

The streets were crowded. At times we had to move behind each other, like couples who seem to have nothing more to say to each other.

Total silence all the way to the café.

The back room was empty. No takers for the cracked plastic booths, the sinister lighting. Claire looked at the place, said nothing, but wiped the seat off before she sat down. It was just like her. So was wearing a white skirt in mid-December.

I took off my parka. She kept her jacket on. She didn't look good, mauve around the eyes. She glanced in the mirror, sighed, "I look awful." The waitress came up, acting put out. We ordered a chef's salad and a grilled cheese sandwich. And an extra plate.

Chin on her hand, Claire looked at me silently. I remarked, "You don't look happy."

"Happy?"

She blurted out in amazement. As if there was no question of happiness. It made me so sad I protested, "Then why keep it?"

"It's the only thing I could do," she said firmly.

I didn't understand. There was something else she could have done. Charles wouldn't have been in favor of it but he would have helped her. He'd never have let his daughter go just anywhere, to anyone. Even Mom would have cooperated once Claire made up her mind.

"You know it isn't."

She turned away. I saw the letter hidden in her drawer. Antoine's name burned on my lips.

"Do you know what they told me at the hospital? That when they suction it out of you, they have to put the pieces back together to make sure nothing's missing. That they haven't left anything inside."

"The creeps. They just say that to scare women away."

"Maybe so. But it's true. It's the law. A jigsaw puzzle of a baby."

She looked deep into my eyes.

"For the first time in my life when I had to make a decision, all by myself, it just couldn't be that."

A teenage couple came in. They went to the farthest table, and as soon as they were seated, as if they'd been waiting centuries for that moment, locked in an embrace. Say what you will, it was good to see the two of them. The one of them.

I asked, "What about Antoine?"

I'd caught her off guard. She was speechless. Her face closed as if I'd hit her without warning. I've never laid a hand on Claire. Cécile, I have. Swung at her.

"What does Antoine have to do with anything?"

"If you heard the way he talked about you to Mom and Daddy . . . to him you're a — "

"A phantom," she said in a dull voice, "an idea, a zombie. That's it. A zombie."

She turned to look at the waitress bringing our plates, the sandwich and salad. She grabbed her fork. Backing away from me. But I wasn't easily discouraged.

"Don't make fun of him. You know he cares about you."

He *cares*. Why had I watered it down? Just like me. Afraid of everything, even words. Her fork clinked against the table. She looked at me for a few seconds, from far off, defiantly. She was going to let me have it, get up, go back to her flowers. I'd ruined everything. She'd said, "I can feel it move." Shared something wonderful with me. And I came back with "Antoine." Why had I done it?

But then her expression disintegrated. She covered her face with her hands and her shoulders slumped. She was letting go: all the seeming indifference of the last few weeks. I didn't know what to say. I was overwhelmed.

I'd thought, "Maybe she loves him." Deep down I didn't believe it. And now I could see her love, alive and well, almost naked. This was the closest I'd ever come to touching Claire. Which Claire?

Without looking up, she reached for her bag, took out a handkerchief, and blew her nose noiselessly, discreetly, princesslike, her hair hiding her face. I had a terrible lump in my throat. I put my hand on her wrist. I have a hard time making gestures like that, only because they're so inadequate, get across so little of what you're feeling. But they're all we have.

"Claire!"

She finally looked up. Her eyes were superb, deepened with tears, royal blue, living blue. "Don't you think he could have . . . cared about me *before* we went to America? Before Jeremy?"

She managed a smile. Because before America, before Jeremy, we didn't know Antoine. Because without our trip there, he never would have come to La Marette. He wouldn't have known us, much less "cared."

My eyes begged her to keep talking. Perhaps it had nowhere to go, but like any story of unexpected love, it was worth hearing. Only a few months ago she had been so sure she didn't want to be in love. Tied down, as she put it. To a man or a job. Now look. My poor Princess.

She said softly that for the first time she felt someone understood her, totally. Understood, accepted the real her. I felt a smile coming on. The real her? A Christian martyr?

"I felt like . . . like . . ." and I didn't understand the note of distress that crept into her voice.

"It was at the beginning. When we got back from the States."

Every night, when she'd walk into the living room, Antoine's eyes sought Claire out, and a warm, strong feeling washed over her, a mixture of certainty and amazement.

"It felt so good. I told myself that if it wasn't for Bernadette, we'd never have met."

When you're in love, you like to think how you almost didn't connect, how love almost didn't happen. Because there are so many men and women, so much loneliness, because it's so hard to meet. There you are, going your separate ways, and then . . .

"I couldn't get really worried about Bernadette. When I

went to the hospital, I thought about Antoine and told my-self it would all work out. Talking about her every night brought us closer together. And then one night . . ."

A shadow flitted over her face and now she was staring at a point over my shoulder. One night?

"Do you remember when I spent the night with Bernadette? At the hospital? Antoine came to meet me there. He stayed until morning. We didn't sleep a wink."

She closed her eyes. "And that was the end of everything."

The end? I didn't get it.

"He told me about his childhood. It wasn't easy for him to talk about, let me tell you. I could feel how important it was, as if he were giving me a gift. Well, when he was seven his mother took off with another man, left him with his father."

I saw Antoine and his silences, his slightly distant look, as if he wasn't quite there, not quite back from someplace else. His childhood?

"He got over it eventually," Claire said. "Then he had to meet that Philippine."

"That Philippine." She sounded resentful, upset. So she knew about Philippine before her surprise visit? I was beginning to understand about the letter.

"What happened?"

"They were both very young. She was his first love. Then she started working in television. You can guess the rest of it. She said he was the one she loved but she couldn't resist temptation. He broke it off before last summer."

Claire twisted her bracelet. Her face was soft now, re-signed, but so sad.

"He told me all that and I realized he was talking to someone who wasn't me. To a girl who'd never had an af-fair, who'd attach the same importance he did to waiting, being faithful. I thought he saw the real me, and in fact it was just the opposite. Mom and Daddy told him I was a loner, that I didn't go out much. So he figured I was a virgin. He kept telling me how important it is to find someone serious. How casual affairs, easy women, don't interest him and never will. 'Easy . . .' as if making love defines everything about you."

"Didn't you say anything?"

"I tried. But I couldn't get it out. I was too afraid he'd leave."

She laughed sadly.

"He didn't even try to kiss me. We did have Bernadette six inches away, though, snoring to beat the band."

"And the next day, wouldn't you know, I had my first morning sickness."

The red eyes, the silences, the questions we asked ourselves. It was all so simple, so ordinary, like any life crisis.

"So," she said, "you wanted to know and now you do."

The sandwich was congealing on my plate. I couldn't touch it, even though I was hungry. Death, disaster, setbacks, nothing ruins my appetite. I was truly sad for Claire. But there was a bright side, a sparkling side. In one sense, it was nicer that she loved him. There was hope.

She put her hand on her stomach. There was the baby, too. I kept forgetting.

"And you still decided to have it?"

"What do you think I should have done? Get rid of it without saying anything to Antoine? One more lie?"

"No," I said, "of course not."

The way she looked at me I felt guilty for even thinking it. Besides all the good qualities attributed to the Princess, there was one more she did have: honesty.

"Especially since to him, abortion must be a crime. I didn't think they made men like him anymore. Old-fashioned."

"But you love him!"

She didn't answer right away, but looked into herself. The past.

"I've never felt so good with someone. I felt like I was where I belong. Understand? Where I belong. I'd like to . . . to sleep beside him."

"Are you sorry about the past?"

"I don't believe in regrets. It means looking backwards. Telling yourself that what you did wasn't worth it. But I don't know, the others didn't count. In a way, they showed me that with him it's different."

"So go tell him that. Now."

Her eyes opened wide.

"Never. I can't. I don't want to hurt him."

"You already have. And he's bound to find out sooner or later."

"The later the better. But first I want to make him think . . . I don't love him."

She picked up her fork. Her face went blank again. I could feel her struggling to regain control of herself. She was leaving me.

"Let's not say any more about it. Please."

It was already half past one. The clock on the wall said so. We hadn't noticed the young couple leave. They didn't have much time, but they'd made the most of it. Now there were only two empty cups on their table. Cups that spoke of absence.

I bit into my sandwich. Around us life grew dense: it was overwhelming and beautiful. I felt it all around me. Claire's pain had awakened it. And I hurt too.

I hurt for the day I rode my moped over to Antoine's, almost two months before. When I planned to seduce him. Went braless. What a joke. Claire, I'll never tell you about that day. But I offer you my useless trip, the calendar of hearts on the wall, the naked-looking dog, and my head swimming with anticipation.

Gifts can be something we keep to ourselves, too. Antoine gave you what's saddest inside him. If it somehow works out for the two of you, my silence about my dream that day will be my engagement present to you.

❦ 17 ❦

The Message

RIGHT after dinner I said I was going up to finish packing and slipped out the kitchen door instead. Everyone was busy getting ready for the trip to Montbard. And if they did notice I was gone, so what?

The night was dark. It was quite mild out. So far the winter had been hesitant, soft and damp, shot now and then with long shivers of wind. The kind of weather that's full of wonderful smells, but it makes people nervous because they know the cold is bound to come and they'd rather just get it over with.

I pushed my moped a little ways out beyond the gate so no one would hear me, but a dog still barked as if I were a gang of burglars. Our street is a dead end and it's very quiet at night.

On my way out to the road, I saw Roughly Speaking in his kitchen, reading his paper, and I felt a kind of tenderness for him. He might still be there when I got back. When the bridge would be crossed. Having an appointment with him made me feel better.

The church seemed to be watching over the village, swathed in all the prayers that have been said inside it.

"God, make everything work out," I wished to myself. I treat God pretty badly. I only appeal to him when things are going badly. When everything's all right, I'm not even sure he exists.

It seemed to me I was rousing the whole countryside with my motor, and I didn't feel especially safe. Mom and Daddy don't like us to go out alone at night, and when we do, one of them takes us, the other picks us up. But not for one minute was I tempted to turn back.

I didn't have any trouble finding my way and I made good time, even though it was a full five miles. From a distance I spotted Antoine's car; a streetlight reflected off the bumper. His yard still wasn't fenced in, but it looked less like a public dump. As I walked in, I noticed the bench we'd sat on that day was still there.

A light was on in the main room. He must have finished dinner and been reading or working now. I could never live this way, with no one to talk to, give anything to, or simply a familiar face to look at now and then.

There was no answer to my knock. The door wasn't locked. I went in.

The room was empty. Suddenly I imagined finding a body hanging there. Visions like that just come over me sometimes.

Antoine had painted all the walls white; a grainy plaster white that tempted you to feel its roughness. Almost no furniture. The big farmhouse table, a sideboard, a few cushions by the fireplace. No fire or music.

A hiss of frying came from the kitchen just off the main room. That was where I found him.

He didn't hear me come in. He was frying eggs. I think that was when I realized I was going to hurt him. Because of the eggs. And the little slices of bacon and the tomato he'd put on the plate and that I was going to keep him from enjoying. Unless I waited for him to finish dinner before I started talking, which I sincerely doubted I'd be able to do.

I coughed to get his attention, like they do in the movies, and scared him half to death. Granted, I was only two inches away. You're minding your own business, fixing bacon and eggs, and suddenly you're face to face with a frizzy-haired girl, all teary from the cold, wearing a tragic expression because she's just imagined you hanged in your own living room.

First I told him everything was fine, well, pretty good. He put his hand on my shoulder and asked me to give him a second to finish the eggs.

I hadn't seen Antoine for more than a month because Claire had achieved her goal; he didn't come to the house anymore. Now he seemed different. Maybe it was his clothes; he was dressed in what looked like ski clothes and it was only then I realized the house was chilly and that he probably didn't have any heat yet.

I reached for one of the potted herbs he had in the kitchen and pretended to examine it, just to have something to do with my hands.

"That's thyme," he told me. "I put it in just about everything. It's really good." He pointed to the frying pan. "Would you like me to put in a couple more eggs for you?"

No thanks. I'd already eaten.

Something in his manner held me at a distance. I'd said that everything at home was "pretty good," with no reaction from him. He didn't ask why I'd dropped by after nine at night, as if it were the most natural thing in the world. Maybe as if he wanted to keep me from talking.

I summoned all my courage.

"I've come to talk to you about Claire."

He didn't react right away. He kept working on his eggs, carefully poking the bubbles out of the white as it cooked.

"Well? How's the flower shop going?"

"Not too well. She's tired."

"Tired?"

His voice was incredulous, ironic, too. I said, "Claire isn't exactly a tower of strength, you know."

He laughed. "Oh, but she is. Beneath that Princess exterior, your sister is incredibly tough. I'd never have suspected it."

He didn't try to hide his bitterness. I saw that by "tough" he meant "hard." He believed Claire had rejected him for no reason, or for the young man he saw her with the last time he stopped by. I couldn't let him keep on thinking that, so I said, "She's having a baby."

That sounded less drastic than "she's pregnant," but it had the same effect on him.

He whirled around and I thought he was going to hit me. I backed away.

"No," he said. "That's impossible."

I could only nod yes.

"The blond guy?"

"No, an American, Jeremy."

I was getting ready to add that she didn't love him, that he meant nothing to her, but he didn't give me time to. He hurled his fork at the wall and walked out of the kitchen.

For a minute I didn't move. My heart was pounding as if I'd been running too fast. I picked up the fork just to do something. I couldn't put two thoughts together.

Then all at once I was afraid he'd headed for our house and I rushed into the living room.

He had the door to the yard wide open and was standing on the doorstep, taking in deep breaths of the night. I'd thought it would hurt him, but not this much. Not his two hands gripping the stone doorjamb as if he wanted to pull the house down around him. Not this breathing like a drowned man. It was so violent it seemed theatrical.

I went up to him.

"She doesn't love him. She doesn't want to marry him."

He didn't respond. His eyes were closed. I felt like leaving. I might have if he hadn't been blocking the door.

I went over to the fireplace, the burnt-out hearth like a dead love, and I waited. When he came over toward me, his face was closed, hostile.

"If she didn't love him, didn't want to get married, why?"

I looked at him uncomprehendingly.

"But it was an accident. She didn't do it on purpose."

"Did she make love with him by accident? Not on purpose?"

"Sex is no big deal to Claire."

And I added, stupidly, "A lot of girls feel that way."

His face was even harder.

"I guess I thought you and your sisters weren't just any girls."

A strong smell of burning came from the kitchen. It must be the eggs. It didn't seem right to think about bacon and eggs at a time like this, but that didn't mean Antoine wanted to wreck his pan and spend hours scrubbing it. So I went into the kitchen. I walked stiffly, as if the whole world were watching.

It didn't look good. The pan was black and bubbling. I turned off the gas, stuck the pan in the sink, hissing and sputtering. While I was at it, I threw the eggshells in the garbage. I found a half glass of wine on the counter. I downed it. Sometimes it feels good to do something that's bad for you.

When I got back, he was sitting in front of the fireplace, leaning forward, staring at his hands, which dangled between his legs. I've noticed that people often look at their hands when they're upset, as if expecting them to do something. Their hands, at least.

I sat down a little ways away. I was afraid my breath would smell of wine.

"If giving your body, yourself, is no big deal, can you tell me, Pauline, what *is* a big deal to you?"

Basically I agreed with him. Giving myself *is* an important thing for me. I hope it always will be. But if I told him so, I'd be siding with him against Claire. So, stuck in the middle, I couldn't find a thing to reply and he misinterpreted my silence.

"Do you think your family would be what it is if sex was 'no big deal' to your mother? Don't you think your parents were ever forced to say no to someone?"

Anger rose in me like an incomprehensible despair. He had no right to talk about my parents. They had nothing to do with this.

"We're talking about Claire," I said. "For my parents, it wasn't the same thing."

"I don't see why not. We're all made the same way. And if you don't learn to control your impulses, you'll never be able to build a solid relationship."

Waiting, virginity. Claire was right. Old-fashioned. Oh, the good old days when girls saved themselves for men who hurried out to cheat on them with wanton women. Claire had to have it better than our great-grandmother, Rose, who was found huddled in the closet the morning after her wedding night.

That was when I stopped feeling sorry for Antoine. I can't stand people who are judgmental, speak out of turn about your parents, and fixate on the past. It seemed perfectly natural to bring up Philippine. Because Claire may have had her Jeremy, but as far as I knew, Antoine hadn't "controlled his impulses" with Philippine. He was just lucky she hadn't gotten pregnant too.

"What about Phillippine?"

That got him. But good. I laid it on thicker: "She came to our house. All worked up. She was looking for you. Even left you a note."

I took it out and handed it to him.

He read it, crumpled it up, and waited a minute before responding.

"It's all over between Philippine and me."

"It's all over between Claire and Jeremy."

I was just waiting to hear him tell me that for men it wasn't the same. That would have been the icing on the cake. But he simply looked at me and suddenly I felt ashamed.

"With Philippine it *was* a big deal. It was no accident. It was a mistake. A painful one for us both."

He spoke curtly and I felt his contempt for me. He was right to feel that way. I wanted to wind things up, say what was left to say, and leave. Claire loved him but would never admit it. Admit that she cried at night. That with her sunken eyes, swelling breasts, her fatigue, she was hardly like a princess at all anymore. That if it's true a welcome pregnancy produces a happy child, Claire's baby was out of luck.

I wanted to tell him all that, but I couldn't. Something was holding me back. I guess I was mad at him: for acting a hundred years old. For mentioning my parents. For loving Philippine. I didn't feel like being nice.

He got up. He went to get a bottle and a glass, poured himself a drink. He almost started to drink it before he remembered I was there.

"Would you like something to drink?"

I pointed to his glass. "I'll have some of that."

He hesitated. There was no label on the bottle, and that always means it's some kind of home brew, and strong. I drank it down in one gulp, like the wine in the kitchen. For a second I almost blacked out.

"What's she going to do?"

"She'll figure something out."

"Figure something out?"

I guessed what he was thinking and quickly added, "She plans to keep it."

He seemed relieved. In a way.

"All by herself?"

"All by herself. That's why she started working."

For the first time, I felt something a little different in him, a trace of tenderness. It started in his voice.

"A baby. Does she know what she's getting into?"

"Of course she does."

But he didn't seem any more convinced than I was. We stayed silent a minute. I was cold in front of his empty fireplace, in his joyless room.

He looked at me. He disappeared into the bedroom and came back carrying a blanket he tossed on my lap without a word.

From that moment on, with the blanket that gave me permission to stay, in spite of everything a sort of well-being stole over me. He sat down too. He still didn't say anything. Stared at the wall. I stared at my glass, the clear liquor still burning in my throat. I waited calmly. The worst was over for him now.

Then, as if talking to himself, Antoine told me about Frédéric.

He was a resident at the Center for Disturbed Children where Antoine worked. A boy of ten. Autistic. Frédéric didn't talk. He ate just enough to keep from starving. When he walked, he tied his feet together so that he only inched along. He refused to live because life was too threatening for him.

I whispered, "Why?"

"His parents never accepted him. He got in their way. They let him know it."

"What can be done for a child like that?"

I felt like I was asking the question of myself, too. I hoped Antoine wouldn't notice.

"You can be there," he said. "That's all. Really be there. And maybe someday when your eyes meet he'll see a light. A message."

I'd pulled the blanket up to my chin. I thought about the message that might never be gotten across. In a softer voice,

Antoine said he didn't know why he was telling me all this. Wait, yes he did. Probably to make me understand how important love is. All a child needs to feel at home in the world is a loving look. There's a direct link between love and life. It must never be forgotten. That was all.

I wonder if I didn't fall asleep. I saw Frédéric inching along, his feet tangled up in his shoelaces. I tried to keep pace with him. I didn't make it.

"You have to get home," Antoine was saying suddenly. "Do you know what time it is?"

He was standing over me and he looked gray. That was exactly it: gray. He pulled the blanket off and I felt cold.

"Does your family know you're here?"

I said no. I hadn't told anyone I was coming and would rather nobody knew. Especially Claire.

"Don't worry about Claire. I'll make sure she doesn't find out."

That meant he wouldn't be seeing her. I still could have told him she loved him, but again I couldn't get the words out. I was too tired.

He decided to follow me home in his car. He didn't want anything to happen to me. My parents must have enough worries as it was. He sounded like an old man.

Before we left, I turned around and looked at the room I'd probably never see again and where more than once he must have imagined my sister living. Then, as if reading my mind, he said, "I guess I won't be hanging around here long."

Before he got in his car, I informed him we were leaving for Montbard in the morning. We were taking the Princess. She'd had two dizzy spells this week and Daddy was making her quit her job.

It didn't seem to make any special impression on him. He started his car before I was even finished.

With Antoine following me, I screamed that Claire loved him, the whole thing was stupid, that jealousy, possessiveness, demands, only got in the way of building uniquely on love. I screamed that I'd never be jealous and yet I would like to be someone's first love.

The lights were out at the Taverniers', and La Marette was dark except for my bedroom light, which I'd purposely left on. Luggage was piled in the front hall. I tiptoed up and opened the door without making any noise.

There was Claire.

She stood up and I immediately knew she knew. Her face was a mixture of fury and disgust. I'd never seen her look like this. Like she might hit me.

She walked up to me.

"Where have you been?"

I didn't have to answer since she already knew. Her face grew even tenser. It frightened me. Made me feel guilty. I saw myself in it.

"What did you tell him?"

"About the baby."

"What else?"

"That you don't love Jeremy."

"Why," she asked, "why did you do it?"

"To help you."

She laughed. Then she looked at me with profound contempt. Mostly I remember her delicate lips pursing together. Lips are the best at expressing disgust.

"If you wanted to help me, you wouldn't have done a thing. You went to see him for yourself. To make yourself feel good, because you stick your nose into everything, because, I don't know, but you're a little bitch."

She didn't slam the door. She simply left the room, leaving it wide open as if I didn't exist.

And the rage that surged through me, almost to the point of hatred, made me realize she was right.

18

The Smells of Childhood

WINTER for real. I was going to say "at last." White on the mushroom-hunting forest over that way. White on the plum trees and meadows where the River Brenne slithers, so warm and gentle on your shoulders in summertime, with long grass on the banks to stroke you lightly.

White on the rooftops of Montbard, working up to the top of the hill, where we find our own rooftops beneath the twin towers of the park named for Buffon, the famous naturalist. We feel proprietary toward the towers, named Aubespin and St. Louis, since our family's house once belonged to Buffon's friend and collaborator, Daubenton.

The car skates up the hill. Melted snow splashed the sidewalks. Noses pressed to the car windows, we counted the shops.

There was the bakery where we put in our order on Sunday morning. There was the beauty shop where Madame Lecoeur always called her husband in to consult. Forget about the banks and insurance offices. But here was something worthy of our interest: the cheese shop with wonderful *crème fraîche,* and around the corner the local department store.

"Childhood memories sure are neat," Cécile said, her eyes shining.

She clapped when the walls of the lowest terrace came into sight. Our terrace.

Grandmother has five acres of grounds, a series of terraces, once Buffon's kitchen gardens: seven of them in all, on each one a well, and at the bottom of each well, death holding its mirror up to you.

The gate was wide open. We went up the drive leading to the twin houses, one Grandmother's and the other belonging to her brother Alexis.

And just at the moment Charles stopped the car at the bottom of the stairs that branch off in the middle, one set leading to each house, the dinner bell started ringing its head off.

It was Uncle Alexis's way of letting Grandmother — and the whole neighborhood — know we were there. Mom shot out of the car, flung herself at the old gentleman at the end of the bellrope. He dropped it and hugged her, eyes closed, overcome with emotion. Mom always was his favorite.

Eighty-three years old, with a young man's shock of hair still mysteriously red, a child's temper, and, according to Grandmother, an enormous ego, Alexis was the oldest child. Then came Thomas, eighty-two, a retired priest, then Hélène, who'd died ten years ago, and finally Charlotte-Marie: Grandmother, the only one of the four children to marry, for which we gave thanks.

"That old Charlotte is really getting hard of hearing," Alexis announced to Mom, but not looking too annoyed since he thinks his own hearing is fine. "Nothing but the bell gets through to her, and that's only because it's right under her window."

And with that, "old Charlotte" made her appearance on the balcony, her lap robe over her shoulders. Without wasting any words of welcome, she ordered us to come up at once.

"Get back in there this minute," Alexis roared. "Your throat!"

"Your back," Grandmother roared in reply, "and don't any of you let him touch the bags. Poor Alexis doesn't know when to stop."

The door slammed. Flushed with anger, Alexis stared at the empty balcony. No one knows why, but all her life Grandmother has referred to her brother as "Poor Alexis," and it's always infuriated Alexis, who thought he was destined for great things.

"Know when to stop," he grumbled. "We'll just see who ends up in jail."

"Jail!" exclaimed Mom.

"She's at it again," Alexis said, "even though they gave her a warning."

Grandmother likes her home brew. Every fall she and her accomplice, Aunt Nicole, Mom's older sister, can be seen stripping the plum trees along the roads. The result is a huge bottle of clear plum eau-de-vie out of which she takes two fingers every night at bedtime, in her cup still warm from herb tea. But one day she made the mistake of offering a shot to the local gendarmes.

We took turns giving and receiving the three kisses on the cheek dictated by local custom. Our great-uncle's nose was freezing. On his cheeks I recognized the fresh scent of shaving cream.

He settled for shaking hands with Charles. Alexis never quite forgave him for taking their "little girl" away from him and from Burgundy. Especially for taking her to Paris, that dreadful place where all you smell is exhaust fumes. Smells are a prime necessity in Alexis's life; I take after him in my need to sniff out things and people.

Our father declared he was going to get the bags and put the car in the garage. Mom had already started scaling the steps. When I handed Claire the bag she'd left on the seat, she wouldn't look at me.

We were supposed to go in the main upstairs entrance that leads straight to the parlors: the smaller front one, with the piano where great-uncle Thomas practices chanting the Mass when he's visiting, then the big back parlor, presided over by our ancestors, arranged two by two on the wall in gilded frames. But we've always preferred to go in through the kitchen.

And the smell hit us smack in the face, smack in the heart: the smell of the house, intimately connected to our childhood vacations. It seeps out of the walls, sings in the gleam of copper cookware, it's in the lamp that pulls down to touch the long wooden table. The smell of everything that's simmered here, of course, but also of the cut flowers that have been strewn on the table before they're arranged; the endless pitting of plums for canning or making into jams; the smell of herb teas: thyme for the liver, St. John's wort for constipation, violet for colds, and wild pansy . . . and meadowsweet . . . and all the soothing or invigorating concoctions known only to Grandmother and Henriette.

Henriette! There she was, by the big wood-burning stove that heats the whole downstairs. She deliberately stood in its shadow so we'd seek her out and find her there. But I could tell it was a special day for her from her two clean aprons, one on top of the other, and her freshly coiled chignon. A real smile? We didn't expect one. Henriette never lets her happiness show; heaven might punish her for it.

Misshapen, hunchbacked, taken in at sixteen by Grandmother (only five years older herself), she never left her. She claims she's the one who raised Mom, Aunt Nicole, and Uncle Adrien. Didn't her poor crippled legs pedal for miles during the war to find butter, honey, the piece of meat they needed to keep growing? And slowly but surely, over the years, by dint of meals and the schedule they imposed, washdays, keys to the linen closet, Henriette had taken possession of the house. She reigns as its mistress. Does it make her happy?

For the moment, Mom was in her arms. Cécile, next in line, seized the opportunity to see what smelled so good in the pot on the stove, but Henriette snatched her hand away from the cover.

"Sneaky as ever, I see."

And she's still secretive as ever about the food she serves until the moment it appears on the table.

After the kisses, she inspected all three of us. Her eyes came to rest on our jeans.

"Talk about China, we're not in much better shape. Everyone in uniform."

I don't know whether it was because I'd grown or because she no longer frightened me, but she seemed smaller.

Sitting on a bench, Alexis watched the reunion; his happiness was touching. Henriette, pointing to him, told Mom, "Your uncle must have asked me at least fifty times when you'd be here, it was driving me crazy. Not to mention that every time he did, he swallowed one of the eggs I had out for the mousse."

Cécile, all innocence, slipped in, "A mousse for Christmas Eve dinner?"

"What dinner is that?" Henriette asked with a frown.

"It's tomorrow. We always have a special dinner," the Pest protested. She hadn't forgotten the rules of the game.

"Ah!" said Henriette, "I thought Christmas was the feast of Jesus, not of the Holy Stomach."

A cane tapped furiously on the ceiling. Grandmother was getting impatient. We all headed straight for the stairs.

She was standing in the middle of the parlor, next to the Christmas tree with its star touching the ceiling, as promised. Presents were piled at the bottom. The fire in the fireplace lit up the trimmings, and on the mantelpiece, a crèche. The plump and dimpled baby Jesus lay between an ox and a donkey that didn't look undernourished either. Mary and

Joseph were in front of him, then the shepherds and some of their flock. Farther off, the Magi, whose great riches made them less dear to the heart of God.

"What were you doing down there?" Grandmother asked, her eyes shining with happiness. "You took your time getting up here."

"Henriette . . ." Mom explained.

I felt like falling into one of the Regency armchairs I wasn't allowed to sit on as a little girl because the upholstery might get dirty. Collapse and not move again. It was all too good. Too essential. Montbard, Grandmother, the crèche, everything. Just looking at them, seeing them again, filled me with the feeling that things would fall back into place. Starting with Christmas, a shaft of light in December, a frail joining of present and past, a warmth. At La Marette, the light didn't shine anymore. Here it waited for us. Intact.

Claire felt good too. Standing stiffly when we came into the room, she now looked wide-eyed at the fire, the crèche, the tree, and Grandmother, so small in her best pearl-gray wraparound skirt, by the green branches. And in the Princess's eyes, in the way she craned her neck, was a cry, a hunger, that was heartrending. As if she'd just discovered that Montbard, this house, held a truth she hadn't lived up to. Now she had only the shadow of it. And regrets. I remembered Antoine's words of the night before: "build a solid relationship." Is that the truth this place holds, what makes us feel so good here?

Grandmother stood still. She watched Claire staring at the tree, her face like a call for help. She slowly pushed Cécile aside and walked over to our sister. Only when she lay a hand on her arm did the Princess seem to come back to earth.

"I know people my age shrink," Grandmother said, "but I didn't think I was completely invisible yet."

It was said gently, to make her smile. And Claire obeyed the summons. She touched her lips to the forehead Grandmother proffered with a feigned expression of annoyance. But she'd barely finished when Grandmother took her face in both hands and turned it toward the light.

"Are you sure you're feeling all right?"

Silence. Claire didn't like to lie. She's never been able to. And Cécile and I had been given a solemn warning, in the car. With the Princess's consent, Mom would be the one to tell Grandmother about Claire, when the time seemed right. It was bound to come as a shock to her. Grandmother has very strict principles. She's never left Burgundy, so to speak. She's always refused to have a television. In a nutshell, Grandmother isn't modern. It wasn't going to be easy.

"Claire took a job," Mom explained in an unnatural voice. "It's been quite tiring. She's on her feet all day."

"What kind of job?" Grandmother asked, knitting her eyebrows.

"At a florist's," Mom answered. "Just until something better comes along, of course."

"Something better?" said Grandmother. "I'll tell you what's better." She went over to the tree, rearranged an ornament, and came back to the Princess's side.

"How old are you again?"

"Twenty-one," Claire said, perfectly aware that Grandmother knows the date, time, and particulars of all our births by heart.

"At twenty-one," Grandmother declared, "I'd already produced your Uncle Adrien, and Nicole was on the way. I don't have anything against flowers, but you'd be better off having children."

As Grandmother spoke her part, Daddy made his entrance and almost went into cardiac arrest, especially when his mother-in-law flung open her arms and asked him how he'd like to be a grandfather!

To hide my nervous giggle, I headed up the staircase. It was white stone, worn down in spots. Aunt Nicole often complains about how hard it is to clean. Says dust gets into the pores, builds up into ridges you can trip over. Suddenly I saw the dust as the precious leavings of past hours and seconds, all we've lived through in this house, before, when Claire was still speaking to me, when she'd come into my room at night begging me to get rid of a terrifying moth, when we'd lie in bed and tell ghost stories.

I stopped in my tracks. Sometimes childhood gets a hold on you. It's too strong. Since the previous night, Claire hadn't looked at me one single time.

The stairway leads to a long hall with three bedrooms off it. The nicest one, Grandmother's, is at the very end. A tall pine tree caresses the stone railing of her balcony. The middle one I usually share with Cécile, and the front bedroom with its own sink and mirror is Claire's choice, of course. Nicole sleeps over at Uncle Alexis's. He has central heating and modern plumbing, everything Grandmother has always turned her nose up at. Wasn't there plenty of wood stocked up for the winter? And stoves in every room, and a hot water bottle at the foot of every bed? As for bathrooms, Grandmother considers that too much time spent soaking in hot water or looking in the mirror makes you lose sight of important things and lowers your defenses.

And what was more, Poor Alexis was always catching colds.

My room hasn't changed, with the two four-poster beds. I got a running start and landed in the middle of the enormous down quilt. The wood stove sputtered. Here the smell is of wallpaper, flowers on a background of green, the color that helps you sleep.

Between the two beds is a crucifix, the holy water font beneath it filled with a supply Grandmother's friends bring her back from their annual pilgrimages to Lourdes.

I got closer. A crown of thorns wreathes the bloody forehead of the figure nailed there. What always impressed me the most is the feet, so lifelike, the toes so real, with the nail through them and the drop of blood trickling out like a tear.

I touched it with my finger. The first time I'd dared to, it seemed like an act of sacrilege because of the equivocal, incomprehensible pleasure I'd suddenly felt. It was almost like siding with Jesus' executioners.

"Whew," said Cécile, suddenly surfacing behind me, throwing the bag of presents on the bed.

She told me Claire almost got sick right under Grandmother's nose and Grandmother gave Mom a dressing-down about how she didn't make sure her daughter ate right. Meanwhile, it was decided that Claire should sleep over at Uncle Alexis's.

With a glance, Cécile took possession of our old room, sighed a sigh of contentment.

"If I get cold, I'll come sleep in your bed."

Then she turned to the crucifix and tenderly stroked the face with her finger, the way she might have greeted a long-lost friend.

"The thing that makes me really sad about Jesus," she said, "is that just before he died he thought his father had forsaken him. Just imagine Daddy! It's the kind of thing you'd never get over."

❧ *19* ☙

A Precious Envelope

"**B**LESS us, O Lord, and these Thy gifts," Grandmother said. "Give bread to those in need and make Adrien stop driving like a maniac so they'll get here in one piece."

"Amen," the family responded, Nicole's voice rising above the rest with conviction.

We sat down. Daddy was on Grandmother's right, Mom on Uncle Alexis's, the rest of us wherever we felt like sitting. As usual, during grace Charles stood up straight to show he respects others' belief, but didn't say "Amen" or make the sign of the cross. And as usual, Grandmother blessed herself with a flourish, watching him out of the corner of her eye, since she's still hoping for a miracle. She's been praying so long for her son-in-law's conversion!

"Why does Uncle Adrien drive like a maniac?" asked Cécile.

"As if you didn't know," Grandmother said. "He'll do anything to get Philippa's goat."

Philippa is Adrien's wife; Adrien is Mom's older brother. We were expecting them later in the evening with Gaston, their eleven-year-old. They live in Dijon. *They* haven't deserted Burgundy.

Aunt Nicole, who came in as we were going into the dining room, wanted to catch up on all the news. So it was true Bernadette was spending Christmas with the Saint-Aimonds and wouldn't be here until New Year's Eve? Did Daddy really have to go back to Paris the week between Christmas and New Year's? If doctors worked themselves to death, who'd take care of their patients? And how did his family rate?

"Dead last," Cécile sighed.

Nicole laughed. Two years older than our mother, never married, a social worker, lover of life. Just looking at her was like a breath of fresh air.

Uncle Alexis had eyes only for Mom, saving the crust end of the bread for her, refilling her wineglass, finding a way to take her hand every couple of minutes. Nicole was telling us the talk of the town: Démogée, the well-known writer, youngest of the Prix Goncourt judges, with his name in the press almost daily, had agreed to chair a Christmas Day round table on problems of contemporary living, and sign his latest book.

Démogée was born in the area but had long since severed his Burgundian roots. It was really a great honor for the city and the Senior Citizens' Center where Aunt Nicole works.

"Senior Citizens' Center!" Grandmother said indignantly. "What will they think of next to corral old people together? Nobody knows what to do with us anymore, so they treat us like we're still youngsters and get us out of the way. Isn't that right, my poor Alexis?"

Poor Alexis grumbled something incomprehensible and concentrated on the dish of *oeufs à la tripe* Henriette had just set on the table. The "tripe" is really onions, and I was just as glad. A smile shone in Mom's eyes as our great-uncle gravely pulled his knife out of his pocket and lay it on the right side of his plate, pushing aside the one that had been set for him. It was the Swiss Army knife he'd been given for his high-school graduation at sixteen. He's never let it out of his sight since. In places the red has rubbed away, but in others it's darkened to almost maroon. Age does strange things. The knife has six blades, a corkscrew, a leather punch, and is a source of additional arguments between Grandmother and her brother, since even when attending the most formal dinner parties, he's true to his Swiss Army knife, to her great embarrassment. For my part, I like to run my fingers over the eighteen notches he carved in it, one for each month he was a prisoner of war. It feels like touching his life. Being true to his knife is Alexis's way of thanking the fates that let him return home. And I have an inkling that the day he loses track of his knife, it will mean his death isn't far away.

Speaking of death . . .

"Do you know what poor Alexis has gotten into his head?" Grandmother asked.

"Charlotte!" Alexis protested, "my private life is of no interest to anyone."

"Oh, yes, it is," Mom begged with eyes shining.

"He's convinced his organs will be snatched away from him when he dies," Grandmother announced mischievously.

Alexis turned to Daddy with an accusing look.

"There's only one thing left they can take away from us: our own bodies. And now that's settled. Pretty soon you'll be able to borrow against your heart or your kidneys. Maybe your lungs, why not?"

"At the risk of hurting your feelings, Alexis," Grandmother remarked, "I must say I don't think they'll be waiting in line for yours."

"I'll bet my lungs are better than a lot of Parisians'," Alexis countered.

"So how about taking off your jacket?" asked Nicole, mugging at us.

Uncle Alexis clutched at his lapels. We're told that pinned

inside his jacket is an envelope to be opened "in case of emergency."

"That's where he says he's not giving anything away."

"Oh, yeah?" shouted Cécile. "I'm donating everything: my heart, lungs, kidneys, eyes, and whatever else they'll take."

"Maybe you'll see things differently when you're my age," Alexis said, "when you understand that *you* have never gotten anything for free."

Daddy was the only one not to laugh. I knew he had something to say when he took off his glasses and looked at them a minute before setting them on the table.

"In my hospital," he said, "there's a little six-year-old girl who'll die within a few weeks if a donated kidney isn't found for her. And of course, she's only one case among many."

Alexis looked both glum and, judging from the glance he shot over at his sister, grateful. Daddy hadn't said he was too old to be a donor. It was sweet of him.

Henriette, who'd just put the roast on the table, stationed herself next to Grandmother.

"I have only one request, ma'am. To be buried in warm clothes: my gray wool stockings, my slippers, gloves, and my regular coat. All my life I've been too cold. I don't like to picture myself wearing a nightgown in my casket."

Grandmother exchanged a knowing look with Nicole. Poor Henriette. She'd never change.

"Of course," she said agreeably, "your coat and your wool stockings, dear. Instead of gloves, I think we'll use mittens, though; they're easier to get on. No need to worry. I'll see to it personally."

Reassured, Henriette went back to get the cheese-topped mashed potatoes. Even though she's five years younger than Grandmother, she's convinced Grandmother will outlive her. That she must have a right to.

"The way I see it," Cécile remarked, "unless you go

straight to heaven, which must not happen every day, you're more likely to be too hot in the next world."

We all laughed. Except Claire. I caught Nicole watching her closely. I could tell she was wondering what was wrong. It wasn't that Claire was talking less than usual, but that her silence was different. No longer the silence of someone skimming the conversation, riding on a daydream, but that of someone burrowing in.

I looked the other way. Through the window, the sky touched the garden, heavy with snow. This morning at home it had been raining. It started just after midnight. "A little bitch . . ." Stretched out on my bed, I heard the drip of the rain and the word Clair spewed at me. A bitch? I didn't know. I wasn't sure anymore. All of a sudden I couldn't stand the idea that Antoine should be hurt without knowing why; that he should love my sister for nothing. So I hurried to him. I didn't want to come between them. But I did want to see him, talk to him, feel good with him, and deep down I must have known that telling him would be the end of Claire for him. So . . .

The conversation was about life in Montbard. The town is growing. There are two new movie theaters. A reformatory has opened not far from here. People protested. They're afraid.

The conversation was about the Midnight Mass Grandmother had decided to attend. But the church was awfully cold. Was it really a good idea? Then I heard my father calmly say he'd personally escort his favorite mother-in-law. You should have seen Grandmother's face! And he was off and running. Perhaps it was the Pommard Uncle Alexis had brought up from the cellar to celebrate our homecoming. "There are two good times in life to do foolish things," Charles was saying, "when you're young, because you have all the time in the world; and when you're old, because you don't have very much left." And the devil with being reasonable. A little folly keeps you young.

Uncle Alexis gasped. Nicole reveled.

I know what Daddy is seeing when he looks off like this: he sees all the old people in his hospital, buried alive, who tell him they'd rather be dying just so someone will beg them not to go.

"What I don't want to miss," Grandmother said with a lump in her throat, "is the living Nativity scene. They'll have a real lamb, a real baby Jesus. I suggested Claire to play the Virgin Mary, but they wanted a local girl."

Honestly!

Over coffee, Mom cajoled Uncle Alexis until he opened the notorious envelope for her. After writing with many a flourish that he wished to retain his internal organs, with the most precious ones underlined, he asked to be cremated.

No one would think of making fun of him for that. Our family has good reason not to.

❦ 20 ❦

The Dead Woman's Daughter

O NE morning Grandmother's own great-great-grandmother was found dead in her bed, much to the despair of her husband and two children. She was still young,
in good health, and there was no apparent reason for her to
depart so suddenly: without warning, without benefit of
the holy sacraments, and, in view of her age, insufficiently
equipped for Purgatory with the indulgences she could
have earned by praying and having Masses said.

From miles around they came to the funeral, a most moving one since the young woman was loved by all, and it
made them realize what they had coming to them as well
(this is how Grandmother tells the story). Then came the
sad task of interring her in the family vault.

At the time the household included several servants.
Among them was a rather unscrupulous newcomer who decided to get his hands on the fine gold wedding band the
dead woman's husband had left on her finger, since for true
lovers death changes nothing.

At nightfall, the servant let himself into the vault and
somehow opened the casket. There was our ancestor, looking pale but still lovely. But he couldn't get the ring off her
finger. Not knowing what else to do, the servant took out

his knife and hacked away. That was when, roused from the unconscious state that had caused her to be mistaken for dead, great-great-grandmother sat bolt upright, terrifying the wretch, who took off into the night, leaving his lantern behind. "He's still running," the family legend says.

Now fully conscious and in possession of all her faculties, Grandmother's great-great-grandmother picked up the lantern and walked, still wrapped in her shroud, back to the house, where she rang the doorbell Her husband answered the door and was so shocked he almost took her freshly vacated place in the vault. Again, this is how Grandmother tells it.

Once he came to his senses, he promptly got her pregnant: Grandmother's great-grandmother. She was always called "the dead woman's daughter."

And that is why, wary and little inclined to take risks, Great Uncle Alexis says in the letter pinned inside his jacket that he wishes his cherished organs to be solemnly reduced to ashes.

Grandmother's great-great-grandmother's portrait is in the back parlor. She's old, but still lovely. Her hands are crossed on her lap, the right one covering the left with its missing finger. She looks over at her husband's identically framed portrait beside her. She has the face of someone who knows a secret.

I thought about her smile as I looked out over Montbard from the Parc Buffon, where I walked after lunch. I thought about the mutilated hand hidden under the good one. I shivered. I was about ready to see a ghost! But there's often a kind of aura quivering above the town, rising from the roofs and fields, a distant murmur, a muted something mixed in with the wind, the summer foliage, the smell of the place. Does it come from what the city has lived through? Montbard was once a famous seat of the Dukes of Burgundy. Then came the plague, pillage, sieges. Now it's just an ordinary town with two new movie theaters opening and a well-known writer paying a visit. Still, it can't be that nothing is left of the screams, the death rattles that have sounded over the years.

At times I feel the city's wall give off a muffled echo of these sounds. It makes me dizzy, makes me want to live more intensely, or differently. So now it was my turn, Pauline Moreau, eighteen, my eyes no different from all the other eyes that had come up here to take in at a glance this hillside of tiled roofs, this ribbon of water, these fields, this sky, and feel at home.

I got settled in my favorite spot, with my head leaning against the base of the Tour de l'Aubespin. For a long time I was afraid of the tower, with its perpetually damp stone walls and slits for windows. I imagined people shut up in it.

I'd brought pen and paper: a letter to Claire. I'd put it under her pillow. I'd tell her.

I closed my eyes. When I remembered Antoine, he was framed in his doorway, his arms spread wide as if trying to pull the house down around him. When I remembered him, he was throwing the blanket in my lap, and suddenly I felt good. And what if he'd tried to kiss me? Take me in his arms?

I crumpled the paper. No matter what I wrote to Claire, it would be a lie. Suddenly everything was all wrong. Too complicated. Yet everything seemed fine earlier when I saw the Christmas tree with Grandmother standing beside it like a special gift. Everything had seemed so simple all of a sudden. And now nothing was clear. Philosophy was worthless: Plato, Machiavelli, Bergson. Can you know yourself? The answer is no.

What if I took off without leaving word? Just like that. Into thin air. I felt a lump in my throat. I could see them searching for me, calling in vain. I could see Claire. *She'd* know why. I could see the pain on their faces. "We never expected this. What could have happened to her?"

Nothing had happened to me. That was just it. I opened my eyes. The stone I was sitting on was wet. I felt the dampness seeping through my jeans. I knew I wasn't going anywhere. I'd go home like a good little girl, put another log on, and dry out in front of the fire. That was what I'd do.

I lifted my eyes to look for help, try to forget I was eighteen and didn't know who I was, and that was when I noticed the man.

He was sitting on a stone wall about ten yards from me. He must just have gotten there because I didn't see him when I sat down. You couldn't hear anything with all the snow.

He was thirty, thirty-five. Hard to tell. Dark. Must be tall. Wearing some kind of sheepskin down to his ankles, like a cowboy's coat.

He looked at me straightforwardly, right in the eye, and when our eyes met he didn't look away.

I stuck my nose back in my notebook. All of a sudden I felt unsteady. Fear? Maybe I'm warped but I was sure he was a flasher. Or a mental patient. Probably both. He was going to come up, open his coat, and give me a show. I didn't need to come all the way to Montbard just for that.

He didn't take his eyes off me, as if to confirm my suspicions. My heart raced. Just a minute ago I was ready to take off for parts unknown. Now I was paralyzed. What was he waiting for? We were alone. No one else was crazy enough to come out in the freezing weather to admire a scene benumbed with cold, so still, so quintessentially indifferent.

I uncapped my pen and started to scribble. He'd see I was busy, that I wasn't afraid. He'd go look somewhere else. Or I could leave. But there was a snag: I'd have to pass in front of him. There's no other way out. And before I got to the somewhat busier street leading back to the house, I'd have to walk a good fifteen minutes on a totally deserted road. Plenty of time to be overpowered and raped. He had me.

At least I'd read plenty of advice on how to deal with a rapist. That's all you see in the papers. The other day there was a story about a guy who committed four rapes in a row at knifepoint. I wondered, incidentally, how he managed to hold the knife and do everything else at the same time.

Apparently the best thing to do is submit. Great.

I raised my eyes just an inch and noticed my assailant looking out over the city. My heart pounded. Now or never. On your feet!

My legs were jelly. I hadn't gone three feet before he turned around and started staring again. Now I might be heading for the death of a part of myself, as they say in the papers.

Too late to backtrack! And just as I passed in front of him, he pointed and said, "I think you forgot your glove."

I turned around automatically and there, unmistakably red and white, lay my right-hand glove, since I was still wearing the left one. I said "thank you" and went back to get it. His voice had changed everything. He didn't sound anything like a flasher and his face was rather handome, if very somber, especially the eyes.

I picked up the glove and slipped it on. I could see myself making each gesture. Again I walked in front of him.

"Do you know what day it is?"

"The day before Christmas Eve."

He gave a strange sigh.

"Just what I was afraid of."

He knew what day it was. Obviously. And I fell for it. As I walked away, he begged, "Wait!"

I stopped. I almost felt like the prisoner of my mistaken suspicions about him. He pointed to my notebook.

"Poems?"

I didn't know what to answer. I clutched my notebook. He scanned the park, smiled slightly.

"A ruined tower, new-fallen snow, Christmas in the air —
ideal material for a girl."

I hated that! The indulgent, superior tone of voice. It
reminded me of Béa at her worst, when she's trying to bring
you down.

My voice sounded like someone else's when I said, "All
anyone writes about now is war and the seamy side of life.
If nobody but girls will talk about beautiful things anymore, well . . . well . . . I'm sorry you're not one."

It certainly wasn't very clever, especially the part about
being a girl. But it stopped him dead, that was the main
thing. No more questions? I walked off. Head high. A
flasher? Even worse. A snob! It's all the rage to make fun
of what's beautiful in life, to sneer at the feelings you can
have in the fresh snow, beneath a tower, above a city that
has watched you leave quietly, summer after summer, vacation after vacation, for somewhere quite different. A city
with more towers than you can count, streets you were
afraid you'd get lost in, an old park full of ghosts and the
smells of childhood. It was his tough luck if it left him cold.
So then could he tell me why he came up here in the first
place? To tower over the city? To make sure he couldn't be
moved?

Hey, I should have asked him. I felt angry. It felt good.
Warm. Filled me. Angry with him, with myself, because
legal adult or no, senior or no, I still keep dreaming about
things that have nothing to do with life instead of dealing
with what really happens to me.

At the end of the walkway I turned around. Still sitting
by his wall, the snob. But not looking at me anymore. Out
of sight, out of mind, the girl with the poems. So what? He
didn't care anyway.

There was the church where we'd attend Midnight Mass,
the street I was so eager to get to, the house summer tour-
ists take pictures of, and, beyond, the sound of cars splash-
ing slush on the walls. The reassuring rhythms of daily life

lying under the snow. My shoes were soaked, my toes numb. Quick, back to the house, the fire, Grandmother.

Why did he say "just what I was afraid of" when I told him it was the day before Christmas Eve? To be witty? It wouldn't surprise me. But by being witty, weighty about things that are genuinely moving, grownups spoil everything for themselves.

As I slammed the gate, I had the pleasant sensation I was slamming it in the face of the pretentious stranger.

The scene in front of the house was wonderful. Uncle Adrien's car was here, doors wide open, and Cécile was speeding across the lawn, with Gaston chasing her and yelling, "Give me, give me it!"

They were sledding on the plastic toilet seat lid. White on white, it looked like Cécile was sliding on her bottom. Quite a spectacle! At any rate, Grandmother's prayer was answered: the whole family was there.

It seemed Uncle Adrien had brought three jars of snails he'd put up himself. Henriette threatened to turn in her apron, her aprons, if they were served for Christmas dinner. She didn't have anything against snails, but on the day of Christ's birth, really! Especially since they undoubtedly came from the cemetery, our uncle's favorite hunting ground. It's wrong to eat thy neighbor on Christmas day. Wait for New Year's!

❧ 21 ❧

The Storm Bell

*A*DRIEN. Four years Mom's senior, the oldest child, family champion at our version of *billard Nicolas* because he makes you laugh so hard you can't blow through your straw. A self-styled woodsman. He can find you a morel mushroom from fifty feet away, just by the smell. A hunter, trapper, berry-picker, he always seems to have a game bag slung over his shoulder, and when he opens it, what a smell!

He says that in this day and age, if you want to get anything out of life you have to cheat a little, because everything is so regulated, there's no room for the out-of-the-ordinary, the spur of the moment, the spice of life.

According to Aunt Philippa, he overdoes everything. Laughs, smokes, eats too much, spends too much time playing cards, dice, the horses. He leaves his house in the morning, runs over to his neighbor's, and bets him a cold beer that within ten minutes, four red cars will go by, and there they are at the window starting the count. Win or lose, they drink the beer.

It hadn't taken long to figure out that Uncle Adrien's marriage to Aunt Philippa was a complete mistake. You don't match a devotee of well-aged baby boar meat with a tofu-and-wheat-germ addict. You don't put a hail-fellow-well-met who needs to press the flesh together with a woman who wants her children to dress for dinner.

Uncle Adrien realized immediately, I'm told, that he'd been blinded by a passing fancy, but as a good Catholic, he believed in staying married. So he made the best of things. He lets her gripe, whine, vacuum under his feet. When he gets really fed up he, just looks her right in the eye, very serious, very dignified, and says, "Philippa, you're nothing but a pain in the ass." Grandmother loves it!

Gaston is the spit and image of Adrien. An easygoing little butterball. He's always gotten along well with Cécile, no matter how hard a time she gives him. He prides himself on his unshakable belief in the superiority of women. When he grows up he wants to be a "househusband," stay home with his children and bake cookies.

On December 24 I was the first one down to breakfast. The day was a kind of hesitation. Between joy and pain. It made me think of a wartime morning, though I don't know why since I've never experienced one.

Henriette had her wood fire lit and was getting Grandmother's breakfast. She hadn't twisted her long white braid into a chignon yet, and she looked awfully old to me. I thought about her wish to have wildflowers on her grave. Sometimes it's hard to believe that ugly people can appreciate beauty, which makes it even more unfair to them.

I was the one who brought Grandmother's tray up. Her light wasn't on yet, but she was awake. I saw her head turn toward me in the dark. Every morning and every evening Grandmother works on her daydreams. In her favorite one she's a crack shot. She dispatches child-killers, hostage-takers, and pornographers, everyone who preys on the innocent. Gives them the last rites and sends them to heaven.

I opened the drapes and winter slipped into the room. Occupied it. Grandmother seemed happy to see me.

"We may get more snow," she remarked as she sat up to look outside. "Make sure you bundle up for Midnight Mass."

She was reminding herself, too. Getting ready for that happy moment. I sat down on her bed and watched her butter her dry toast. She always started with that, then put the sugar into her cup, the milk, the well-steeped tea. Strong as possible, since she isn't supposed to drink coffee and isn't pleased about it.

Seeing her so relaxed, I was sorry she'd have to find out about Claire. But I hoped it would be over with soon.

She remarked, "Your mother seems tired to me."

I quickly answered, "It's nothing. The holidays."

I could tell she knew better. I was grateful to her for not pressing me. Then suddenly I felt like telling her everything, the same as Antoine. But I'd done enough damage as it was

I asked, "Do you remember when you were eighteen?"

A smile flickered in her eyes.

"It may sound strange to you, but I still *am* eighteen. You don't really leave it behind you, you know. The sad part about getting old is that you stay young on the inside. That you stay young but nobody can tell anymore."

"But what was it like for you?"

She put down her cup to think about it. She wiped her mouth. She always wipes her mouth before speaking.

"Different from one day to the next. Up and down. I was jealous of Alexis; it seemed like he could do everything. And I wanted to do so much, without knowing exactly what it was. Anyway, it's never very easy being eighteen."

"I know," I replied. To hide how worked up I was, I got up and walked around the room.

Grandmother has a lot of keepsakes. Every year she moves them around so they have a change of scene and she can see them with new eyes. The mantel is for pictures: her husband, her four children. I took a close look at the photograph of Claire, Mom's younger sister, who died at twenty. I tried once more to see if you could read her approaching death on her face. They say death is like love, that you never know when it will turn up. She looked like a happy young woman, that was all. A girl who wanted to do so many things "without knowing exactly what. . . ."

The little "storm bell" was on the commode. It's a consecrated bell that Grandmother's ancestors used to ward off thunder and lightning.

I picked it up and rang it, expressionless. When I came back to Grandmother's side, she was smiling.

"What are you chasing away?"

She seemed to understand perfectly.

At breakfast, we stuffed ourselves with buttered bread and honey under the reproachful glance of Aunt Philippa, who followed her diet: tea, soft-cooked egg, fruit juice, dry toast. She wasn't trying to lose weight — she's thin as a rail — she just believes in healthy eating. To her health! I intentionally drank a second brimming cup of hot chocolate just to spite her.

The sun was rising and it was lovely in all the whiteness, timid and unexpected: like having the back of your hand stroked. Daddy asked if anyone was up for a trip to Saulieu to see the famous "kissing *vouivre*."

The *vouivre* is Burgundy's dragon, a winged serpent with a carbuncle in the middle of its forehead. The magic stone lets it see in the dark but also gives it away. For such dragons guard the strong rooms in Burgundian castles.

The kiss in question is depicted on a pillar in the basilica of St. Antoche. We make a pilgrimage there every year.

Cécile, who has a weakness for serpents, volunteered at once. So did I. Gaston joined in because a store near the church sells the black currant candies he eats by the handful. Nicole has seen the dragon a hundred times and had an appointment with her well-known writer to go over the schedule for his day at the Senior Citizens' Center.

When Aunt Philippa said she'd like to go, it dampened our enthusiasm. Daddy could barely repress a grimace; he knew that on the way there she'd want some free advice about her hemorrhoids — she has tons — or her allergies — ditto.

Uncle Adrien said he had wood to cut for Grandmother, and the only kind of serpents he liked were stewed eels.

The expedition couldn't have gone worse. While Charles waxed eloquent about the beauties of Romanesque architecture, Cécile and Gaston held a contest to see who could spit as far as the eighteenth-century fountain across from the church. A little later, trying to win his audience back with a spicy story, Daddy explained that the female *vouivre* bites the male's head off when they mate, and the Pest stared so hard at Aunt Philippa that it was quite clear what the comparison was.

She tucked her folding cane under her arm — lucky for Cécile it doesn't have a dagger-tip — and went to wait in the car, which, to top things off, was adorned with a parking ticket.

The store was out of Gaston's candy.

When we got back, the presents were under the tree: one for each of us. The colored envelopes hanging on the branches held the crisp bill Grandmother gives us now that she can't do her own shopping.

I went up to the tree. My happiness seemed to walk beside me. I recognized it: last year's happiness, the spirit of Christmases past. But I felt I couldn't really grasp it. Watching Cécile's face light up, my smile was hollow. I was afraid that was what it meant to be an adult.

We had a cold lunch, since Henriette was very busy with dinner. The food was still great. Claire didn't join us, saying she had a headache. Aunt Philippa said she was just coddling herself. "That comes from one who certainly ought to know," Uncle Adrien retorted. You could just see Grandmother holding back her applause.

I quizzed Nicole about Démogée.

"He's just like they describe him," she said. "Doesn't go out of his way to be nice. And when he looks at you, you feel like he's seeing what you hide from yourself."

He already had a solid body of work behind him and his name had even been mentioned for the Académie Française. If he were elected, he'd be far and away the youngest member ever.

"How old is he?"

"Thirty-three."

I deplored the fact there were still no women members. Everyone laughed. They'll see.

After coffee, Grandmother beckoned Mom to follow her to her room. As they left, Mom trailing behind, nervous, almost like a child, Cécile, Daddy, and I looked at one another. The hour of truth had come. Grandmother was going to interrogate Mom and she wouldn't be able to keep from telling her.

Their talk lasted a long time. Cécile and Gaston had disappeared into the attic. Everyone else was reading. The wait was killing me. I went down to the kitchen to ask Henriette for asylum. I was afraid she wouldn't need me, but she immediately asked me to unstring some dried mushrooms.

There were three long strands of them on the table. Nicole had picked them in the St. Remy woods in September. There was also a mound of dough beneath a clean dish towel, *crème fraîche,* and heads of garlic.

When I'd finished with the mushrooms, I peeled the garlic. I worked slowly, fully aware of my actions. To Henriette, no gesture is meaningless: everything has unknown implications. The time of day you pick a head of lettuce, the way you separate the leaves, or baste a chicken, all have enormous importance. We didn't speak, but I felt sure we understood each other. I wished she could keep me working all afternoon.

I kept straining to listen. I was truly afraid for Grandmother. Afraid I'd hear her scream. And we did hear her shout down the stairway for a double cup of bluet-and-thyme tea, "for the nerves," Henriette grumbled.

I let her take it up. It was already four o'clock, and there was only a little bit of daylight left. I bundled up and started out for the Parc Buffon. I didn't see why I should give up my favorite place to walk just because some snob I'd never see again was there the day before.

The snow had turned to mud, except for a few disappointing clumps that turned to grainy white lumps in the hand.

There was a lot of commotion around the church, and once again I felt the Christmas spirit. The lamb and the manger might already be in place.

I slowed down a little before the tower. I felt everything acutely: Christmas so near, Grandmother knowing now, and myself on the hill. I had a few intense minutes, as if an adventure awaited me.

A room is supposed to look bigger when the furniture is moved out. The park, though, with its leafless trees, looked very small to me.

The man was there.

22

Counting the Lights

A<small>LL</small> my life I've been told never to talk to strangers. Surreptitious shots of tranquilizers, kidnappings,
white slave trade . . . in Paris, I'd never even think of responding to the men who whistle at me, ogle me, try to
pick me up in the subway. First of all, they turn me off.
They nauseate me. In their eyes I feel myself turn into something empty, anonymous, nothing but surface. They make
me fearful of love.

In Montbard it's always been different. When I was little,
I was taught to greet everyone we met. We went down into
town: Hello! We went mushroom hunting, baskets over
our arms, the baskets we never filled, tokens of hope:
Hello! But don't say "good luck" because of the mischie-
vous spirits lurking in the forest. We took the train: again
hello. Safe journey, come back soon. And of course Grandmother knew everyone.

This total stranger said hello and I answered with a smile.
He didn't seem surprised to see me. It looked like he'd slept
there: the same sheepskin coat, same position, same place.

He looked at his watch. "You're late." I must have looked
surprised. He laughed. "I mean, compared to yesterday."

"How did you know I'd be back?"

He pointed to the tower, the stone where I sat beneath it.

"Because of the spot you chose. It's where I used to sit twenty years ago: the best place. You have to know the park to find it. Really know it."

Twenty years ago I wasn't born yet, so I couldn't be sure he was telling the truth, but I was flattered, as if he'd paid me a compliment. It was stupid. I quickly asked, "Do you live around here?"

"My grandparents used to," he said. "My older sister has the house now. But it's been quite a while since I've been here."

There was something a little forced in his voice, a little too brisk.

"How about sitting somewhere else for once and coming over here?" he asked, patting the wall next to him. "At least you won't get the seat of your pants wet."

I was completely taken aback. The seat of my pants! So he'd noticed that yesterday. Like Grandmother, who sent me up to change as soon as I got in, saying, "It would be so nice to see you in a skirt."

"We can count the lights. It's just the right time of day. You'll see."

That convinced me. Counting lights. I did that as a little girl. I'd come here about this time, take note of each dot that lit up, each house, each life. An exercise in accounting. Each light made me feel a little better.

I sat down next to him, but on the edge of the wall, and looked out over Montbard. I knew the town by heart, but suddenly it appeared strange to me, as if the fact I was gazing at it with this man made it different, a bit hostile: a friend you're about to betray.

"Are you in college?"

"Not yet. Just finishing high school this year."

That brought me back to La Marette, the day before yesterday, Claire, the whole mess.

"I don't feel like talking about it," I said. "I'm on vacation."

"That's right, Christmas vacation," he repeated. "Me, too."

"What do you do?"

He smiled at me.

"I'm in publishing. My title is 'Special Projects Consultant,' I think."

"What kind of projects?"

"I edit history books. They seem to be doing well at the moment."

I wanted to tell him that I wrote. That I felt the urgent call to come to terms with myself, other people, and everything I sensed all around me without quite being able to grasp it.

He looked at me as if he'd heard the questions I was asking myself and was waiting for me to put them into words. It disturbed me. To hide it, I asked him if he knew Paul Démogée.

"I know his books. But I hear he's hard to get along with, a typical literary bad boy."

The "boy" made me laugh. In case he didn't know, I told him Démogée was over thirty and his name was being mentioned for the Académie Française.

He looked amazed. How did I know all that? I told him about the Senior Citizens' Center, my Aunt Nicole, and everything. She though Démogée was hard to get along with, too, but she was awfully glad he'd agreed to come sign his books.

He looked perplexed. "It's strange . . . as far as I'm concerned, having a book signed by an author leaves me cold. It's like meeting someone under false pretenses. What about you?"

"I wouldn't know. I've never had a book signed."

We looked off into the distance for a moment. Where a bell chimed winter, the empty countryside, and Christmas.

It echoed far into the distance, not blending with all sorts of other sounds as it did in summer. It was like a call to assembly.

I took a deep breath. The cold air stung my nostrils.

"While we're on the subject," the stranger said, "have you noticed how people spend their lives looking, hoping, for someone, but almost never end up meeting the right person? It's like a giant game of blind man's buff."

I'd often had the same thought. I can even say I thought about it all the time. So many people, so many lives, so many possibilities. And oneself. I felt a kind of warmth. It was an enormous comfort to know someone else felt the same way, even if it didn't remove the blindfold.

I told him that. He looked at me with a smile. It was the first time I saw his face light up. I noticed details: the deep crease between his eyebrows, a scar near his temple.

He stuck his hand in his pocket and pulled out a paper.

"I found this on the ground after you left."

I took it. It was a sheet from my notebook.

He said, "I used to hide messages under stones: a few lines thrown to the wind or for any stranger who found them. I thought this might be important, so I took the liberty of reading it."

All I'd written was "Claire!" I said, "That's my sister. I came up here to write her a letter."

I looked out over the city again. The daylight was already dimming. You could tell from the more blended colors and the milky tracing of the Brenne between the houses.

I rolled the paper up into a ball. The cityscape in front of me trembled: you can play blind man's buff with those you love most, too.

"In parks," my neighbor said, "people mostly like to write about trees. It seems silly, but it's much more important than anyone realizes."

I knew that: writing about a tree meant a lot of things; for instance, that you didn't want to die.

I told him that, too. And then to get back to his game of blind man's buff, if you were blindfolded, and missed hooking up with other people, it was because basically you were a prisoner of yourself, and in my opinion there wasn't much to be done about that.

It seemed odd to be talking this way to a stranger, almost someone off the street. I wasn't sure which of us had gone first, how it had come about, but it was good.

Though he had his face turned outward, I felt him listening. His hands were still crossed on his lap, rather long, quite nice-looking hands that reminded me of a doctor's.

There was a silence. Then he pointed to one speck among the faraway houses.

"Quick! Look! Know what that little light is that just went on? A child's room. And I can see a little girl putting her shoes by the fireplace."

"No, she's not," I said. "She's putting her boots down so she'll get more presents."

Another light went on a ways off. This time *I* pointed.

"And over there! Look! A kitchen light. No admittance. A *bûche de noël* is under construction, almost a yard long with meringue mushrooms, elves, and a procession of snails."

He laughed. Then there was no stopping us. In the house over there they were setting the good china, in the next one, an old couple was holding hands. And over there . . . we searched all over, on the lookout. Not one house lit up without our entering it.

He exclaimed, "Did you see that one? Three front windows at once, no less."

"The whole family is getting together," I said. "At least twenty people."

"But they won't all fit around the table."

"That's why they're having a buffet. The pâtés are still covered up, but the kids are already getting into the bowl of nuts, even though they've been told not to."

He made his hands into binoculars and put them up to his eyes.

"And what do you think those twenty people are up to?"

"Feeling good," I said. "Well, mostly."

"Just mostly?"

I made a set of binoculars too. It was a game but it was serious, too, almost dead serious.

"One of them has just walked out on her husband. She's young, well, fairly young. She really seemed fed up with family life. She was suffocating. Needed fresh air."

"Like that man all alone over there," he chimed in, pointing to a tiny dot of light on the other side of town. "Except his wife was getting in his way. He's just kicked her out. And don't go thinking he's sad. I think you can see the big tin of caviar and piece of cake on the table."

I looked a little closer. I saw silence and loneliness, too.

"He didn't kick her out. She was the one who left. The caviar was her goodbye present. Deep down she loved him but they just couldn't get along anymore. A total lack of communication."

"If she loved him," my fellow spectator asked, "do you think she'd go off the day before Christmas?"

I looked to the left, nearby, very near, where the big tangle of trees made a kind of bouquet. Behind it were my own family's two houses, the terraces with their wells, Claire. From here you couldn't see the lights.

"You can hurt the people you love most," I said. "It happens all the time."

Now lights flashed on everywhere. A kind of flowering. "Over there . . . over there," we said. We didn't have time now to go into detail about people and their lives.

When all Montbard was resplendent, with an ember here and there in the surrounding countryside, when the Brenne was a taut black banner between the streetlights, he asked me if I didn't have to be getting home. It was 6:30. Wouldn't my family be getting worried?

"I hope so," I answered. "The last thing anyone needs is having no one worry about them."

I got up. My legs were half asleep and my seat had gotten wet anyway. He got up too. He was very tall. Taller than my father. Taller than Antoine.

"If you're not in too much of a hurry," he said, "I'd be happy to go a few steps with you."

I didn't get his meaning until we started to walk. He had one very stiff leg and an unsteady gait. I thought I saw some kind of strap under his right shoe.

His eyes followed mine and as I quickly looked away, he pointed once again, but this time farther off, toward the forest so black that it looked like a hole in the darkness.

"I left my right leg somewhere out there. A hunting accident. I was eighteen. At the time I was what you might call an up-and-coming swimmer. Apparently I was very lucky not to die. So if I tell you that since that god-awful day I refused to set foot in Montbard, you'll know practically all there is to know about me."

❧ 23 ❧

A Living Nativity Scene

THE church was full. It creaked, hissed, and most of all, waited. The large, ancient wood-burning stove snored, its huge pipe twisting upwards, like something in an artist's studio.

The church is small but lofty, rather rustic, with a steeple that can be seen for miles around even when the leaves are on the trees. Inside there's a minimum of decoration, only a few statues, wooden pews with long, uncomfortable kneelers, and a smell of stone, moist and warm as a thought.

We got there early to find good seats and we took up two whole pews. As he promised Grandmother, Charles was there. The nativity scene was to the left of the altar, lit up with a spotlight that made the straw glint. Kneeling, in a long blue dress that looked like a formal, the low-cut neckline draped with a shawl, was Mary, the Blessed Virgin. Claire would have made a better one; her hair wasn't bleached and she didn't wear such revealing dresses. Of course, she had less to reveal, under normal circumstances, at least.

In front of Mary, in a basket set on the straw, was the baby Jesus. He was sleeping, blowing little bubbles. No Joseph in sight, but Mary seemed to be expecting him because she looked anxious and every time the door creaked open she leaned over to see who it was.

The shepherd was there with his sheep on a lead, a young ram that must have been freshly washed. He was looking around with his lovely yellow almond-shaped eyes, complaining sadly now and then, as sheep will.

Aunt Philippa held a handkerchief over her nose. Just like her! As if a sheep smells of anything but wool, warm straw, sweet grasses. Maybe she was just afraid of germs. The Three Wise Men would be along later.

It seems the congregation used to be separated by sex so the men and women wouldn't distract each other, and Mom told me she never came to Mass without a hat. That's a thing of the past, except for Grandmother. Her hat was so big that Gaston, sitting behind her, had to twist his neck to see anything.

Swimming in a fur coat that must be a hundred years old, Grandmother sat between Daddy and Claire. Daddy, in case anything went wrong, and Claire, because since early this evening Grandmother had appropriated her.

It had started in the parlor, where we all drank a big mug of bouillon before leaving for Mass. When I got back from the Parc Buffon, I was afraid I'd find Grandmother changed by what Mom had announced to her; afraid her eyes wouldn't look quite the same; but it wasn't at all the case. She was smiling in her armchair, all dressed up in a gray skirt and silk blouse with a big bow at the neck to hide the signs of age. She asked the Princess to serve her bouillon, and when it was time to go down the steps, very slippery at night, it was Claire's arm she took.

I saw the look Claire shot at her, then Mom. Claire knew Grandmother knew. I wondered who was supporting whom.

Grandmother was praying. Some people pray only to themselves, but she puts her lips, her eyes into it; she leans into it. Like her, I was looking at the statue of Christ above the altar. When I pray, it means talking to someone I'm not certain is there, though I'd very much like him to be. It would simplify everything. At least there'd be someone who, blindfolded or not, would see you as you are. "Dear God, please exist!"

Meanwhile, in came Joseph! St. Joseph in his carpenter's robe, a sort of burlap affair with a rope tied around the waist. It looked strange next to Mary's blue formal, and it was too bad his sneakers stuck out from under it.

"That's the Quidors' son," Aunt Nicole whispered to me. "Father Gosier forced him into it . . . to make sure he got to at least one Mass this year! He claimed he was too big a sinner. But Father said, 'That will make God all the happier to see you here. And do you think Joseph didn't have his faults?'"

And there the poor guy was, blushing beet red, kneeling next to Mary, sneaking peeks at the congregation, and furiously chomping on a mouthful of gum. Mary kept hiking up her shawl when it slid off her shoulders to reveal a splendid cleavage. There was music and chanting. Father Gosier's solemn entrance, preceded by choirboys and the bleating sheep, startled Jesus awake and into his own powerful chorus. Off to a good start!

A murmur swept through the congregation. Aunt Philippa was triumphant. She's resolutely opposed to Christmas pageants. She'd told us over and over all evening: it's a distraction, a disturbance, it keeps people from thinking about heaven.

Jesus was screaming bloody murder. It was a mistake putting him in the spotlight: it was shining right in his eyes. Mary grabbed a bottle in the hay. "All we need now is the ox and the donkey!" Adrien told his wife just to annoy her. Everyone tried to sing louder to cover up the noise. Needless to say, Cécile was pulling out the stops. I must admit she has a nice voice. Sometimes the people around her stop to listen.

I've heard that these days people are more likely to pray to Jesus than God the Father. He seems closer to them. I always thought I'd have better luck with God. "Dear God, if you do exist, make things work out for Claire."

Aunt Philippa followed the Mass with her prayerbook full of holy cards from baptisms, communions, and funerals. Some of the funeral cards had quotations such as "She was the soul of kindness," or "Her inner light shone on all those around her." I tried to imagine what they might put on Philippa's card. "Her life was devoted to wheat germ and soybeans," or perhaps, " 'You're nothing but a pain in the ass,' her husband said of her." A fit of giggling. Surprised look from Mom. "What's going on?" Cécile asked, intrigued. I buried my head in my hands. I felt really bizarre, tingling. Life?

His name is Paul! Earlier, as we left the Parc Buffon, I'd told him my first name. He laughed: "Same as mine." The only difference is that he likes his. Or rather, doesn't care one way or the other. He said, "Watch out. If you don't like your name, it means you don't like yourself." Indeed! But once he said that, I felt relieved. There's hope. When I tried to help him into his car, he brushed me away. "Don't." And in answer to the question I was silently asking, he said, "This car was designed especially for me. A sort of handicapped street machine."

I wasn't sure whether or not I was supposed to laugh. He said, "See you tomorrow."

The Three Wise Men, at last. They walked solemnly down the central aisle of the church, bearing their gifts: a chest of gold, wonderful-smelling frankincense, and myrrh. Their robes rustled. Melchior, Caspar, and Balthazar in blackface. No matter if Nicole told me they were two of the butcher's helpers and an apprentice tile-layer, my throat tightened seeing them kneel before the minuscule infant and proudly lay their gifts at his feet.

Something was slipped into my hand. A folded piece of

paper. From Cécile, in back of me. It read, "Can you promise me your Christmas money from Grandmother? Need it fast. Pay you back with birthday money. Write yes and sign."

My Christmas money from Grandmother? I turned around. The Pest's eyes implored me. But what did she need it for? She'd get her own envelope. I didn't understand. What was the rush?

I sent the note back unsigned. We'd see. Typical of the Pest to try taking advantage of you during a Midnight Mass when you're feeling sentimental.

Father Gosier was preaching about joy, true joy, the kind that stands your hair on end, makes you walk on air. Mary and Joseph were sitting on two yellow inflatable cushions. Joseph must have had hay fever. He couldn't stop sneezing. Jammed together on a bench, the Three Wise Men listened sleepily. Balthazar's makeup was starting to run. Grandmother had nodded off.

She didn't wake up until it was all over, sprang straight up, and proclaimed to one and all that the Mass was wonderful and she couldn't believe how fast it had gone.

Everyone got up. Handkerchief to his nose, Joseph fled toward the sacristy, while the Three Wise Men, twirling in their skirts, shook the parishioners' hands on the way out.

The baby's mother, picking him up, discussed the pageant with Mary, who'd given up and tied her shawl around her waist. They seemed to be having a hard time removing the halo attached to Jesus' baby bonnet. Philippa, a horrified look on her face, watched the sheep relieve himself on the straw.

Charles led his mother-in-law out. This was no time to catch cold. On the way out, people greeted us. I felt recognized. It was nice. Henriette had gone ahead. It must have been starting to smell awfully good in the kitchen.

And when we got back to the dining room, a holiday table was set. Holly everywhere, a beautiful tablecloth, silver, the best china. If you chip a plate, you're wasting a fortune. King Louis-the-I-forget-what ate off them once. Respect.

Uncle Alexis made his entrance, carrying with the utmost care a basket full of bottles covered with dust, the signature of time. Daddy was at Grandmother's right, as usual. No one understood when she motioned Claire to come to her left. That was Adrien's place. Adrien didn't seem to mind. Everyone was standing, waiting for grace. Just because we'd been to Midnight Mass didn't mean we were excused from it. Quite the contrary; we needed to stay in touch with heaven.

Alexis had already set down his knife, the corkscrew blade ready. Always ahead of the game, Gaston took a bite of his bread. Henriette stuck her head in to see if we were finished with grace.

"Stay here with us," Grandmother said to her.

Henriette stood still. Slowly, with a flourish, Grandmother blessed herself. Then it seemed like a century went by. She had her eyes closed. She was centering. When she opened them again, they shone brilliantly and in her voice was a plea.

"Bless us, O Lord, and these thy gifts, give bread to those in need, and help us all to joyfully welcome Claire's baby."

❧ 24 ❧

A Splash of Wine

*T*HERE was a silence so total you could hear the butter sizzling in the pan down in the kitchen. My heart beat wildly. With a strange "ahem," Henriette left the room. Calmly, Grandmother sat down and unfolded her napkin. Everyone followed her lead. A huge scuffle of chairs. I didn't dare look at anyone.

"Well, why don't you get busy and serve the Montrachet?" Grandmother asked Alexis, still as a statue, his hand on the corkscrew.

Everyone watched our uncle regain the use of his limbs, but not of his brain, taking the first bottle he lay his hands on out of the basket beside his chair.

"It appears to me, my poor Alexis," Grandmother said gently, "that you're about to serve us the Clos de Vougeot that goes with the roast of boar."

Beet red, Alexis switched bottles. Adrien let out an unnatural laugh. Straight as a rod, Claire stared at Mom, who looked at Daddy, who gazed at his mother-in-law as if he'd just discovered an unknown species of human.

I saw Cécile squeezing Nicole's hand. Cécile was the only one who dared look Philippa in the eye.

Philippa's eyes went from Grandmother to Claire, then

came to rest on Mom. She didn't seem to get it. To understand Philippa's attitude toward sex, all you need to know is that every time she has an appointment with her gynecologist, she breaks out in hives.

She opened her mouth to phrase a question.

"Have you picked out names?" Grandmother asked Claire. Claire instantly turned as red as Aunt Philippa at the gynecologist's.

"I'm not sure. That will depend . . ."

"You could call it Alexis," Cécile suggested, coming to Claire's rescue. "They're aren't any in my class." She turned to our uncle. "Would you allow your name to be used, or is that the same as your organs?"

Alexis swallowed the Montrachet he was swishing in his mouth and looked at the Pest very seriously.

"My name, yes. Because I'd be giving it during my lifetime, or at least I hope so."

He looked at Claire as he said it. Grandmother held out her glass. The ice was breaking.

"Welcome Claire's baby . . ." I felt like I'd never forget the moment, the second when she said those words, or the silence that followed.

Nicole gestured at Mom, who answered with a shrug, looking at her mother. Once the initial shock was over, Adrien was all smiles. I saw him give Claire a wink of encouragement. Just like him! Adrien and Grandmother are the two gamblers in the family. That is, they always expect the unexpected.

"May I ask . . ." Philippa began.

"My dear Philippa," Grandmother interrupted in a warm tone of voice, "if you won't drink with us tonight, to this great news, we'll all feel very hurt."

Philippa, her hand covering her glass as usual, eyed the bottle of Montrachet Alexis held out to her, then looked at Grandmother as if she were setting a trap for her. And she was! Drinking to the news would mean accepting it, toasting Claire and her baby. Philippa pursed her lips so tightly her chin wrinkled.

"Well?" said Grandmother.

Stiffly, Philippa held out her glass.

"Just a splash."

"Like the one Claire's baby will make," Nicole toasted.

"I'll drink to that," said Adrien.

"To get back to the name," Grandmother continued, "we'll have time to find a slew of them before April twelfth."

I admired the way she worked in the due date.

"April twelfth? Why, that's just around the corner!" Adrien exclaimed, all smiles.

And Gaston, slow on the uptake as usual, finally seemed to get the picture. He trained two eyes big as saucers on Claire, popped a huge piece of bread in his mouth, as if to fuel his courage, and resolutely put both feet in it.

"But Claire's not married!"

"Don't talk with your mouth full," Grandmother thundered, dismayed.

Philippa stared at her glass as if she were sorry she drank it. Cécile threw a killing look over at her cousin.

"Marriage is out of date anyway," she declared, "a dying institution. Haven't you heard?"

"What?" roared Philippa.

Now she focused her damning look on Mom for not having taught her daughters to respect the holy sacrament of marriage. Mom hunched over.

"That dying institution is still the best place to bring up children," Grandmother told the Pest. "But I agree that it's better not to enter into it if you have to start off on the wrong foot."

Philippa looked crushed. The only thing she had in common with her mother-in-law was principles, virtue. She was lost. And even Nicole seemed astonished by her mother's reaction.

"And since it appears," Grandmother went on, turning to look at Claire, "that it's legal now to stop this sort of thing once it's under way, I congratulate women who have the courage to see it through. Even if it would have been better not to get started in the first place. And I've sent a telegram to our Minister of Health stating my views."

"A telegram to the Minister?" Daddy repeated, incredulous.

"Saying the law should only be applied when women's lives are in danger, not so they can just go out and do anything they want. Mademoiselle Bureau at the post office agreed with me completely."

Upon which Mom took the wineglass Alexis had just refilled for her, drank it straight down, and looked amazed to find it empty.

The appearance of Henriette's *pauchouse* — river fish in a white wine sauce — brought us back to reality. Henriette trod carefully so the sauce wouldn't spill over. She presented the platter to Grandmother.

"Rather than carp, I bought pike this time," she said in a husky voice.

And she added mysteriously, looking at Claire: "Seeing what goes on, I'm not sorry . . ."

Her pike was cooked in Montrachet, flamed with cognac, the sauce thickened with cream, garnished with onions and garlic: the garlic I'd peeled in the afternoon while Mom, fearing the news would kill Grandmother, told her ever so cautiously about Claire's condition.

Grandmother had her nose to the platter.

"It seems like there's something new in your sauce."

"Could be," Henriette said, dabbing at her eyes with the corner of her all-purpose apron.

"Don't put another drop of anything in your sauce, dear. It's perfect the way it is."

Laughter all around. Well, except for Philippa. Henriette's *pauchouse* was smooth and strong-tasting at the same time. I don't know how she did it, but there weren't any bones in her pike.

"Of course," Grandmother sighed, "in America they wouldn't know how to make a sauce like this."

Claire blushed again.

"In America?" Adrien queried.

Nicole caught on, though. "Puligny-Montrachet and Coca-Cola don't mix," she said, pouring herself a healthy dose of the former.

"Or snails and popcorn," Daddy chimed in. It was the first thing he'd said since the beginning of the meal, and he didn't seem at all unhappy with it.

"And an American besides!" exclaimed Philippa, sounding so put out that we heard Claire's laughter for the first time.

A nervous laugh, like the one gaining on Mom — who'd just downed her third glass of wine despite signals from Daddy — but a laugh all the same.

"But don't take me for a chauvinist," Grandmother said.

"Oh, come on!" said Nicole.

No one's more chauvinistic than Grandmother. It's quite simple: in her eyes, only those who appropriately roll their *r*'s, are natives of the department of Côte-d'Or, and know how to make *boeuf bourguignon,* are truly worthy of interest.

"Let me add just one thing," she said. "If anyone feels inclined to say the least word against my first great-grandchild in my house, he or she can leave immediately."

Grandmother didn't look at anyone in particular. But Cécile did. We all imagined Philippa getting up from the table and disappearing into the cold, leaving her big footprints in the snow.

The leg of wild boar had been flambéed in cognac after marinating for three days. With the utmost care, Alexis opened the Clos de Vougeot 1973. We were already full. After the wild boar, we'd have the chicory salad with truffles, a boursault cheese Grandmother would take a good chunk of, and after that the long *bûche de noël*.

At the end of the meal everyone was wiped out, having drunk the following: eau-de-vie in the *pauchouse* and Montrachet with it; cognac in the wild boar and Clos de Vougeot on top of it; a touch of liqueur in the cake; plus champagne to top things off.

Grandmother got up, quickly followed by the rest of us. She made the sign of the cross before the prayer of thanks. Silence you could cut with a knife. Nervous glances.

"Thank you, O Lord, for this meal, Amen."
Whew!

❦ 25 ❧

Grandmother's Envelope

W E opened the presents the next morning about nine and I must say no one was very bright-eyed.

Henriette had a big fire going. Everyone was in nightclothes, except Alexis, and we all knew why. He sleeps in a nightshirt, and even for an audience he wouldn't switch to pajamas.

Philippa was wearing her crimson velvet bathrobe with satin trim; Adrien, his pajama top and regular pants. Grandmother was dazzling: powder, cologne, the works. She was even lovelier after she put on her present: a hostess gown of fine white wool.

I got a handbag, an oversized sweater just the way I like them, a bunch of little things, and the famous envelope with a big bill in it. Henriette was there too, so touched to get a transistor radio that she wept.

I mainly remember the endless sound of crumpled paper, exclamations that seemed a bit forced, I'm not sure why, and the feeling that time had stopped. It was neither morning nor evening; it was, suspended somewhere, a Christmas morning, period.

I sat down on the sofa next to Grandmother. Her eyelids were lowered and at first I thought she was asleep. Then I noticed her eyes were open just enough to watch Claire opening her presents.

When Claire opens a package, it can take hours. She undoes each bow, taking care not to wreck her nails. She folds the paper with the greatest care, even if it would only be thrown out afterwards.

Grandmother watched Claire through her barely opened eyelids and her face was very different from the one she'd worn last night at dinner. It was no longer taut with defiance, or firm with the desire to pull off a coup. It was the face of a woman alone, an old woman, pondering what life is.

She felt my eyes on her and I saw her smile and the light in her eyes pull her features together again. Her head came right next to mine and she said, "You see, Pauline, the storm bell still seems to work pretty well."

It was a little later, during breakfast, which lasted until eleven, that we noted the first thing missing: Henriette's matches, the big box of kitchen ones.

Henriette always seems at odds with her matches. She uses them until there's nothing left but a little black stub. Making a box of matches last as long as possible, she's winning some kind of bet.

As soon as she came into the dining room we could tell something was wrong. She headed straight for Alexis.

"Would Monsieur Alexis mind giving me back the matches he took for his pipe?"

Alexis, his pipe in his mouth, brandished his own box at her. So no, it wasn't him.

Henriette didn't seem convinced. She walked around the dining room two or three times, looking everywhere; but since she couldn't actually search us, she had to resign herself to opening an extra box.

We didn't give it any further thought. We did have other topics of conversation.

First of all, Nicole announced she had business to attend to in Paris and asked Daddy to take her with him that evening; she'd spend the next day there and take the train back.

Daddy didn't have any objections; quite the contrary. His sister-in-law's conversation would keep him awake, and if she'd rather sleep between clean sheets than under a bridge, say the Pont de la Concorde, she had a slew of beds to choose from at La Marette.

Daddy was in a very good mood. Claire and Mom, too. Everything was lighter all of a sudden: like an afternoon at the seaside when all at once the rain stops, the gray breaks up, it's blue out, smells waft, it's full of mirrors.

Philippa didn't breakfast with us. Gaston brought some herb tea up to her room: she'd overindulged last night. I wish I were like that. The more I eat, the hungrier I get.

After breakfast I went back to bed. I love being in bed when I'm not supposed to be, watching the slate-colored winter laid out on a garden I'd seen swarming with summer.

Cécile was getting dressed. Usually she made a hundred round trips between the sink and the chair where she draped her clothes, so her audience wouldn't miss seeing that, anatomically speaking, she was catching up with her sisters.

But today she didn't. She threw her clothes on in record time with sighs intended to warn me something was up. And it didn't take long for it to come out.

"I really need your money from Grandmother."

She was standing at the foot of my bed, her sighs exchanged now for a tragic face.

"I'll pay you back when I get my birthday money."

The fact her birthday was only a few weeks past, and she'd spent all her money on Christmas presents, didn't seem to faze her. Nor did the prospect of devaluation.

"You just had a birthday."

"I swear you won't regret it."

"Then tell me what it's for."

She began to stare at the brass ball on the bedpost, a stubborn look on her face.

"I can't. But Gaston knows. And he gave me *his* money."

It was a goodly sum, and it must be important if Gaston gave in, since he never had a penny to himself. Aunt Philippa is so stingy that if you got hives from being a tightwad, she'd be a real redskin.

Cécile was quiet now. Generally, when you won't do what she wants, she tells you such selfishness is unheard of. That it's inadmissable to attach so much importance to material things and it's a good thing private property is on its way out. Then she'd slam the door in your face and find a way to get her hands on what you wouldn't give her anyway.

Today she settled for pursing her lips, staring at the brass ball. She obviously wasn't going to slam the door, and when I asked her to hand me my new bag, where I'd put the envelope, she sounded so excited I hardly recognized her voice as she promised to pay me seven-and-a-half-percent interest.

She left the room at a stately pace. But since I didn't hear her steps on the stairs, I suppose she was faithful to her habits and slid down the banister.

My morning was ruined. I wondered what kind of prank she'd pulled now. I didn't dare talk to Mom about it because of Claire's saying I stuck my nose in everything. I was mad at myself for giving in to her. I don't know how to say no. It's not even generosity, usually just weakness.

In any case, not for a moment did I make the connection between Cécile's plea for money and the missing box of matches.

After lunch, we all gathered in the parlor. All that was left under the tree were Bernadette's presents and the package for Stéphane. I wished we'd hurry up and replant the poor tree. It was starting to shed its needles seriously, despite the fact it was watered twice a day.

There were various plans for the afternoon. Daddy proposed a visit to the Abbey of Fontenay. We all knew it by heart: "its striking proportions, triumphal arch, blind nave, spare façade, its pure, heartrending beauty . . ."

And when you get outside again, the need to make noise, run, hear the leaves rustle on the trees, because those old stone walls are superb but dead, dead; dead for seven hundred years, like seven hundred shovelsful of dirt on your heart.

All Nicole wanted was to take me with her to the Town Hall, where her good old Senior Citizens' round table with Démogée was being held. Reporters and TV cameras would be there; she was sure I'd have a good time.

I said I'd be along later; right then my head hurt too much.

Part of the family took off for Fontenay. I stayed a minute alone with Claire in the parlor. I asked, "How's it going?" She didn't even answer.

A little before four o'clock I put on the blue scarf I'm told goes with my eyes; a touch of makeup and I walked up to the park.

The church was locked. All that was left of Midnight Mass was a lot of mud where people had trampled the ground.

At first I thought that if Paul wasn't there, it was because I'd arrived too early. I sat down on the stone and tried to write a superb poem that would make him gasp in admiration, editorial consultant or no. But I wasn't inspired and despite my new gloves my fingers quickly froze.

I walked around so it wouldn't look like I'd been there forever. The square was still empty when I left: night was falling like a catastrophe, Christmas or not, and the lights went on all over town.

What hurt was not knowing among all those lights which way I should turn to find his.

❦ 26 ❧

Under False Pretenses

Two long blue trucks were parked in front of the Town Hall. Cables came out of them, twisted toward the steps, went up, disappeared, full of power, full of mystery.

Boughs of holly were all over. The spotlights made them shine. A huge poster announced the round table, with Démogée's name in enormous letters. I don't know why, but I imagined a bitter-looking old guy. Probably because of his reputation in the media. But bitter or not, today the great writer wasn't camera-shy.

People entered and exited, better dressed than usual. Earlier, as I was waiting up in the park, the party had already started here. And I hadn't imagined anything of the sort! There's one wish nobody ever makes in fairy tales: to be in several places at once. That's my wish.

It was six o'clock. The round table was supposed to be over about four. I don't like the term. A "round table" is all surface, instead of getting to the heart of things. So now it must have been the second half of the program: a reception and autograph session. I remembered what Paul said about it: for him, having a book signed was "like meeting under false pretenses." So he'd spoiled that for me, too. Without him, I would have been happy to meet a writer. Without him, I would have come at three with Nicole and not wasted my day.

I was mad at him and mad at myself for being mad. After all, he hadn't promised me anything. I was the one who threw myself head first, heart first, at the least outstretched hand.

The steps led to a stone-floored, somewhat formal entryway. Groups of people were talking and laughing. The doors to the reception hall were open. Inside, a big wave of people surged with an impressive rumble. It was like walking through a wall.

"So she finally made it!" Nicole exclaimed. She navigated toward me, took my arm. "Headache better?"

There was a note of irony in her voice, so I said too loudly, "All better. But I took three aspirins."

That's one too many. She smiled. "Let's wash it down with a glass of sangria. Come on."

If she'd believed my story, she wouldn't offer me liquor. If I stuck to my lie, I'd turn down the sangria. But I followed her over to the table, and to get back at her for my weakness, I told myself she didn't look right in her nice new dress. Nicole is at her best in pants, a big sweater, the casual look. This way she looks like an imitation lady.

She handed me a glass full of red and gold, redolent of oranges.

"Drink this. You know, it went fantastically well. Démogée was wonderful. He doesn't take himself seriously after all. He had us all on the floor laughing."

People came up, surrounded us. She introduced me: "My favorite niece." I chimed in, "My nicest aunt." The "golden agers" didn't look so old after all. But they laughed a little too loudly. They seemed intimidated by their own happiness; they needed approval for coming to this party, laughing, trying to act a little younger again. A trembling, candle-flame happppiness.

With the sangria, the warmth returned. To think that a

minute ago I'd hesitated to come in. A voice, a few smiles, and everything was fine. We were part of the wave. To hell with Buffon, his park, his light, and his missed appointments.

Naturally, a whole lot of people noted a resemblance between Nicole and me. It's what we call "the family eyebrows." Two little bushes over the eyes. All that's missing is the birds.

"Now come with me," she said. "I have to introduce you to our author."

"Where is he?"

"I put him in the mayor's office. That way he can talk to people. Signing books isn't all there is to it."

First I saw the President on the wall, then, a little lower, behind a tall stack of books, the writer's head bent over. I stopped in my tracks. I felt the breath knocked out of me. I couldn't. I didn't want to believe it. I didn't want to believe I could have been so naive, so stupid.

"What are you waiting for?" Nicole said. "Go ahead."

And like an idiot, I went up instead of running the other way. You couldn't see his legs behind the desk. It was probably also because of his handicap that they put him here, away from the milling crowd, in a comfortable chair.

A grandmother was sitting across from him. He was writing in her book.

"My niece," Nicole announced.

He looked up at me and smiled. Without surprise. He was expecting me. I'd never seen his face in the light. He was someone else. Younger. But hollower, too. And he was someone famous; I wouldn't be able to forget that from now on. From now on he'd never be the man who'd counted the lights with me in the park.

He looked at his watch. "Pauline! It looks like you're late again."

Nicole smiled. I could tell that she was in on everything. He'd told her about our meetings in the park. She'd figured out it was me. Not too tough. And I supposed they'd had a good laugh over it. They'd led me into this trap.

The grandmother got up, clutching her book. She couldn't let go of his hand. She'd be able to say, "I shook his hand." I felt the tears welling up and I was ashamed. So ashamed of everything: confiding in him, being taken in by Nicole, feeling betrayed, not being able to hold back my tears. If only sadness were all. But when I cry, nine times out of ten it's because I feel like lashing out and I can't.

Monsieur Démogée's smile disappeared. The way he was looking at me — half-serious, half-intrigued — didn't help matters. He had gray eyes. He was handsome. I hadn't realized that.

He handed me a book.

"I wrote something for you."

I ignored him and wheeled around. I dove into the crowd, rushed for the door. I seemed to hear someone call my name. So what.

The way back to the house was straight uphill. I still had the sweet taste of sangria in my mouth. "My favorite niece . . ." What a laugh! And Démogée's book should have been called *Betrayal*. He could just go back and wait for me in the park. He wouldn't be going anyway. It was all just to set up this superb joke.

If Nicole said anything at all to the rest of the family, I'd never tell her anything personal again.

Daddy's car was in front of the house and when I went in through the kitchen everyone was around the table, eating the wild mushroom omelette that would get our travelers in gear.

He raised an eyebrow.

"Where have you been?"

"At the Town Hall."

"How was it?"

"All right."

168

He didn't care. He was just being polite. Daddy was already far away. Back at the hospital where he'd stop as soon as he got back, to see a patient they'd called about several times.

He caught Henriette by the apron strings.

"Are you absolutely sure there's no garlic in this omelette?" He wouldn't inflict garlic on his patients.

"If there is any, I didn't put it in," the cook protested.

At his side, Mom was fussing over him. It's "Do you want a little wine?" and "I left you plenty to eat, and there are clean napkins in the drawer. . . ." You might have thought they were going to be separated for six months. It's like that every time. Even before they're apart, they miss each other. Love? Habit? The love of habit?

I barely noticed the only important fact that came up in the conversation. Daddy had lost his razor. His beloved electric razor. He had used it that morning. And he was sure he had put it back on the dressing table.

We really couldn't figure out what had happened to it. Alexis has a shaving brush and straight razor, and we girls only use shaving equipment in the summertime.

Mom promised she'd look for it. He had another one at home. Subject closed. No one made the connection with the missing box of matches. I'd remember that later. Too late.

Nicole got back five minutes before their departure time. No omelette for her, thanks; she'd done justice to the buffet. As soon as she threw two or three things in a bag, she was ready to go.

Everyone was there to say goodbye to the two of them. Nicole took Claire by the shoulders and looked at her a minute before they kissed. The Princess didn't know what to do with herself, especially since she had a mouthful of wild mushrooms (Henriette had just slipped her a little extra).

When she got to me, I turned away. I felt my aunt's lips against my ear and she whispered, "Really, Pauline, you're a strange one."

"A strange one." I didn't like being called that.

❦ 27 ❦

Planting Christmas

THE "strange one" decided she'd had it and she was going to take life easy. She crossed romantic walks off her schedule, along with light-counting, dreams of communication, philosophical reflection. On the attic shelves she found novels she'd read during summer vacations, novels where one and one always made two, which isn't at all the case in real life; where people's eyes were the mirrors of their souls, which proved they had one; and where, if you were sinking, there was always a hand outstretched to save you in the last chapter.

The strange one settled down by the fire. She decided to knit a scarf as long as her afternoons, and didn't go out again until the twenty-seventh, at 12:10 P.M., with her mother, to meet Bernadette and Nicole at the station.

We chatted on our way back up the main street to the house with our travelers. The snow was over. It was too cold: a dry and luminous cold like the blade of a knife.

At La Marette, Daddy and Nicole had already told Bernadette all about Claire, but she wanted to hear it again from Mom. She'd never forgive herself for not being there when Grandmother announced the news. Oh, how she would have liked to hear Philippa ask for a "splash of wine." Why not a "drip"? And how was she doing now?

Now it was all right. Philippa hadn't mounted an offensive, but sometimes her eyes were frightening. Especially since Adrien went back to Dijon, where he works as a stockbroker and dreams of hunting snails.

The only man we had left then was Alexis. We couldn't wait until Friday, two days off, when Adrien would return, and the thirty-first, when Daddy would bring Stéphane down with him.

"How's the service?"

"Not too tough, but boring as hell," Bernadette summed up.

I laughed. At her categorical, colorful way of putting it. With pleasure at having her back. The moment I saw her getting off the train I realized how much I'd missed her. She studied the platform, the station, as if looking for a fight, about to spring. Bernadette is a fighter. And when she talks, the sun comes out. The opposite of Philippa.

The two of us carried her big bag, one hand each. Nicole and Mom followed behind. Bernadette's eyes were everywhere; she breathed in deeply. "My God, I can't believe how much it smells like Montbard!" Just before we got to the gate, she looked at me more deeply and asked, "And how about you? Doing okay?"

I answered, "Business as usual."

And immediately regretted it. But it was already too late. Bernadette was off on another topic.

No, I was not doing okay. And there was some funny business: Cécile. If everyone from Henriette to Grandmother hadn't had their eyes glued to Claire day in and day out, they'd have seen that something was out of whack, gradually getting worse, as if something too strong for her was weighing on the Pest. They'd notice the circles under her eyes, the strain in her laughter. Grandmother would be worried to see how she barely touched her meals, though normally she loves to eat. Mom would wonder where she disappeared to all day long.

I didn't know anything. When I tried to talk to her about it, once again she wouldn't answer. And she told me that if I mentioned to anyone that I'd given her money, it would be "even more serious." Blackmail occurred to me. But who'd want to blackmail Cécile? And for what?

Daddy's razor mysteriously reappeared on the dressing table. On the other hand, Alexis's bottle count was off. He was sure some were missing. Of course it couldn't be Philippa! As for Gaston, he was in bed with the flu and had lost his voice, apparently.

Lost or decided to lose? I tried questioning him. He turned his face to the wall. He seemed afraid.

I'd answered Bernadette, "Business as usual." Later Daddy assured me it wouldn't have changed anything if I'd confessed my fears to her that day. It was already too late, it seems. But after what happened, what else could he say?

I forget what happened next. Lunch, thanks to Bernadette and Nicole playing off each other, to Grandmother's delight, was a wonderful time. Even the Pest laughed out loud again for once.

In the afternoon, Alexis gave me a driving lesson on the grounds. He has an asthmatic old car that shakes like crazy, but he assured me that once I master it I'll be able to drive anything.

I avoided being left alone with Nicole. I didn't want to talk about her party at the Town Hall. But that night, just after I got in bed, she came into my room and set a book down on the covers.

"From Démogée. He didn't mean to hurt your feelings, you know. He was very upset when you ran off like that."

The poor thing . . . I made no reply. For a writer, he was singularly lacking in imagination, that's all. I waited until she left to read the inscription and my heart did flutter.

"For a little light on a damp stone in the Parc Buffon."

It was sweet, but incomplete. The light didn't shine anymore. He'd stamped it out.

I slid the book under my pillow so Cécile wouldn't ask any questions. Her covers were rigid. She kept me from sleeping at night.

In spite of everything, we had a nice time replanting the Christmas tree.

Our Christmas pines form a sort of hedge on the first terrace, near the spot where the lawn chairs and Grandmother's beach umbrella are set up in summer.

Certain trees have done better than others, but they've all survived.

First we had to dig a deep hole, which wasn't so easy with the ground frozen. At least no one felt cold after that.

Once the hole was dug, we brought the tree out of the house in its planter, not without difficulty, especially when Henriette started yelling that we were getting dirt all over her parlor floor.

Alexis, Mom, Bernadette, Nicole, and I were the haulers. The others cheered us on, except Philippa, who said we'd never make it and declared that a tree this tall would be death on the chandeliers.

The needles rained on our heads. Everyone was shouting; now and then we stopped to laugh. When Claire offered to help, that took the cake.

Out in the yard, we took our Christmas guest out of the planter and carried it on a wheelbarrow. There was still a little tinsel on the branches; I was eager to help revive it, pat good living soil around its roots; eager to have its branches feel the wind and bear the weight of snow, since that's what evergreens like. I felt I had great power.

As we planted it, Uncle Alexis once again told the story of this spot.

Before our family, Buffon's friend Daubenton lived in the house. Daubenton was a naturalist too, and needed cadavers to study. It was against the law, so he went to get his raw material by night in the nearby cemetery, and when he was finished with it he buried what was left in the first terrace.

But that was only the beginning of the story. During the last war, Grandmother's house had been occupied by German officers. And after they left, seven newly dug graves were found on the same terrace, exactly where we drink coffee looking out at the view, white cows on the hillside and the train that chugged along with our childhood memories.

They were the graves of seven German boys between fifteen and eighteen years old. And what Alexis really would have liked to have seen, and so would I, was the look on those officers' faces when they dug the graves of these children — that's the only way I can think of them — these children who could have been me, with no desire to fight, still marveling at the sky's colors and love's power over the body. When they found all the tibias, skulls, and pelvic bones, not to mention the rest, that Daubenton had buried here.

So that quiet, sunny afternoon of Bernadette's return, we planted the Christmas tree in the ground where the great marriage of the absurd between the French and the Germans had been celebrated.

Cécile hunted for pieces of bone. Uncle Alexis looked contented. Better yet, peaceful. When we'd heaped the last shovelful of dirt around the tree, he lit up a pipe and considered his work, blowing out big puffs of smoke like messages to the past.

I wondered if he hadn't chosen this spot for his Christmas tree hedge on purpose. You never can be sure with Alexis. Or with death.

It crept over the house. It came sneaking in, like a thief. It was already doing its work as we planted the tree, believing we were bringing it back to life.

But before it hit us, a lot of things happened, great and small, to blindfold all of us.

And to start with, the family game of *billard Nicolas* that was never finished, a most unusual occurrence.

❧ 28 ❧

A Game of Billard Nicolas

I T was after lunch, December 28. Uncle Alexıs teamed up with Mom. Nicole was on Grandmother's side. *Billard Nicolas* is a variation on pool. The object of the game is using your red blower to push a little white cork ball into the opponents' pocket. The most exciting part is when the ball wavers near the hole, with both sides huffing away at it.

It went very badly, as usual. Alexis and Mom got trounced. Alexis claimed it was because they'd given him the blower that doesn't work, that sticks to your fingers. For the last forty years, it seems, he'd gotten it every time, and when he started complaining about it in the heat of battle, Mom laughed so hard she couldn't breathe. Grandmother would settle for winning, while reminding Alexis that someone born on the feast day of St. Placide ought to be more in control of his nerves, which made him blow his top. Nicole was lethal: not a smile, not a sound. The only thing that interested her was wiping out the enemy.

Grandmother's team was ahead five to one. Leaving the youngsters to their game, Claire, Bernadette, and I were trying to read. Cécile had disappeared, as usual. Philippa was digesting her meal in her darkened room, next to poor Gaston's. His fever had gone down but he still wasn't allowed out of bed.

I thought I heard a car pull into the drive but couldn't be sure. Almost at once, there was a knock at the door and Henriette poked her head in.

"A gentleman to see you, ma'am," she said to Grandmother.

Grandmother looked up. Mom took advantage of the situation to whack the ball deep into enemy territory.

"No fair!" Grandmother yelled. "Time out!"

And to Henriette, furiously: "A gentleman? What gentleman?"

Henriette stepped aside, the door opened all the way, and Antoine appeared.

He was wearing a lumber jacket, as if he thought he'd be landing on the North Pole. He looked calm. He was smiling. His smile was what struck me first; I remembered him with a gray face. He smiled walking over to Grandmother, who took a minute to recognize him, but then did. He kissed her hand.

"Really," Nicole said in a perfectly phony voice, "I was beginning to wonder if you'd show up."

Grandmother looked at our aunt, bewildered.

"We asked him so long ago," she explained. "In September, when we had that *fondue bourguignonne*."

"A fondue?" Grandmother couldn't help parroting. It was one of her favorite dishes.

Nicole looked at Antoine with mischief in her eyes. "And I believe the invitation was issued on one condition."

"That I'd bring my fondue sauce," Antoine said on cue.

It sounded like a play. Grandmother joined in now. "I don't see any sauce."

Antoine tapped his forehead. "It's in here. You'll know when you smell it."

He finally turned to the rest of the gathering: to Alexis,

178

still holding his blower, Mom, who seemed dumbstruck, to us, to Claire.

Claire was standing by the sofa, holding on to the back of it. She was white as a ghost. Even her lips. She looked at Antoine as if she couldn't believe her eyes. Just when I was starting to wonder if she wasn't going to lose it, Bernadette hurried over and without a word pushed on Claire's shoulders to make her sit back down.

Antoine walked over to us. I felt his hands on my shoulders, his lips brushing my forehead. They were still cool from his trip.

"Well, Pauline!"

He shook Bernadette's hand. Then he was face to face with the Princess. He looked at her for a long time.

"How's everything?" He asked it forcefully, like a question he'd been saving a long time. He said it breathlessly, as if he'd run there to get the answer.

For several seconds, Claire kept quiet. It seemed like too much for her, as if surprise had drained her strength. But that wasn't it. Not at all.

Very slowly, delicately, she placed her hand on her stomach.

"Everything's fine," she said, "and so am I."

Her voice wavered slightly. With pride, I'd almost say. And I remembered our lunch that seemed so long ago, when she tried to explain to me that in a way, it was on account of Antoine that she was keeping the baby.

There was an immense, interminable silence. They looked at each other. Eight of us were in the parlor, not counting Henriette at the door, who wasn't missing a thing; but for the moment, for certain, the two of them were alone.

And Antoine had more surprises in store. He was still looking at Claire in his breathless way.

"Are you happy?"

A sort of smile flickered on our Princess's face. "I'm trying."

Grandmother gaped. She turned to Mom, whose hands were gripping the same table. Nicole was staring at her feet. That was when Uncle Alexis came to the rescue.

Alexis is an extremely reserved man who hates interfering in other people's business, and keeps his opinions to himself.

He stuck his pipe in his mouth, and as he lit up, he headed, paunch first, for Antoine and Claire.

"One thing I've learned from experience," he said, "is that trees you plant when you're happy are ten times hardier and grow an awful lot straighter than if you put them in when you don't feel like it."

In her doorway, Henriette seconded him with big nods. The same for her sauces. She was always telling us that you had to put your heart in your work.

Looking at Alexis, Antoine waited for him to go on, but he was finished. Our uncle went back to the game table, to Mom who looked at him like he was a king.

A log cracked and scattered its embers. Fire and ash. A noise that summed everything up.

Although Claire's eyes were lowered, Antoine was smiling at her. It was fine to see. I think he was smiling at the baby.

Nicole went over to Henriette, still standing by the door.

"How about making us another round of coffee?" She spoke loudly on purpose. To snap us out of it, take us by the shoulders, and plunge us back into everyday life. Nicole is rooted in it.

"It's already on the stove," Henriette chimed in. "Won't take a minute. I'll just run and get it."

But instead of leaving, she went up to Grandmother and said in the authoritarian voice of someone who'd already made up her mind, "Where shall I put the gentleman? In the Green Aunt's room?"

"Do," Grandmother said, "do, dear."

Most of the rooms are named after the ancester whose portrait sits in state there. In her fine gilded frame, the "green aunt" isn't green, but livid, hence her name. She died, poor thing, of the "lingering illness": tuberculosis.

Antoine came over to Mom. I heard him say something about a hotel. Nicole protested. If he wanted a room with the competition, he might as well go back to Paris. And what would Charles say if he didn't find Antoine here in the house?

I learned, we all learned, that the three of them had had dinner together the night before last at La Marette. News to Bernadette, who was at the Saint-Aimonds' that night. Was it a dinner or a planning session?

In came the coffee. I let Nicole serve it. It was so easy to see that she needed to move, get close to us, look questioningly into our eyes.

It was "no, thanks" for me, "two and a half sugars" for Bernadette, just a sugar cube soaked in coffee for the Princess.

I sat down next to her in a complete daze. Couldn't think straight. At the same time I was happy and I felt robbed. Of what? Suddenly I wanted to be in someone's arms. Wanted life to declare for me, carry me off, in spite of myself. It was good that Antoine had come. It was good that once I had thought of him as an impossible love. It heightened everything. It was a sign of things to come, complicated things, the opposite of sleep. What I yearn for and fear.

Claire got up and I returned to reality. She was bright red now. She got up and walked to the door without looking at anyone, without making any effort to conceal her jutting stomach. Quite the contrary. The room screamed with life.

Antoine's cup tinkled on his saucer. He got up too, said, "Please excuse me," and followed Claire out.

When the door shut, there was an awkward silence. We

needed to make light of what had just happened, make it like before. Maybe we could if Bernadette had an ounce of humor in her. But Bernadette's sense of humor . . .

She marched up to Nicole.

"You could have warned us. At least Claire!"

"I didn't know if he'd come," Nicole protested. "I just extended the invitation from September again. Until just now I swear I thought he'd turned it down."

Bernadette still looked wary. "Admit you went back with Daddy just to tell him to come."

"Well, sometimes you have to give a little nudge to get life going."

"With you, it's more like a big kick," said Grandmother.

Finally Mom laughed. Grandmother joined in. Alexis headed for the liquor cabinet. As soon as there's a problem, for him it's time for a nip of the plum brandy. Grandmother summarily held out her coffee cup. Alexis pointed to the game table.

"Don't you want to finish up first?"

"Count yourself the winner for once," Grandmother conceded. "We quit. My poor Alexis, life is definitely full of surprises."

I've always loved to follow the Burgundy canal, thinking about all the loaded barges that once had plied it.

I took an old bike from the garage, pedaled through town, passed the bridge, went along the factory whose whistle we heard four times a day, then the workers' housing, so depressing.

The canal is lined with huge poplars. Their confetti-shaped leaves make a papery noise in the wind. Now that the canal is no longer in use, there are branches on the banks. Shrubbery and flowers have been planted. My dream is for this body of water to regain its freedom and overflow, filling the countryside with the sound of barges, a change of scenery.

When I was far from everyone's eyes, I leaned my bike against a tree, and, walking along the canal, I finished Paul's book.

It was a novel, supposedly a good one. Won a prize. I didn't like it. It was the story of a man — not even a story, there was no plot — the description of a man lost in the crowd, loveless, aimless, hopeless. The portrait of a phantom; a dreary book, composed of snuffed-out sentences, bloodless words; a listing of objects, place names, figures.

At no point did I find life in it. Not once did the book say anything about me, about all of us, what I see, sense, feel each day.

How could I have been so mistaken? I thought I'd met a warm, open man. It was only a mask. What I'd taken as caring and poetry was only pretense and mockery. He only watched the lights come on to shut them out in himself. Now I understood that he'd tricked me, and it was a good ending to the whole farce.

I remembered the log that had cracked open earlier, the burst of life. I would have described the embers. Paul would see only the ashes.

To find an excuse, I tried thinking about his leg. But there was someone in me who refused to forgive, come to his defense. To end this pointless story for good, I dropped the book in the water, and with it the damp stone, the lights of Christmas Eve, and the sadness of missed connections.

❧ 29 ❧

Grandmother Underdrawers

"*L*ook," said Cécile. "Honestly! You've got to have a dirty mind . . ."

Antoine laughed. They were sitting side by side on the sofa. On their knees was one of our most delightful family heirlooms: a big bound volume dating from the sixteenth century. Red and gilded, with a gold clasp. It's a book of reproductions of classical statues. Nothing special about that. But the many-times-great-grandmother who first owned this marvel, shocked by the nudity in it, had invented the bikini in 1520. Painted in india ink is a whole collection of bathing suits: two pieces for the women, briefs for the men. The models are obviously more solidly built and with bigger muscles than today's version, but they pose and show off their best features the same way.

The fantastic thing is how painstaking the work is, the minute detail, the variety. Elegant knots at the sides of the men's briefs, lacy straps on the women's bras, single or double, wide or narrow to fit each set of shoulders. If zippers had existed then, you'd see every tooth. This superb line of ready-to-wear fashion had earned our original ancestor the name of "Grandmother Underdrawers."

"It must have taken her forever," Antoine exclaimed.

He was only half laughing. When we showed him around the house, he was deeply impressed by all the crucifixes, stations of the cross, sacred hearts, and, in antique frames, bones or pieces of cloth that are saintly relics intended to ease our family's passage into heaven.

"I bet she really got off on painting this. Especially when it was the men she was bowdlerizing."

"Bowdlerizing . . ." guffawed Aunt Nicole.

"Just what do you mean by 'she got off on it'?" Bernadette asked hypocritically.

"Well, it must have turned her on," the Pest specified. "Just look at all these little straps to undo. And never anything showing, just think about that. Too bad she didn't use cloth instead. We could look under it."

"We could try to get the ink off," Bernadette suggested, "but there's no guarantee it would work. We might bowdlerize them for good."

Gaston tried to stifle his laughter. Aunt Philippa was pretending to read, but she dutifully shot a frown over at him. She has no idea her son is quite knowledgeable about the naked female form. Two years before, the woman from the pastry shop had come to complain to Uncle Adrien: Gaston was paying her daughter to go up to the attic and let him look at her, no underdrawers or anything, when she came with the weekly order.

Uncle Adrien had a good laugh and pointed out to the mother he'd done the same thing with her thirty-five years ago. She backed down. Philippa never suspected a thing. Now the shopboy made the deliveries.

"If you don't stop making fun of your ancestors," Grandmother threatened, "I'm locking up the book."

Sitting in the lamplight, she was playing solitaire, under the watchful eye of our mother, who'd promised to keep her from cheating. She's rather proud of the fact that given the choice between the book's market value and her own values, Grandmother Underdrawers had chosen the latter.

Cécile kept turning the pages, holding her laughter in. Earlier, when she came into the parlor and saw Antoine, she stopped in her tracks in amazement. Then she flew to him. Since then, I thought I read something like relief on her face. And it was a long time since we'd heard her laugh so freely.

Claire watched them out of the corner of her eye. It would be hard to know what she and Antoine had said to each other during their two-hour walk, at the end of which she'd gone directly to her room. Good sign number one: she was listening to a Mozart opera on the radio. Number two: she was wearing lipstick.

Five to eight. In five minutes the dinner bell would ring, Henriette clanging away. I quietly left the parlor and went up to my room. I felt rather guilty about what I was planning to do, but I was so concerned I had to.

I left the door open so I could hear if anyone was coming. My heart was pounding. The room seemed different, hostile. I began by searching the closet, without finding anything. Nothing under Cécile's pillow, either. I opened her dresser drawer. A bunch of socks, underpants, and hankies. I must have been mistaken in thinking I'd seen her hiding something when I walked in on her earlier.

I poked around. I was about to give up when I felt something like paper inside a sock. It was an envelope.

I expected to find a blackmail letter, or threats. An object of some kind, perhaps. But this, never.

It was a plane ticket. Dijon to Marseilles. Leaving December 31. The next day. 4:10 P.M. Passenger: Mr. Moreau.

Mr. Moreau? There was only one person by that name here: my father. And there was one thing I was sure of. He had no intention of flying to Marseilles the next day. He was driving here then. He'd just assured Mom on the phone that he'd be bringing the *foie gras* for our New Year's Eve dinner, a fantastic *foie gras* we ordered from Sarlat, in Dordogne. For Cécile there would be a slice of smoked salmon, as usual, because she can't condone the torture of geese.

Mr. Moreau. Dijon-Marseilles. December 31. 4:10 P.M.

I stuck the ticket back in the sock and closed the drawer. My head swam. Tomorrow . . . I collapsed on the bed. This was serious.

When I heard footsteps on the stairs, I had just enough time to head for the sink, I splashed water on my cheeks. Yes, it was Cécile. She leaned against the door and watched me. How tired she looked.

"What are you up to?"

"Just what it looks like. It's so hot down there with the fire."

The dinner bell rang. She kept eyeing me warily as I wiped my face. We went down together. Not a word was spoken. But what could I say? It was too soon. We wouldn't have had enough time and I needed to think. I was dying to tell Mom everything. I was angry with her for not noticing. But I remembered Cécile's words: "If you say anything, it will only make it worse."

The family was in the dining room. They were waiting for us to say grace. Everyone noticed that Antoine made the sign of the cross.

One of the terrible facts of life is how easy it is to hide your troubles from those closest to you. I was very natural. I ate normally. Besides, I was hungry and the food was good. I listened to Antoine explaining to Grandmother that an autistic child is one who cuts himself off from the world. I thought about Frédéric. I tried not to look at Cécile. She hid things well, too. She was just a little too well-behaved . . . that was what should have tipped Mom off. But what Antoine was saying was so much more interesting.

At one point I caught Alexis watching the Pest closely. He'd sensed something. His knife pointing upwards, he seemed to be questioning her. But it was quickly over.

The evening seemed endless. All I could see was the plane ticket. Tomorrow . . . Cécile excused herself right away. Philippa was being charming to Antoine, who'd examined Gaston's throat and pronounced him in great shape.

I thought about confiding in Antoine. I should have. But I remembered the night I'd gone to betray Claire's secret. What would he think if now I told him Cécile's?

Uncle Adrien arrived about then. He was introduced to Antoine. I took advantage of the commotion to go upstairs.

The Pest was already asleep. Sound asleep, the covers drawn up to her chin. I opened the drawer again. So what if she woke up! I hoped she would. The ticket was gone. It didn't surprise me.

I went over to her bed and looked at her for a minute. What had she gotten herself mixed up in now? And how? She looked really little, I mean young and defenseless, with her smooth face that made it hurt to think about the future.

It was later, when in her sleep she threw off the covers, that I saw she was fully dressed.

I made up my mind not to sleep that night.

❦ *30* ❦

Gabriel

A creak of the door awakened me. It was pitch-black. I felt like I'd just gotten to sleep; my heartbeat echoed through the room.

Nothing else. Yes. A slight sound of breathing, breath being held; another heart beating. I didn't move a muscle. I even closed my eyes. You never can tell.

The door was opened ever so carefully. I couldn't see it but could sense it; I felt it like a tingling inside. The door was open. My night's sleep was over, obviously. And yet every bone in my body protested. I didn't want to get up.

This time there really was nothing else. I waited a few more seconds and then turned on the light. It was six o'clock.

I slipped out of bed. I'd slept in my clothes, too. It's awful how grubby it makes you feel. I picked up my shoes and went out of the room. Fate is gray, it tastes of dust. You resist it, but know you'll end up giving in. This moment awaited me. The last few days had been building up to it. I couldn't do anything about it; in a sense, I'd even asked for it.

A small light disappeared at the bottom of the staircase:

Henriette's flashlight, I supposed. I went down the stairs. The steps were ice-cold under my feet. They almost seemed wet. I used the banister to guide me. Cécile was in the kitchen. She had left the door open a crack, not enough for me to see anything.

There were sounds: a match being lit, a pot banging. Could it be the Pest was simply hungry? She'd practically stopped eating. And no one in our family sees any harm in a midnight snack, "one of life's little extras," says Daddy, who insists the sausage tastes best when everybody else is asleep.

But if hunger was what brought Cécile here, why didn't she turn on the light?

Standing against the door, holding my breath, I hesi tated. Though this would be the right time to go in. I'd have her cornered. I'd mention the plane ticket and demand an explanation. But I was tired; I had no desire to fight, and if there was a chance, even the slightest chance, she was going back to bed now, I wanted to let her.

I slipped into the pantry where Henriette puts empty bottles and keeps the cheese, especially the heady *époisse* Antoine cut into yesterday under orders from Grandmother. I leaned against the wall. Here there was a different kind of cold. In the trapped air was a kind of sunshine of dust. What was Cécile up to? And what was I doing there, hiding like I'd seen it done hundreds of times in the movies or on television?

The kitchen door opened and, light first, like a ghost, Cécile finally emerged. I was afraid she'd see me; I closed my eyes. I heard her go up the stairs. She stopped on the main floor. I knew deep down she wasn't going back to our room. And when I heard her open the door leading to the outside — it's always squeaked — I felt obliged to leave my hiding place and follow her.

On my way out the hall, I grabbed at the coatrack. As luck would have it, I pulled down Antoine's lumber jacket.

I put it on with a kind of revenge. It weighed a ton. It smelled old, used, and there were shreds of tobacco in the bottom of the pockets.

The cold took my breath away. Everything was motionless, as if congealed, killed. The night was in the sway of frost.

Farther off, on the walkway leading to the terraces, the small light was dancing. It wasn't headed at all in the direction I expected — toward the gate, the streets of Montbard. It was going deeper into the grounds. First terrace. There were a few lights on over near the station, the two streetlamps, and here and there a light in a window. It still smelled of fresh soil near our newly planted pine tree. Cécile took the walkway leading to the lower terraces.

They're connected by small stone stairways. One of the wells is historic. Buffon's B and Daubenton's D entwine on the stone. All kinds of vegetables used to be grown on the terraces. It was wild how much was produced. Wild, the multicolored jars on the kitchen shelves: peas, tomatoes, beans, and sorrel, because nothing goes better with fish.

When the old gardener died, they couldn't find anyone to replace him. So now only one terrace is gardened, with Nicole and Alexis fighting over it, and the others are planted with fruit trees. Yielding tarts, fruit salads, cakes, crêpes, fritters, wonderful preserves with the occasional pit to crack a tooth on.

As I followed the light, I repeated all that to myself like a litany, as if all the tarts and preserves in the past could protect me from the present, this frozen early morning, following my sister down to the third terrace, kneading Antoine's tobacco shreds between my fingers — and suddenly the light disappeared.

It was way at the back of the third terrace. I sped up. I could see a little, thanks to the streetlamp farther down. When I got to the wall, I realized Cécile had gone into the shed where the gardener used to keep his watering cans, wheelbarrow, and tools. And besides, I could make out the light between the slats.

I stopped. So there I was. I'd go in and then I'd know. Know what had been upsetting my sister, about the plane ticket, this icy outing. Now I was afraid, horribly afraid of what I'd discover, what Cécile would say when she saw me, and it took some courage, of which I had very little, to push open the door.

Cécile was crouched in a corner. She screamed in terror, and I realized she was expecting someone much more threatening than me to appear, since when I got closer and she recognized me she seemed infinitely relieved; so relieved that her eyes closed and I half expected to see her swoon.

I went all the way in, and to snap her out of it, prove that it was really me, I stammered, shivering all over, "What on earth are you doing here?"

She didn't answer. The flashlight, held between her knees, made her face a mask with bottomless eyes.

She was wearing her parka, her gloves. She clutched a thermos to her chest, the one we use for taking coffee on picnics. A very unpleasant odor filled the shed.

"Shut the door," she whispered.

I did as I was told and came closer. Against the wall, a tiny gas heater gave off a blue light. Beside her, what I took for a pile of old sacks was a person.

He was curled up under a stack of covers. All that showed was his hair, cut very short. The blankets rose and fell with his breathing. My heart started to thud. Cécile didn't move but her eyes beseeched me.

"Who is he?"

Just as I asked the question, he tossed restlessly and the blanket slid off. I recoiled. I felt like I was going crazy. He had on a steel-gray uniform jacket, the uniform of the Pontifical Zouaves. He'd stepped straight out of one of the picture frames in the parlor. All he needed was that hat and the mustache, and he could have been the defiant young man over the piano. Zouave ... we thought that was a funny word. It made us laugh. And yet it was a tragic story. Our two great-granduncles, the two difficult children no one in the family could manage, but for whom the Curé of Ars had predicted great things. The two boys volunteered in 1810 to go defend Papal territory. Volunteered for death.

"He was so cold," Cécile explained in a dull voice. "All he had on was a pajama top and an old raincoat that wasn't even his."

I understood, recognizing other items from the attic: old rugs, moth-eaten blankets, a rickety chair. How had she managed to get all this stuff down here without anyone noticing?

He looked at me. Or rather, he looked through me for something or someone. His eyes were very dark, yet ablaze, with a wild, searching expression.

Cécile finally moved; she carefully unscrewed the top of the thermos and knelt next to him.

"I've brought you something hot to drink. It'll make you feel better."

She sounded like Mom does when we're sick, with the voice you use to coax children.

The stranger's eyes were on her now, and he seemed to be asking his question of her. When she slipped her hand behind his head and lifted it, he moaned.

Cécile's face was determined. She pursed her lips as she stuck the rim of the bottle up to his rigid mouth and started pouring. He twisted his head, and the liquid went everywhere except where it was supposed to. I recognized the smell of yesterday's vegetable soup.

"Please drink some," she begged. "Please drink some, or you won't be strong enough to leave."

I knelt down next to her. He had very long hands. They gripped the blankets as if he were sinking. I tried to get the thermos away from her.

"But he can't. Don't you see he's choking?"

Then Cécile turned her angry eyes on me.

"His fever went down yesterday," she whispered. "He really was getting better. I swear it."

But as if to contradict her, he started to cough, and it took everything out of him. He couldn't stop. I was afraid I'd see blood. I was afraid of what she'd done, what would happen.

"We have to tell someone. He can't be left here like this. You're crazy! He's sick. Who is he?"

She got up. Now her expression was nearly one of hatred.

"I can't tell anyone. I promised."

I was silent. She repeated: "I promised! I promised!" And then the sobs came. From far off. She must have been holding it in a long time for them to be so strong, so deep. She sobbed as he coughed; and fixed his covers, and stroked his hair, and, when a new fit of coughing shook him, threw the thermos in the corner and went to the far side of the shed with her hands over her ears so she wouldn't hear him.

I went to her. I held her close. I pleaded, "Calm down." I promised, "I'll help you." We fell to our knees by the blue light that did give off a little heat. She shivered in my arms. Under his covers, he was breathing hard, fighting for each breath.

Then I remembered and I looked at my watch. It was nearly seven. I told myself Henriette would be down soon to light her stove. I imagined her gray braid, the smell of coffee and toast, the smells of the everyday.

Cécile finally decided to talk.

❦ *31* ❧

The Code of Secrecy

IS name was Gabriel, like the angel. She found him with Gaston, the day after we got to Montbard, on their first walk. Yes, they went for walks at first.

He was hiding in a tunnel: an abandoned tunnel with moss on the walls, full of mystery and strange smells, where Cécile and Gaston had always liked to go get scared.

Scared? They nearly died when they ran into him. And so did he. They thought it was an animal until he had a coughing fit that echoed off the walls like thunder. It was because of the cough that she stayed, while Gaston, panic-stricken, was already halfway back to the house.

She offered him some cough drops she had in her pocket. She saw he ate them out of hunger. She had a chocolate bar, and it went down the hatch too.

Then she tamed him. When she tames someone, Cécile always thinks of the lesson the fox taught the Little Prince, and she takes her time. She sat down next to him and waited patiently. He eventually told her his story.

He was twenty. His parents had abandoned him. He ended up in a reformatory, not far from there. He couldn't stand it. It got worse and worse. He was in the infirmary when he saw his chance to escape, at night, wearing a guard's raincoat. Either that, or he was a goner.

She said "a goner" a little softer, looking at him as if afraid he'd hear.

He wanted to get to Marseilles. But he didn't have the money, or the right clothes, or anything. The right clothes were important. She'd get to that.

He didn't dare leave his tunnel. He'd almost died of cold the night before. The worst part was the water, the water all over the ground and the walls; he said it was like being in a river. But when she suggested taking him back to the house, she thought he was going to bolt. That was when he made her promise not to tell anyone about him.

"You should have seen his eyes! They look like Madame Cadillac's dog, you know, Poulbot, the one his first owners mistreated." Poulbot had been beaten as a puppy, and when approached he backed away with eyes that said, "Please don't kill me."

Cécile remembered this shed and she suggested it to him. At least he wouldn't be sleeping in a river. And she'd get him clothes and a razor; he really needed one. He said yes, but just for one night. Gaston was the lookout while she led him into the garden. It threw a scare into them when Henriette passed right in front of them on her way to pick some bay leaves.

It didn't work out for the clothing. Uncle Alexis kept his room locked, for fear someone would swipe a pin from him; Daddy had only brought one change of clothes; she had to make do with the trunk in the attic. The uniform jacket was the only woolen garment and he could wear it on the trip if he put his raincoat over it.

But the next day his fever went up and he couldn't get to his feet. Christmas and Grandmother's money weren't here yet, so Cécile dipped into Henriette's hoard of five- and ten-franc pieces, even two fifty-franc ones, she keeps in an old canning jar, saving for her tombstone. With that Cécile bought what was most urgently needed: the little heater and decongestant tablets.

As if she didn't have enough to worry about, dumb old Gaston was getting more and more frightened and wanted to tell Grandmother all about it. She threatened him with the direst consequences, so to get out of helping her he did something she'd never forgive him for. He took the thermometer she'd used for Gabriel and convinced his mother he had a fever, seeking asylum in his bed.

So Cécile was left all alone. The day before yesterday she told him Gabriel was gone. She was too afraid he'd betray them. Gaston was instantly cured. She'd never speak to him again in her life.

I looked at the heap of covers. I murmured, "What now?"

"He has to get to Marseilles," she said stubbornly. "It's very important to him. I've made all the arrangements."

She got up, went to slip her hand beneath the covers, and retrieved an old wallet, bringing it over to me. She took out a picture. We bent over the lantern to look at it. It was a little girl, rather homely but not at all unpleasant-looking.

"His sister. She's been in a foster home down there for the last four years. He's afraid they'll tell her he's bad. He wants to find her to set things straight. He says after that the world can blow up for all he cares."

She put the picture back. She didn't seem to realize her Gabriel was incapable of leaving. Unless she was just talking like this to make herself feel better.

"Why by plane?"

She didn't bat an eyelash, figuring I must have discovered the ticket.

"He's afraid they may be watching the train stations. He's leaving this afternoon."

Her voice wavered a little. I prodded: "But how will he get to the airport?"

I thought it would hurt her, but suddenly her eyes lit up. She'd just had a brainstorm. You can always tell what Cécile is thinking.

"What if you took Alexis's car? You wouldn't have to tell him. We'll just slip away. It isn't that far to Dijon. We'll both take him to the airport. And who cares what happens after that?"

I turned away. Her eyes were so hopeful.

"I can't drive that well. And he'll never be able to get on the plane. We have to tell somebody. He needs a doctor."

"Somebody?" Cécile said. Her eyes turned somber once again.

"If they send him back to the reformatory, he's had it. They get him better, and then what? A month of being locked up for attempted escape. It's the rule."

Locked up! She sounded terrified, as if she'd experienced it herself. Cécile has never been able to stand the thought of people being put behind bars. When she was tiny, we'd find her in the closet. She wanted to know what it was like. Prepare herself. Prepare herself?

I didn't know what else to say. Under the covers, he looked like he was strangling when he coughed. I wanted to run to the house, ring the bell, cry for help.

"How about hiding him in the house?" Cécile suggested. "We could use the wheelbarrow to move him. He can't be much heavier than the Christmas tree."

"That won't do any good. He needs a doctor. Listen: let's tell Antoine."

I suggested it without conviction. I knew she'd refuse. She didn't respond. She turned to Gabriel as if to ask his permission. Once more her tears fell, but differently, without defiance. I think she'd reached her limit. Couldn't take it anymore. She'd held out as long as she could. It's often that way. You feel like people will never give in, but all they need is a chance, a nudge, to break down. Break down, meaning be themselves again. At last.

Cécile turned back into a twelve-year-old girl who was afraid for Gabriel; who was frantic about what she'd done.

"Doctors are bound by the code of secrecy," I told her. "Antoine can't reveal confidential information about a patient."

She got up. "Are you sure?"

I nodded. She went to lean over Gabriel.

"I'll be right back. If someone new comes with me, don't be afraid. Remember the code of secrecy."

We left the shed. She locked up with the big key with a tag on it that Grandmother's gardener always carried on him, afraid someone would take his tools. I liked the way he used to say "my tools," as if he meant "my life."

It was gray out now and the silence was less profound. Everything was damp. We ran. Before we got to the house, she whispered to me, and there was the hint of a smile in her voice, "I put all Henriette's money back in the jar after Christmas, but I didn't have time to get change. Think she'll believe it's a miracle?"

Antoine was sound asleep. It took him a minute to realize who we were. He finally got up, looked at his watch, and made a face. "What's going on? You certainly look like you're up to no good."

Then he must have noticed that the smaller miscreant couldn't get a word out, that her mouth was all screwed up like when you're trying to keep from crying, and that her accomplice wasn't doing much better. His smile vanished. He sat down on the bed.

I told him. Not too loud, because Alexis was sleeping next door and people who are half deaf always hear what they shouldn't (but not what they should). As soon as I said that Gabriel had a fever and a bad cough, he got up again.

"Go on. I'm listening."

He grabbed his pants and put them on in the adjoining bath, leaving the door open. By the time I was finished, he was dressed. If he only knew what awaited him. He got his bag and off we went. He didn't say anything about his lumber jacket.

On our way, we saw that the light was on in the kitchen. Henriette! We walked fast. The sky was lightening. It was healing. Cécile had gotten her voice back and was talking nonstop, mixing everything together: the police, the reformatory, Jesus, the soup, the airplane, the cough. She mentioned the code of secrecy several times. Antoine didn't respond. He laid a hand on her shoulder.

When she pointed to the mist-shrouded shed, saying, "There it is," he made no comment. He left the door open. With a sweeping gesture, he cleared everything off an old crate, drew it over to the pile of covers, and sat down. He touched Gabriel's forehead, lifted his eyelid, took his pulse, and that was all. He didn't even open his bag. He immediately stood up and turned to the Pest.

"Go wake Alexis up. Tell him to get the car out. We have to get him to the hospital."

Cécile was paralyzed. She looked at him and at me, holding her breath. The hospital?

"Can't we take care of him in the house?" she stammered.

"We wouldn't have what he needs," said Antoine in his calm voice. "He's very sick. Hurry now."

She took off. I saw her running up the walkway, stumbling. I felt guilty. When I told her we should tell Antoine, I knew it would lead to the hospital.

"Help me," he said. "We'll bring him up."

He lifted him up to roll him in the blankets. It was no time to think about such things, but the smell was horrible.

"They'll change him when we get there."

Gabriel groaned. His hand clutched at Antoine's sleeve.

"Don't worry, son. You're going to be taken care of."

Antoine's voice was different from the one he'd just used with Cécile. More commanding. But darker, too.

"You're going to pull through. Soon you'll be in a nice warm bed."

I wondered why he was explaining it to someone who couldn't even hear. Then I remembered what Daddy told me: you can never be completely certain someone's not hearing you. Some people who're given up for dead and then resuscitated can even tell you everything you said, which can be embarrassing if you've been discussing what to wear at the funeral.

I helped Antoine lift him up. The blanket was around his head, too. Like a mummy. Of course he couldn't stand up. Antoine took him by the waist. I did my best on the other side. He was heavy, my hands were frozen, I felt like we'd never make it. I gritted my teeth. I wanted so badly to go higher, higher than myself, than anything, for once.

We went up the first steps. One day they had picked Paul up along the road and taken him to the hospital, too. And perhaps he, too, had moaned. I hurt for him. I hurt ten years ago. I forgave him somewhat for disappointing me.

We paused before the second set of steps.

"All right?" Antoine asked.

"Yes."

"At least you won't catch cold."

"With your lumber jacket, you mean?"

He looked at me, deeply, and everything was there. My two visits to him, what I'd dreamed of. Claire. Everything. Even what might have been. Even what never would be.

The sound of Alexis's car shattered the moment. "Let's go!" We went straight up the last few steps.

Alexis was wearing his heavy hunting jacket. His car steamed. So did he. He came right over to take my place.

"It's already warmed up," he said briskly. "Where do we put him?"

"In back," Antoine ordered.

Cécile already had the door open. It's hard to get someone completely limp into a car. I worked on his feet. The blanket had slipped off and the uniform showed. Alexis saw it, narrowed his eyes, but said nothing. Yet I'm sure it was a shock to him.

"Is it far to the hospital?" Antoine asked.

"Not very," Alexis said. "And I know a shortcut."

"You drive. I'll stay back here with him."

Before he got in, he remembered Cécile. The Pest was staring at Gabriel. Or rather, she was staring at a point between his shoe and his pant leg, his naked ankle, so slender, white, and fragile. Anyone's ankle. The ankle of all children, with or without parents, in a reformatory or not. She didn't move, but the tears ran down her face.

"The only thing that counts," Antoine told her, "is getting him over this, right?"

"Right," she hiccuped.

Alexis was already behind the wheel. Antoine hesitated.

"Get in front," he said suddenly.

Cécile jumped in. He turned to me.

"*You* go and explain to your mother."

The car took off. Antoine's "*you*" stood still, abandoned, chilled to the bone. The engine noise wound down the drive, got lost in the mist on the grass. The tree trunks were dark brown. It was hard to believe it would ever be summer again. They were out on the street now. Soon they'd make a right turn. They were going by the department store. Passing the cheese shop. Then the bakery.

When Alexis used to take us down the drive in his car, we'd scream, "Faster, faster, Uncle Alexis!" and he'd speed up around the curve to give us a thrill. In the orchards, I'd always eat a fig first because of the color and its velvety sheen.

Faster! Faster, Uncle Alexis!

❦ *32* ❦

The Right to Asylum

I told Mom that for the last three months, since the end of September to be exact, no one had cared about anything but the Princess. That even if her situation *was* exciting, thorny, and every other thing, that didn't mean no one else had problems. That keeping your eyes glued to one person and cooking up Lord knows what with Grandmother the rest of the time blinded you to important, vital matters.

I pointed out that the whole time we'd been in Montbard, not once had she asked Cécile, or me for that matter — though I wasn't concerned about myself — what our plans for the day were, and how things were going, if we were happy. Not that we would have told her, necessarily, but still! Taking an interest in what others do is part of living together.

Mom didn't say anything. Without makeup, her face showed her fatigue and her age. She was sitting on her bed and kept stroking the two lovely embroidered initials on the sheet.

I told her everything, from the dripping tunnel to the freezing shed. I still had Antoine's damned lumber jacket on. Now I was stifling in it, and I don't know why, but it wouldn't have been a good idea to ask me to take it off.

We heard Nicole go softly down the steps. She always leaves for work early. She says that for her caseload, early morning is usually the worst part of the day.

Then the breakfast bell announced it was already a quarter to nine. We didn't move. It was good to see we could at least agree on not sticking to the day's schedule.

When I was finished, Mom simply said under her breath, a little like a prayer, "Let's hope he pulls through. Let's just hope." "Pulling through" meant more than getting better, since she added, "We'll help him as much as we can when he's over this. Don't worry."

She asked me his age. I subtracted a couple of years, for some unknown reason. I said eighteen. My age. I saw his ankle again as I said it.

She got up, still looking tired, and put on her travel bathrobe. It's nicer than the one she wears at home; we always wonder why. Did I agree that we should tell Grandmother at once? She'd be pretty mad if she heard Gabriel's story from an outsider first. Grandmother has always thought that people who share their bread should share everything else, too.

I agreed. Except with the Princess, for a while we'd been sharing nothing *but* bread.

When we went in, the drapes were already open, and Grandmother was getting ready to go down. All she had left to do was put on her cologne: an old lady's first duty is to smell good. Her breakfast tray lay untouched on the bed.

Henriette had just left, fit to be tied. Practically everyone was missing downstairs, it seemed. The only ones who'd answered the bell were Bernadette, Philippa, Adrien, and Gaston. She could understand if Claire wanted to stay in bed. But Alexis, Antoine, Cécile, Mom, and I?

Henriette hates us to be late, because the bread gets hard and the butter gets soft, not to mention the skin on the warm milk and the coffee that never tastes as good reheated. And that wasn't all. This morning, she'd found a dirty pot in her sink, and three wasted matches. She could accept the fact that her meals weren't filling enough, but she wished we'd at least wash up after the snacks we ate to keep body and soul together.

Mom made Grandmother sit down in the high-backed armchair with an immaculate doily for a headrest, and after making her promise to keep calm, she told her everything, omitting only the Zouave uniform, which is a sacred family relic.

First Grandmother got angry with me. Didn't she matter to me? I slept next door to her, nothing but a wall between us, and didn't breathe a word? Could it be I thought she was nothing but an old fogy?

I didn't answer. I wished I could put a blanket over my head and stop breathing.

At that point we heard the car in the drive and all three of us ran to the window.

Alexis was already out of the car, but Cécile's side was still closed. Before she finally appeared, Alexis had to open it himself and hold his hand out to her for quite a while. She stared at the ground. He didn't let go of her as they walked side by side up the steps.

"Let's go!" Grandmother said.

She led Mom to the door. I brought up the rear with the tray.

In the dining room, total silence. Under Henriette's reproachful glance, Alexis spread his napkin on his lap. His jacket hung on the back of the chair, something Grandmother doesn't generally allow. His eyes watered from the cold. His cheeks were stubbly, his hair windblown. He looked like he'd been in an accident.

Cécile still had her parka and even her gloves on. Bernadette looked at her as if trying to figure out what was going on. Philippa sat in state as usual between her husband and son, her special jar of honey and salt-free melba toast in front of her. The most interesting one to watch was Gaston. Beet red, he gawked at Cécile. He seemed to be asking her something, but the Pest ignored him. He no longer existed for her.

Mom went ahead, straight to Cécile, took her forehead in her hands, and gave her a big kiss, looking into her eyes. That was all.

When Grandmother came in, everyone rose. She gave a blanket greeting and went to sit down at her place, as if she ate breakfast with us every morning.

I set her tray in front of her. She pushed it aside and beckoned to Henriette.

"Henriette, dear, today I'll have coffee."

The way she said it no one dared object. Clearly in charge, Grandmother turned to Alexis.

"What's the news?"

"Not so good," he said. "Pleurisy. Antoine's supposed to call us."

"What's going on?" Bernadette asked. "Who are you talking about?"

Cécile's anxious eyes implored us not to give anything away.

"A young man," said Mom, "who had to be taken to the hospital. An emergency. Antoine's taking care of him."

Bernadette sensed it was better not to press us. Her melba toast poised in midair, Philippa looked at us one by one.

"A young man? What young man?"

Gaston was still staring at Cécile, who was still ignoring him.

"A nice guy," he said.

His voice was incredibly husky with emotion. Cécile looked up, incredulous. He'd run from trouble, and now he was sticking his neck out.

"Very nice," he repeated stubbornly.

Uncle Adrien, always on his guard when his wife's around, eyed his son with new interest.

Aunt Philippa put down her toast and turned to Gaston, looking down her distinguished nose at him. *Her* family's nose, so narrow she can't smell a thing.

"What do you know about it?"

"I was with Cécile when we found him in the tunnel," he said, "and . . ."

"Shut up!" Cécile broke in. "Too much is enough."

Philippa flinched with indignation. She thundered at the Pest: "What? What is he supposed to hide from his mother? What aren't we supposed to know?"

Alexis's bowl clinked against his saucer.

"Great God!" he roared. "We waited long enough to have breakfast. Now can't we enjoy it in peace?"

Grandmother frowned at the Lord's name taken in vain, but approved the idea. It made a curious mixture on her face.

Philippa turned back to Cécile.

"So you found this young man in a tunnel."

I could tell that Cécile didn't feel like crying anymore. Philippa was doing her some good. Over at the hospital, Gabriel, struggling. Here, this narrow-minded idiot.

"That's right," she said. "And since it's winter and it's cold out, we brought him back here."

"Here?" Her indignation was almost comical.

"Well, to the grounds," said Mom.

"With my son's help, I suppose."

"Naturally," Gaston said, still staring at the Pest. "I was the lookout."

Philippa looked at each one of us. She's always screened her offspring's acquaintances carefully. She has her "set" and everyone outside it is to be kept at arm's length. Gaston's little friends wear ties and kiss matrons' hands — yes, it's still done. Even if they do compete to see which one of them can whisper the worst insult in so doing.

"And where did this young man come from, before the tunnel?"

"It's so hard to know, with people out of work all over," Grandmother said.

She has nothing against lies as long as they're white ones.

"It's no use knowing your missal by heart if you do the opposite of what it says," Cécile told Philippa. For the last few seconds she'd looked like she wanted to break every last dish on the table over our dear aunt's head.

Mom tried to smooth things over.

"They were just trying to help someone in trouble. It's only normal."

"If you think it's normal for your daughter to bring just anyone into your home," Philippa said through her clenched teeth, "feel free. And I'll feel free to refuse to have my son dragged into it. I suppose you haven't heard about delinquents and drug addicts . . ."

"Philippa!" Grandmother said in a fearfully soft voice. "We hear what we want to. You should learn to judge with your heart, not your ears. Personally, I have only one regret: that Cécile didn't tell me sooner about this young man. I would have been delighted to welcome him at our table."

Philippa's eyes widened.

"With the children?"

"You don't think," said Uncle Adrien, "that children stay tied to your apron strings all their lives, do you?"

He said it very calmly, but his eyes flashed. Gaston let out an astonished laugh. You can't hold it against him. It's the age he's at. He laughs anytime and at anything, generally at the most inappropriate times. I suppose he imagined himself and his mother's apron strings, her meager haunches.

Philippa looked at her dolt of a son. She was about to bawl him out when something occurred to her. Something serious, apparently.

"Your throat! You caught your sore throat from him."

Following his father's lead, Gaston rose to new heights.

"I wasn't really sick. I just pretended because I was afraid of you."

Such naked truth, so simply put, made the whole family fall silent, a silence full of disbelief and stifled laughter.

Philippa got up. You could tell she was close to her breaking point, and I did feel sorry for her. She was terribly upset. And when that happens, you turn nasty if you have it in you.

"First Claire!" she hissed, looking at Mom. "Pregnant with no husband in sight, and you think it's perfectly fine. And now this . . . this vagrant."

She turned to Gaston. "It's a good thing you didn't say anything to me about it. I would have called the police."

Cécile's eyes appealed to Grandmother for help.

Grandmother was half-standing, her fist clenched on the table. Beneath the softness of her voice, a storm was brewing.

"My dear Philippa, if I remember correctly, the ancestor you're so proud of, Anthime de Verdorin, considered the right to asylum his family's prime responsibility. Could you have forgotten that?"

Cut to the quick, Philippa blanched.

"I won't take any more insults."

She beckoned to Gaston.

"Come on."

Gaston reached for his bowl and plunged his whole face into it. He didn't surface.

There was a moment so intense with embarrassment and pleasure that it was almost palpable.

"You're not coming?" Philippa asked threateningly.

His bowl got a notch closer to his face. Then Philippa turned to her husband.

"And you? You aren't going to do anything about it?"

Taking his time, Uncle Adrien fished his car keys out of his pocket and handed them to his wife.

"I'd advise you to go back to your mother's in Dijon.

Haven't you been wishing you could spend New Year's Eve with her? I'm sure you'll have a better time there."

His voice was calm, but his eyes were murderous.

Henriette, who kept making purposeless trips between the kitchen and dining room to follow the action, nodded with her whole being. She doesn't like Philippa because she always scrapes the croutons, garlic, *crème fraîche,* mushrooms to the side of her plate — everything that makes food good.

Aunt Philippa turned to Grandmother.

"Your son . . ."

"At times like this," Grandmother interrupted, "it's indispensable for everyone to agree. My son is quite right."

Philippa took the keys and went out, leaving the door open, which was her way of slamming it. We heard her steps in the hallway.

There was a sort of general sigh of relief. Gaston lifted a flushed face from his bowl. Only then did we see how afraid he was. Uncle Adrien tousled his hair with both hands. But it was Cécile who had Gaston's attention. The Pest still had her parka zipped up to her neck. She condescended to smile at him before taking off her gloves.

"There's one thing I'd really like to know," said Henriette thoughtfully, "whether the *foie gras* the doctor is supposed to be bringing is for tonight's dinner or tomorrow's lunch."

"First we need to be sure the doctor doesn't forget it," Grandmother sighed.

She grasped her cup of coffee.

"At least I'm sure I just made somebody up there really happy," she said, lifting her eyes heavenward. "Good old Anthime de Verdorin."

Bernadette's laughter set us all off, even Cécile. And all things considered, breakfast ended on a note of something resembling hope.

✿ 33 ✿

The 4:10 Flight

*I*filled the bathtub with nice hot water, with peace and oblivion, the doors and windows bolted, and in I dove. I soaked a long time, eyes closed, trying to be in the sea, long ago, when Daddy, the story goes, had to drag me out because I liked it so much, liked the water, sky, sand, and being rocked.

The house was completely silent. If I opened my eyes a crack, I could see Uncle Alexis's shaving brush, his tortoise-shell hairbrush, and on a hook behind the door, his famous nightshirt, ecru cotton. Gabriel slowly became an impossibility.

Around eleven, I think, Bernadette came in to make sure I hadn't drowned. I let her in. My fingertips were red and shriveled; it doesn't take long to deteriorate. She remarked on a big beauty mark under my right breast.

"I bet you'll get a lot of comments on that."

I laughed. "It makes a good landmark."

She said that from now on she was going to call beauty marks "landmarks."

Apart from that, she told me Philippa really had left, though no one could quite believe it. They were afraid it was just for show, even if she'd taken her special jar of honey. Uncle Adrien was more than a little nervous about his car; she'd already wrecked several transmissions on him.

I also learned that Nicole was home and she and Claire had heard the story at the same time. Nicole was familiar with the reformatory Gabriel had escaped from. A good one, apparently. But good or not, the kids who ended up there felt deep down that they'd been given up on.

Outside, blue skies, and sun all over the grounds. Always a good sign. In the drive, we ran into Alexis and Claire. Since they hadn't heard from Antoine, they were going to look for him at the hospital. They'd try to bring him home for lunch. I thanked Uncle Alexis for the use of his bathtub.

"It's all yours," he said laughingly.

The rest of the family was in the parlor. Sitting on the stool in front of the fireplace, still wearing her parka, Cécile was throwing kindling on the fire and watching it twist and burn. Flat on his stomach on the rug, Gaston didn't take his eyes off her. You could tell they were friends again.

Mom called me over. She explained that what I called "cooking something up with Grandmother" was a plan they had for Claire. Grandmother wanted her to stay in Montbard. She thought that from every point of view it would be better for her to have the baby there. Claire seemed quite interested but had asked to have time to think it over.

"By 'every point of view' you mean she should have it in secret," the Pest grumbled without taking her eyes off the fire.

"It means she'll have it in peace and quiet," Mom corrected. "As for hiding the baby's arrival, there's no question of that."

"So can I tell Roughly Speaking when we get home?" the Pest asked defiantly.

Telling Roughly Speaking meant that within a few hours the whole town of Mareuil would know.

"Why not?" Mom said. "But if you don't mind, we'll tell him the good news together."

When Antoine came in, we saw right away that things weren't going well. He looked too collected, as if he'd been rehearsing what he was going to tell us. Claire's eyes were red; as for Alexis, he went to the window and started flipping his knife with his back to everyone.

Antoine addressed himself to Cécile. Yet she hadn't asked any questions. She'd just looked at him briefly when he came in.

He told her that when Gabriel ran away from the reformatory, he was already very ill, taking large doses of antibiotics, and about to be transferred to a sanatorium in the mountains. The transfer was probably the reason he decided to take off.

"He escaped to go see his sister in Marseilles," Cécile said bluntly. "And when he's straightened things out with her, when he's shown her he's not a bad guy, like those jerks who don't understand anything about it must have told him in there, then the world can explode for all he cares."

"I didn't say that wasn't the reason," Antoine murmured.

I thought: "See his sister before he dies." It was very clear. When you die, in one sense, the world does explode. Gabriel realized he'd had it. That was the thought that hurt most. If you have to die young, it should be without knowing in advance, by accident; in any case, not a slow death.

Cécile got up.

"So is he going to die?"

"They're doing all they can for him," Antoine answered. He went up to Cécile and tried to put a hand on her shoulder. She jerked away.

"I know what you mean. That's what they always say when it's hopeless."

I looked at Claire and saw that the Pest had guessed right. Mom was awfully pale. She must have been thinking of our friend Jean-Marc, who'd also died, died young and a slow death too.

"I guess three days in a drafty shed didn't help matters."

"I'm sure it was worse in the tunnel," Antoine said with feeling. "And he didn't have anyone to care for him there."

He spoke a little too fast, a little too loudly. Cécile stared at him, and he looked away first. Then she turned her head every which way, as if searching for a way out. Grandmother opened her arms. But the Pest headed for Alexis.

Uncle Alexis was still staring out the window with his knife open, as if wondering which end of the impassive landscape he'd start stabbing first. The Pest took his knife from him; she ran a finger over the notches.

"In your prison camp, there must have been a lot of guys with TB. You said there wasn't any heat or anything. I bet the Germans didn't give them medicine. Probably tried not to help them. But didn't some of them make it?"

Alexis didn't answer right away.

"Some of them did. But don't kid yourself. Not very many. Not many at all."

She gave him back his knife and they stayed like that for a moment, facing out toward Gabriel. No one had any idea what to say. Cécile turned around, and when he saw her face, Gaston buried his own in his hands.

"Honey," Mom said. She'd gotten up; she walked over to Cécile with Antoine. The Pest pushed them both away.
. "When's Daddy getting here?"

"Soon," Mom said. "Around four or five."

"He'd better make it fast," Cécile said. She looked at Antoine defiantly and went out, slamming the door behind her. Bernadette followed.

"Sorry about that," Mom said to Antoine.

"Can't you see she thinks it's her fault?" Claire exclaimed. "We have to do something."

"We're all to blame," Grandmother said.

Then Alexis turned around. He wore an impossible look. He went over to Antoine.

"If there's anything the boy needs!" he said in his rough voice.

"There's not much that can be done for him now," Antoine replied.

"I just mean," Uncle Alexis continued, "I thought I heard you mention something about kidneys back there."

Antoine nodded.

"So I was thinking that at my age, one would get me as far as I have to go," Alexis went on.

Antoine waited a few seconds to answer. His voice was full of warmth.

"Thanks for the offer. But it wouldn't change anything."

He couldn't have known about the antidonation envelope. No one could find a word to say and now Mom left the room. Grandmother got up; she walked over to her brother, who looked at her warily. She laid her hand on his arm.

"Why don't you stop playing with that open knife? What will I do with myself when you finally manage to stab yourself?"

And time turned sick. Turned limp. Was weightless. We were there like astronauts floating above the surface of the moon.

We were waiting for something impossible: the death of a young man who wouldn't have had the chance to be happy. Grandmother had said it: we all felt responsible.

After lunch, Mom proposed a nice, long walk. Bernadette and Uncle Adrien signed on. I went down to the kitchen.

Henriette had pulled the light down very low over the long wooden table and was going over her accounts in the big black ledger so stuffed with receipts she couldn't get it closed

I sat down across from her and waited. She shot a look at me over her glasses, then plunged back into her calculations. Here, time existed again. It was flowing for her, and I didn't tire of watching her form her figures.

When she finished the last column, she drew a thick

line and then shut the ledger.

"It was time for the year to end. This poor book has had it."

She showed me where the edges were wearing away; on the inside, it looked like sawdust.

From the drawer she pulled out the new one, the one she'd start tomorrow: January 1. Exactly the same, but shiny, with the year stamped in gold.

"You see, every time I start a new one, I tell myself, 'Well, old girl, will you make it to the end? Will you add up the last column?' And every year, here I am at this table with your grandmother holding the fort upstairs. And it's gone on like that for so many years that you might almost believe it will never end."

I didn't respond. I was thinking, "If only Gabriel had been able to sit here, even an hour, one hour of his life, nice and warm, across from Henriette . . . if he only could have . . ." I felt like it would have saved him.

She got up with some difficulty — despite her claims — and went to put on her second apron.

"Don't you think it's time we started thinking about New Year's Eve?"

"The dinner?"

"All we need is to usher the New Year in like this. Since you're here, you can help me."

First I got the ingredients ready for her *oeufs en meurette:* onions, shallots, thyme and bay leaf, parsley.

Henriette always keeps a sprig of parsley on her blouse; says it prevents cancer. "If parents gave their children some to chew every day, they wouldn't end up in the hospital, believe me. But first there have to be parents. Now they're afraid of their children, so they just throw them out."

The flour and the strainer for the sauce. The wine, she'd get from the cellar with Alexis. By the way, she wondered if there was any connection between a wine cellar and a salt cellar. I was in school; she hoped I'd know

Then we went to work on the turkey. She picked it out herself at a local farm: a hen, it's more tender. I don't usually appreciate that sort of detail, but coming from Henriette, I don't know why, it's not the same thing.

There were all sorts of ingredients for the stuffing. But the special one was the truffle wrapped up in a cloth, a big, dark brown truffle.

I was entrusted with cutting it in slivers, with clean hands and the utmost care, if you please. Now time was passing for me, too; I could touch it. If truffles weren't worth their weight in gold, I'd gladly have sliced them for her all day long.

When I finished, she mixed the slivers in with the rest and ground it all together: my truffle, the bacon, pork, liver, veal. So why all the ceremony?

"Ceremony? If you just chop your truffle up, squash it, squeeze out the juice, with no regard for it, what you're cooking won't have any taste to it."

She stuffed the turkey herself. I was a little uneasy watching her jam the stuffing inside, not minding if she got her fingers in it. I didn't think it would all fit, but it did. Afterwards, as she sewed up the opening, I told her she would have made a good surgeon.

"A surgeon? What do you think I do? This is my operating room. Do you really think it's medicine that keeps your grandmother going? The best medicine is what you put in your stomach. Where do you think cancer comes from?"

She almost looked angry. And Paris got her all worked up, too. Was it true the fashion was to serve fish hash, beef with raspberries, lamb broth? She'd really like to know if people realized they were being duped.

Cécile stopped in around four. She turned down a cup of hot chocolate. She went to station herself at the gate, waiting for Daddy.

I found out later he got in about five with Stéphane. Cé-

217

cile stopped the car, said nothing but "the hospital," but in such a way that Daddy dumped his future son-in-law and took off with her again. We have quite a father.

As she waited, Cécile asked the time and that brought everything back. Because, just by chance, it was 4:10 P.M.

It was 4:10 P.M. at the Dijon airport. I heard a voice in the terminal paging Mr. Moreau. "Mr. Moreau, please report to the gate. Mr. Moreau, final call for boarding."

Mr. Moreau was my father, me to some extent, and it was Gabriel. I had the feeling I was hearing life's final appeal to him. With the plane door, the door to the world would close for him. I got on the plane. I saw the empty seat. The flight to Marseilles goes over the snow-covered Alps, it seems. It's superb. A lot of people, blasé, read their newspapers.

"My goodness," said Henriette, "I think I'm going to run out of garlic for my croutons."

She took a ten-franc piece out of her change purse and ordered me to go out right away and get her a head or two.

She always gets her garlic at Bouton's, at the end of town. It would give me a chance to get out, put some color in my cheeks. And she wanted me to walk home slowly, admiring the store windows, mingling with the crowds, with life. I'd bring her back pictures of what was prettiest. I should take a good look for her.

That was all her New Year's Eve dinner needed: a little holiday spirit.

❦ 34 ❦

The Source

THE holiday spirit was everywhere! Well, attempts at it. The main street was all lit up. The shop windows still had their Christmas decorations, the lights, the artificial snow; but now, instead of the department store or toy store, the delicatessen owner was king: with his *foies gras,* sausages, pâtés in their golden crusts; with his eggs in aspic, adorned with a little pink corkscrew tail and two truffle eyes.

His shop was crowded. So were the streets: people buttoned up to their ears, lingering, admiring, conversing. You could feel how important midnight was to them. A star holding back time. I couldn't stop thinking about time.

For my two heads of garlic, I stood in line half an hour. I was quite sure I'd seen a good supply of garlic in the pantry, though. But I felt better now, so thanks, Henriette.

"Pauline!"

Heart racing, I wheeled around. Yes, it was Paul. He was in his car, the door on the passenger side open. He leaned out.

"Can I give you a ride?"

I hesitated. I was completely at sea. I really hadn't expected to see him. And once again he seemed different to me: neither the disturbing stranger in the park, nor the traitor at the book signing. Younger. Or less old. His turtleneck, perhaps. His smile.

A group of girls stopped, whispered among themselves. I was sure they recognized him: Paul Démogée, the writer.

I got in. I couldn't help but feel a certain pride after all.

The interior of his car was very nice, special. The seats were real leather, there was lacquered wood, all kinds of buttons. A handicapped street machine?

He smiled at me.

"I was looking for you."

"Me?"

"I called your house. You'd just gone out. I spoke to your aunt." He paused. "She told me."

"What did she tell you?"

"About the boy. Your little sister. I thought you'd probably gone up to the park. I was on my way up there."

Aunt Nicole talks too much. She doesn't need to go telling everyone all our family's business.

On the sidewalk the three girls kept gawking at Paul.

"Where to?"

"Home."

He started up slowly. He didn't seem to have any trouble at all driving. I was careful not to watch his feet too closely. His foot. Apparently there were only two pedals.

"This isn't the way."

"I know," he said. "But what would you think of a little detour to say goodbye to our friend Buffon? I'm leaving tomorrow."

Buffon? But he didn't head toward the park, either. We drove by the big bookstore. There were decorations and lots of people. Books are a popular holiday item. Books and perfume. I like bookstores. But I feel almost swept away in them. In this flood tide of words, what will be the weight of those I write? As for perfume, it doesn't "take" on me. Will my words "take"?

Place Buffon! So that was where he meant. He stopped the car by the grassy island where the frock-coated statue stands, turned off the engine, put on the interior lighting.

"I'm going to play something for you."

A cassette. I don't know how the speakers were set up, but the sound was fantastic. We were eaten alive by music.

"Schubert!"

Tenderness. I was surprised he liked it. Now, he slid his arm behind me, let it rest on my seatback, and looked at me.

"Did your aunt give you my book?"

"I didn't like it."

It came out spontaneously. Revenge? He didn't look hurt, hardly even surprised.

"Why?"

"It's cold."

I waited for him to trounce me. Paul the writer. For him to explain to poor, ignorant me all that I didn't understand or read into his words.

"What do you mean by 'cold'?"

"Lifeless. Unfeeling. Your hero seems like nothing affects him."

"Do you really think so?" he asked. "And what if he's simply 'done it all' and decided there's no interest in making a show of your emotions?"

Who said anything about making a show? At that point I saw Alexis's face, when he didn't know how to offer to donate his kidney because he's so reserved. My old, grizzled, shabby Alexis, who said it all when he made a show of his knife blades, one by one. I felt like Paul had just attacked him.

"Is that all life means to you? Repressing your feelings? Staying in your shell? That's all you have to offer people? A dreary, pointless tour of things?"

He didn't answer. Didn't smile, either. Thank God. And I told him that I didn't agree. Not at all. That I pitied him with all my heart if he'd "done it all" and thank God not everyone had come to that. Told him people are constantly transfixed, bruised, buffeted by joy or pain. They tough it out. Try to soar. They crash and they dream, dream, and keep on dreaming. And his hero, his Blaise Something-or-other had nothing to offer them, no support, no mirror, no love.

I knew I was overdoing it. It was childish to get so worked up. I was ruining my chances with him once and for all. And so what? "Done it all" was definitely not the thing to say to me today. Had Gabriel ever had a chance to do anything? Since his birth it had all been done *to* him. How heavy he felt that morning as we carried him through the dawn, Antoine and I. Heavy with all the love he'd missed out on, heavy with so much emptiness, so much struggling, not counting the little sister he had to set straight.

In conclusion, I told him everyone at home felt guilty. Cécile, for the obvious reasons. Me, for not saying anything. Mom, for not sensing anything. Grandmother, because she realized she was a more likely candidate. Antoine, because today medicine had failed him. Alexis, with his secret envelope. Every one of us. And it was good that we did. Remorse was our contribution, our way of saying goodbye: a last look, a little wave of our handkerchief.

"I've often thought," Paul said, "that without knowing it, we must all be responsible for someone's death."

"All the more reason to cry out."

He didn't pursue it. In fact, his book was the opposite of crying out; barely a sigh, a vague breathing.

We looked at Buffon on his pedestal. The hardest he was ever looked at, I'm sure. It would have made him happy, since he's supposed to have had a monstrous ego. But in his own way, two hundred years ago, he cried out too, this egomaniac in love with birds, flowers, and the gentle sex (he had his hair waved twice a day).

The cassette was over. End of Schubert. Exit Pauline. He was going to open the door and kick me out.

"A little while ago," he said, "I was packing, and I suddenly wanted to hear your voice. I found myself looking up your number in the phone book. Now I wonder if what I was expecting of you isn't exactly what you've just told me."

I didn't understand. What had come over him?

"The fear of making a show of emotion can turn a writer into nothing but a sort of conjurer," he said, "a more or less agile juggler of words. It can make him forget what's essential: the source that flows inside us all, the place where human beings truly meet. At your age, that was where I wanted to cast my net. Thanks for reminding me."

I couldn't believe it. I didn't know what to do next. Should I smile? Stay serious? I insulted him and he thanked me. He must have been kidding. In a minute he'd laugh. This time I wouldn't fall for it.

"No," he said, "don't laugh. Listen to me, Pauline. Listen. Don't you know yet that everything in life depends on meeting people? It's been so long since I met anyone . . . real."

He put his hand on my knee. My old jeans have been through so much the knees are almost white. I wasn't even smiling now. He put his hand on the knee of my jeans and told me that one of these days they'd put up a little statue in the Parc Buffon with a wet pants seat and — he'd insist — a coat of many colors. Because up there, on the hill like an island above the water, he learned to see things again: lights, for example, which were merely lights to him again for so long.

And now, would I please try to understand? He didn't know anything about young girls. He pictured them as giggling, wearing colored barrettes, and smelling reasonably good. Thanks a lot! Since his accident, he'd lived like a hermit. Alone or surrounded by people like him. Head people, not heart people, who considered anything sweet in life to be outdated.

And then one night he ran across a bizarre young girl with one eye full of enthusiasm and the other of fear; a girl with one foot stepping forward and the other back. Who was dying to express herself, yet struggling so hard with her inhibitions that it was touching. And thanks to her, he was not quite sure how, it was a holiday, a warmth he'd forgotten.

When he saw me later at the book signing, saw my eyes, tears, anger, and saw himself at his table, playing the juggler with his inscriptions, he wanted to chuck it all and run after me. With both legs, he would have. He believed, like an imbecile, that I'd be rather pleased to recognize him at the Town Hall, flattered, in a word. But I saw the only important thing: he'd toyed with the truth.

Since then, he went up to the park almost every day, and each time he was disappointed not to find me there, but thought I was absolutely right not to be.

He pressed his hand to my knee one last time, let go, smiled.

"This is my New Year's wish for you: don't change, Pauline, not even a hair."

He didn't wait for a reply. Lucky for me! I couldn't find a word to say, even a comment about Schubert, so profound and tender, the opposite of his book; Schubert, the purest part of the source he talked about.

He started the car again. I was eager to be alone in my room. To think, sort out the feeling of uneasiness and the something that sings and speaks of adventure and transforms things. How had I been able to live so flatly?

"Now I'll drive you home," he said. "But only if you promise me one thing. Call me in Paris. I need Christmas lessons."

And he did something as funny and appealing as what he

just said: he took my wrist, pulled the sleeve back slightly, and with a felt-tipped pen wrote seven digits. Then he covered it all up. It was over.

We were already on our way up the hill. And there was the gate. Montbard is really only a very small city. A very small island.

He excused himself for not getting out, didn't hold out his hand for me to shake. I weighed a thousand tons as he watched me run toward the gate, stumble, naturally, and hurtle into the grounds.

My father's car was in front of the house. Alexis's, too. It smelled good in the kitchen. I realized as I went in that I'd left my garlic in Paul's glove compartment. Points for me when he finally discovers it!

Henriette wouldn't miss it too much, anyway. There was a whole dish of garlic, minced with parsley. And on the kitchen table was a long tin of *foie gras*.

Everyone was in the parlor. I'd completely forgotten Stéphane was coming. He looked strange with his short hair and long neck. Bernadette's face was pressed to his shoulder.

Mom got up when she saw me. Charles looked at me gravely. I understood. While I was sprouting wings, at the hospital someone was taking off for good.

❦ 35 ❦

Happy New Year

CHARLES was fantastic. So was Cécile.
He said they'd come to a joint agreement to have
our New Year's Eve after all. It didn't mean forgetting Gabriel; quite the contrary. Isn't it a custom to send flowers to
those who can no longer smell them? We'd send Gabriel
this party we would have liked him to share with us.

Grandmother looked just awful. She was all huddled up
in her shawl, as if crushed by the injustice of her being there
while Gabriel . . . Grandmother has never been able to
stand the thought of young people suffering.

Charles walked up to the sofa; he bent over this poor,
guilt-stricken old lady and looked at her severely.

"I'm given to understand you believe in God?"

Everyone was stunned.

"I thought you could plainly see," Daddy went on in the
same vein, "that something comes after . . . that there's a
chance, when you've led a miserable life, of making up for
it in your heaven."

Grandmother lifted her head straight up. She looked at
Charles defiantly, as if he were casting doubt on her entire
existence, even to her presence here.

"I can only tell you one thing," Daddy concluded: "that

when it was all over, the boy's face amazed everyone. He was almost smiling. It was like a fist unclenching."

He stood back. That was when I noticed Cécile's face. Yes, her fatigue was there; yes, it was literally black with dirt, with streaks from the eyes down; but in spite of it all, her face, too, was like an unclenched fist. Like an act of faith.

Mom came close to her husband; she slipped her arm under his; he covered her hand with his own, and she looked happy. I understood her need to touch the man who'd spoken those words.

He simply added that the funeral would be the day after tomorrow and that we'd attend it before we left for La Marette. Nicole would arrange with Father Gosier to hold it in the church of St. Urse, the Christmas one.

And that was all. I looked at my watch. It was only seven-fifteen. Barely an hour before, Paul had bared my wrist and written seven digits on it. I smelled the inside of his car, the strong aroma of the leather seats, the little cigar he lit at one point, after asking if I minded, and a strange, a very strong sensation rushed through me, as if I were touching life.

Henriette came up to Daddy.

"Did the doctor remember my *foie gras?*"

She's always addressed him in the third person, and he's still not quite sure what to make of it. He looked dismayed.

"Dear me! The *foie gras!* What could I have done with it?" He slapped his pockets comically.

"It's on the kitchen table," I said. I looked Henriette right in the eye. "But I forgot your garlic."

Everybody laughed.

"Everyone makes mistakes," Henriette said. "Luckily I found an extra head or two lying around." She left the parlor.

"Why don't we all freshen up?" Nicole suggested.

"Don't mind if I do," said Daddy.

The hospital, the car trip, all he could think about now

was a nice warm bath, with a willing woman to hold out a toasty robe to him when he was done. In the tub, if no one had any objections, he'd gladly drink a finger or two of Scotch.

Grandmother grimaced. She'll never understand his taste for British beverages, when Burgundy produces everything a person could want for any occasion.

Daddy headed for the door. Then the Pest got up. She still hadn't said a single word, and it must have been a good twelve hours now that she'd been wearing her parka zipped up to her chin.

She positioned herself between Charles and the door.

"I don't know what the heck I did to this zipper. It's stuck."

Without a word, Daddy pulled her over to an armchair, sat down, parked her between his knees, and went to work on the zipper. Cécile stared down at his head, brown in places, graying in others; at one point she raised her hand, and I thought she was going to stroke it, but no. She just held it poised in the air a few seconds.

When the parka was finally unzipped, Daddy told her that if she didn't shower now, she'd have to wait until next year, which would be a shame.

And that occasioned the last howler of the year: how long it took to dawn on Gaston that next year was just around the corner.

Just before she left the room, the Pest turned around. She said, "I really want to believe he's at peace now and everything. But still, Gabriel is such a nice name. A name that didn't deserve to die."

In a sense, that was her goodbye.

"If I may make a wish, my poor Alexis," said Grandmother, "it's that you'll stop frowning just half a day a week!"

"And if *I* may," said Alexis, eyebrows knitting furiously,

"it's that from one end of the week to the next you'll stop putting 'poor' in front of my name."

They looked at each other, smiled. Alexis took Grandmother's shoulders in his big paws and they planted kisses on each others' cheeks.

It was midnight! Beneath the mistletoe, it was like a ballet. There was the *pauchouse* again, the turkey with celery root purée, broiled cheese with the salad, ice cream. Too much! The *foie gras* we would save for tomorrow. It made me feel strange to think about all the people kissing as they rang in the New Year. All I can say is, the current was flowing.

"I wish that you'll graduate with honors," Nicole said, grabbing me by the waist.

Not too original; she was the third one to wish me that.

Daddy came up to me. Every time he kisses me this way, soundly, after trying to look deep in my eyes, I get the feeling he's asking my forgiveness for having forgotten me somewhat, being so absorbed in everything besides me and me alone.

"Happy New Year, sweetheart!"

I thought I also heard a "thank you." Very softly I repeated, "Thank you?"

"For Cécile."

I buried my head in his shoulder. One wish per person, that made ten to give and receive. Some people, like Mom, prepare in advance. Others do it on the spur of the moment. Men generally lack imagination. It's "Happy New Year," period. To Henriette, everyone mentions her prize-winning cooking. It seems a little ridiculous to me. Well, if it makes her happy . . . I saw her black ledger again. What does she do with the old ones? I'll have to ask her.

Mom smiled at Bernadette.

"I wish you a part of what you desire."

"Why only a part?" groused our equestrienne.

"There has to be something left over for later on!"

Antoine leaned over me. He simply said, "Be happy." And I don't know why, but it felt like a farewell.

"We'll wish each other a color TV," Cécile suggested, "okay?"

Check. Not much chance we'd get one, but nothing to lose by wishing. My lips brushed her cheek. "Happy New Year."

Alexis and Adrien were chuckling over their wishes. They had to do with underbrush, fishing streams, snail tracks. I'd have so much to say to Claire!

Grandmother was the serious one. Each of us took a turn sitting beside her on the sofa. Somewhat confessional. All we wanted to say to her is, "Stay around a long time."

"Have a little more faith in yourself," she whispered in my ear. "You don't want to haul a storm bell around in your pocket all your life, do you?"

Then Mom.

"Keep your high standards."

I liked that. Something good to think about. "Don't change a hair," Paul had told me. Mom's wish went with his. I was going to get a swollen head.

Seeing Bernadette walk up to me on Stéphane's arm, I realized he was taking her away from us. This year! I blurted out, "I wish that you'll spend next New Year's Eve with us."

My sister laughed. "Isn't that just like you! We're here for this one. Enjoy it!"

"Not if it has to end."

"The cycle just begins all over again," philosophized the soldier with his shaved head atop his long neck.

His kiss on my forehead was light. Bernadette's was a smack. Then she turned serious.

"My wish, dear Paul, is for you to become a famous writer."

"Dear Paul." I felt dizzy for a second. But she often used the nickname, and she didn't know about Démogée.

"Count on it."

"What will you write about?" Nicole asked, half-smiling.

"Everything. Absolutely everything. And caring."

"Why not about us?" Daddy proposed. And he wasn't being sarcastic.

I saw them all coming closer. They surrounded me.

"Your sisters," Bernadette said.

"Your wonderful cousin," said Gaston.

"Your beloved uncle," said Adrien.

"What's going on?" cried Grandmother, abandoned on her sofa.

"No one would want to read about us," I said.

A chorus of "thanks a lot" rained down on me.

"And I don't know if I'll be able to . . ."

"You can try!"

I thought about juggling words, conjuring. I thought about the source. What counts is what flows deep within us, what we all have in common. I felt it like a light inside me.

"Talk about Gabriel," Cécile commanded, "and fix it so he keeps on living."

❧ 36 ❧

Claire and Happily Ever After

"WHAT are you doing?"

There was the Princess, leaning on the door to the shed, in winter boots, a muffler up to her eyes.

She was looking at me as though nothing had ever been damaged between us, broken.

"You can see. Making a clean sweep, I guess."

Everything that fit went into the wheelbarrow, then onto a big heap over by the well, where grass clippings are burned in the summertime. When I got it all over there, I'd set a good fire: I'd brought down the bottle of charcoal lighter we use for barbecues.

"Can I help?"

She pitched right in and picked something up off the ground: a book.

"Alain-Fournier. *Le Grand Meaulnes,*" she read.

"Just imagine. Cécile wanted to educate Gabriel."

I took the book from her. Hardbound or not, it went into the wheelbarrow with everything else. It would go on top of the heap. A story of escape, a fantasy world, celebrations, disillusionment, death. Perfect. Except for the celebrations, obviously.

The moth-eaten blanket, sagging pillow, old clothes. The

mattress was hardest. It wouldn't stay on the wheelbarrow. It should be carried, but I couldn't handle it. I hugged it, heartsick, and dragged it along the ground. Now the winter grass was dotted with balls of fuzz.

Antoine had returned the Zouave uniform to Alexis, recommending that he have it disinfected.

Telepathy was in the air. The Princess frowned.

"If Daddy saw you, he'd be furious. Have you thought about the germs? Alexis said he'd take care of all this."

I knew. But I had something to make up to myself here. And I couldn't have foreseen that this need to eradicate would overtake me. This need to defy, too, I don't know what or whom. To do something out of the ordinary, forbidden, the way you shout when you've been told to be quiet.

"Let's go!"

All that was left in the shed were the crates and broken tools. We'd air it all out and that would be the end of it.

The garden crackled, breathed, you might say. It had rained that morning, and the rain had drowned the cold. Droplets trembled on branch tips.

Claire walked beside me. She put her hand on the handle of the wheelbarrow, not far from my own. A little late to say "Happy New Year!"

"Did you know I'm staying in Montbard?"

"Mom told me."

"I don't want you to think it's because I'm a coward."

"You?" I laughed. Fishing for compliments, my word.

"I need to get away from La Marette."

She helped me empty the wheelbarrow. She took some junk in her gloved hands and placed it carefully on the heap. Some flowered paper plates brightened things up. A towel and a cloth napkin. A comb, newspaper, and lots of wrappers from chocolate-hazelnut bars, Cécile's favorite, cookie wrappers too, lined with tinfoil.

When it was all in place, I poured out the charcoal

lighter. I tossed the match. It took like a gust of wind.

"I need to get away from Antoine, too."

"Why?"

"To get some perspective."

"On what?"

"He wants to marry me and give the baby his name."

"What else are you waiting for? Don't you love him?"

The fire took right away on the inside of the mattress. A blue flame.

Claire looked at me in amazement, almost shock. "Do you think that loving someone automatically means getting married?"

"In your case, you have to admit it would be more practical. And don't you think it would be better for the baby?"

"If the father and mother get along," Claire said. "Look at Uncle Adrien and Aunt Philippa. What an advertisement for marriage!"

"You're not like Aunt Philippa! And I'd be more inclined to look at our parents."

The fire had taken on the embroidered seat of the stool. The plates twisted as they burned. Nasty plastic coating, it made weird green flames. To think we eat on that!

"A life like Mom's? Thanks but no thanks," Claire murmured.

I resented her saying that. And I didn't understand.

"Mom is great."

"Who said she isn't? But she's great to other people, not to herself."

"But if she's happy like that . . ."

Claire waited a minute before responding, looking at the toes of her wet boots. Our fire didn't smell very good. Nothing like the living smell of dried grass clippings, the funnels of smoke rising to the skies like genies out of fairy tales.

"Can you understand," she asked, "that in a certain way

it's possible to be afraid of happiness? A certain kind of happiness?"

I didn't feel like answering.

"Of living happily ever after? Being limited? Isolated?"

She looked out toward the street. The rooftops darken when they're wet. Some of the tiles take on a greenish cast. That little cloud down there could have broken your heart.

"You're afraid of having it too good with Antoine, is that it?"

"Maybe. Either 'too good,' and in a sense I'd die. Or not good enough, and I'd make *him* die."

Her voice was dull.

"How can you tell what you'll be like in ten years? Or even two? What your needs will be and all that? Marriage is too long."

"When you love someone, you don't ask yourself all these questions," I said. "You start off together and see what happens."

"If I'm asking myself all these questions, it's because I do love him," she said. "I don't want us to tear each other apart someday . . . or bore each other."

"So what *do* you want?"

"To sleep beside him. Just live with him, to start with."

She made a face. "But for him, it's marriage or nothing."

That did it. "Marriage or nothing." And the way she said it. I burst out laughing: a laugh that came from deep inside, and that I only half-understood. Something was suddenly singing within me. How to put it? Even if I'm more the type to want "happily ever after," marriage and children, Claire was opening new horizons to me. The horizon of self-confidence, perhaps. A horizon where you aren't afraid to take risks.

"What's so funny?"

"The way you said 'marriage or nothing.' It used to be the girl who said that."

"Because she had no other options. Times have changed."

"But what are your options?"

"I'm going back to school," she announced.

Now I was speechless. For two years they'd been begging her to do this. A hundred times we'd seen poor Charles go into her room with a long face to explain to her that it was in her interest to expand her knowledge, that work is the key to freedom . . . and now she was deciding to! Four months before her baby was due! Now that a man loved and wanted to marry her and she could just put her feet up, with everyone's approval this time, which is what she'd done since high school anyway!

"To study play therapy," she said. "A three-year program. I'll probably have trouble at first. Being rusty and all. But if I try . . . when I'm done I'll work with disturbed children."

"Why children? Why disturbed?"

She looked at me and in her blue, blue eyes was something akin to fatigue mixed with memory.

"Even to me it's not terribly clear. It's because of what happened in the subway. I can't stop thinking about it. I'm not afraid, it's not that, but I keep seeing their faces. . . . Remember? I keep telling myself that I have to do something."

She fell silent a moment, choosing her words. I didn't realize it was still so vivid to her. I'd forgotten, in a way. Erased it?

"After that," she said, "I saw myself differently. I saw differences, injustice. I want to make children happy. I want to make up for it."

A few years earlier, so few, we'd often lean over that well. Throw pebbles into it. The time it took for the water deep in the bottom to answer us was dizzying. Almost as if *we* were doing the falling.

"Your fire isn't doing very well."

No, it wasn't. Exactly what I didn't want: a half-purification. I didn't know if I had something to "make up for" in setting this fire, but it was a failure. Would Gabriel stay inside us like this black smoke hissing, almost breathing?

I emptied the bottle of charcoal lighter. "Stand back." I tossed the whole box of matches on it. But it was no use, really. We were out of ammunition.

"What about your baby? What will you tell it?"

"The truth."

"Even if you marry Antoine and he gives it his name?"

"What else do you expect me to do?"

"And what if he wants to meet his real father someday?"

"And what if he finds out we lied to him someday? If he wants to meet his real father, he will."

She was right. But that didn't stop me from imagining Jeremy's reaction and feeling like laughing again. Laughing with her. Because one morning, by a well, in the garden of your childhood, you can feel ten years old and at the same time on the cutting edge of life.

"You know," said Claire, "at one point I thought . . . I wondered if . . . you loved Antoine too. And why shouldn't you?"

So there it was. You only had to hear her voice. She could make all the high-toned speeches she liked, but she wanted this man. And she'd live with him. No doubt about it.

I looked her right in the eye.

"Antoine? Me? Not at all my type. Much too serious. Remember that I'm in a different generation from you. And these days things change fast."

She decided to laugh, too. She looked relieved. Her eyes came to rest on my wrist. The number had almost faded away now.

"Who's that?"

"Nobody."

"You'll tell me about it," she said. But her smile vanished. "Lord, we're in for it now."

Farther up, on the first terrace, three heads had just appeared, then three torsos, three men: Antoine, Alexis, and Daddy. The smoke was bound to attract attention eventually.

Antoine hurried down the steps. I could already hear him: You're out of your minds! There are some risks you have no right to take. Especially Claire!

But there are times when you have to know how to take risks without considering the consequences. It's crucial.

Claire moved closer to me. "We both decided to set the fire," she whispered, "all right?"

All right.

And I told her, "I'm going to miss you."

"I certainly hope so."

"You're out of your minds!" Daddy yelled. "This is incredibly careless! And Claire, in your condition!"

Antoine didn't say anything. He looked at Claire. He never stopped looking at her that way! Like someone with wings, who might escape from him at any moment.

She laid her hand on her stomach.

"I know it's corny," she said, "but if it's a boy, what do you think about naming it Gabriel?"

❦ 37 ❦

Goodbye, Buffon!

IT seems the arrangements were complicated, but Nicole
and Charles eventually got their way, and the funeral
was held at the church of St. Urse, at three o'clock, before
we left for La Marette.

We loaded the car before we went up to the church. That
way once we got out of the service (since that's what it's
called), all we'd have left to do was drink a good, hot cup
of tea, kiss everyone goodbye, and off we'd go.

The Mass went by in a flash. I didn't believe in Gabriel's
death at all anymore. Or even in Gabriel, for that matter.
Between the rows of pews, near the altar, was a varnished
wooden box on two trestles, and that was it. I'd seen so
little of him, really: a gasp, a shadow beneath a blanket.

What I needed now was to erase the memory of the moment when Antoine and I carried that blanket still full of
life through the morning mist.

Antoine was next to Claire. Like Daddy, he stared at the
stained-glass windows just above Father Gosier's head. I
understood that he was looking toward other children:
Frédéric, perhaps, all children who reject the world around
them, the children Claire had decided to work with. Maybe

ın my sister's eyes they'd find the light that would help them accept life.

Cécile was between Mom and Dad. You could see they'd worked it out in advance, so that she'd feel their presence, their warmth. Groundlessly, I felt left out.

By a column, I spotted a piece of straw. It had to be left over from the Christmas pageant. Midnight Mass had been held there: Christmas, Joseph wheezing, Mary with her low-cut dress, the sheep that went on the straw, Aunt Philippa with her nose buried in a handkerchief. I didn't know how good we had it then. How full. I hadn't enjoyed it enough. Unfortunately, I only enjoy things after the fact, with regret.

Our family took up two whole pews. Besides us, there were only three people from the reformatory, two men and a woman, and an old lady, a local eccentric, who never misses a funeral, cries buckets, and on the way out, knowingly shakes hands all around.

Grandmother sat through the whole service, so small and hunched over her clasped hands that it made us think about when she'd be leaving us too.

Father Gosier spoke about love. He said that Gabriel Marc Levénement hadn't known love on this earth, but that we could rest assured he did now.

He looked very convinced. "What would he know about it?" Bernadette whispered, and I resented her saying what I was thinking.

The little spray of flowers was from Henriette. The larger one, from the whole family. But no wreaths, thank Goa. I wished the flowers could have been all white, like the ones at a christening, communion, or wedding; like when you're celebrating a beginning.

When the Mass was over, no one quite knew what to do. No black-clad family to shake hands with before you step out and take a few deep breaths, back in the fresh air of everyday life. No tearful eyes to meet except the crazy old lady's: she was waiting near the door for the usual formalities, to no avail.

The three people from the reformatory were talking quietly in front of the church. One of the men approached Daddy. He asked, "Did you know Gabriel Levénement?"

Daddy gestured toward Cécile. He said, "She was his friend." Then the man shook hands with the Pest. He murmured, "You know, basically he was a good kid. The thing is, he never had any luck."

The Pest looked the other way with an indifferent expression. The man stayed a minute, on unsure footing, then, since no one seemed to want the conversation to continue, he put his gloves back on and went back to his friends.

Four mortuary employees, dressed in black, put the casket in the hearse. One of them had on workclothes under his pants. They showed at the bottom. It gave the impression the whole thing was a show. I felt like telling him to turn back into himself.

The hearse took off slowly toward the cemetery, stirring the slush on the way down the hills lined with desolate plane trees. Everyone followed on foot, the crazy old lady in the lead. Stéphane was holding Bernadette's hand, and Antoine had taken Claire's arm. I noticed she leaned against him.

Not-quite-flakes, something between rain and snow, began falling again. Daddy eyed the sky nervously. Mom's night vision isn't very good; he'd be doing all the driving on the way home.

I lagged behind. No one was paying any attention to me I backtracked.

The church was already locked up, like a theater five minutes after the ovation. If you'd told me I'd be back that way so soon, I wouldn't have believed it.

I made a beeline for the park the snow would soon whiten again. I could make out good old Buffon's tower in the back. We'd met so often now I was starting to think of Buffon as a friend. I sent him a friendly message.

I had some trouble lifting up the stone. It seemed soldered to the ground. I slipped the plane ticket under it. A childish gesture, for sure. It would have been more reasonable to take it back for a refund. But no thanks to reason.

I let the stone fall back on Mr. Moreau, Dijon-Marseilles, December 31, 4:10 P.M. At least we could give Gabriel this piece of paper that might have been the nicest thing he ever held in his hand, even if he didn't use it. This ticket that meant both leaving and love.

After that, anything could happen and I wouldn't care. I'd come to sit down on the spot where Paul and I met. He must be back in Paris now. The number had completely faded from my wrist. Montbard stretched out beneath me, full of everyday life. Neither Gabriel's death nor Christmas could change this sky, the rooftops, or the course of the river. All I could hope was that my way of looking at this river, these rooftops, this city, would never be quite the same. I hoped!

They must have been lowering the casket about then. What if Daddy hadn't paid? If Nicole hadn't pulled strings? Where would Gabriel have been buried? And what did it matter, really? When it's over, you drink a steaming hot cup of tea, hit the road, and doze off, telling yourself that winter is far from over.

I couldn't convince myself to leave my stretch of wall. It seemed to me that night was refusing to fall. It was true that for two weeks now, the days had been growing longer. Five minutes a day. A tremendous amount.

I summoned Paul's voice from inside me. "My wish for you . . ."

With all my strength, I made a wish to forget nothing, to hold within me the face of the newly dead boy, and the being my sister's womb was preparing to come to life.

And the force of it all made me feel like crying out, without knowing if it would be from pain or for joy.

W24   A 9/11/00
LC 12/27/16   TC 8

10-17-84

F   Boissard, Janine
          Christmas lessons